Also By the Author

The Menmenet Series
The Jackal of Inpu
The Lion of Bastet
The Bull of Mentju

The Founding Fathers Mysteries
Murder at Mount Vernon

The Pirates of Khonoë Series
Hyperkill

Death of A Golden State
The Blockchain Killing

THE LION OF BASTET

A Menmenet Alternate History Mystery

Robert J. Muller

Poesys Associates

San Francisco

To M'Linn and Theo

There is no trap so deadly as the trap you set for yourself.

Raymond Chandler, The Long Goodbye

A man doesn't make your kind of money in any way I can understand.

Raymond Chandler, The Long Goodbye

"Follow the money."

William Goldman, "All the President's Men"
Spoken by Deep Throat

North America

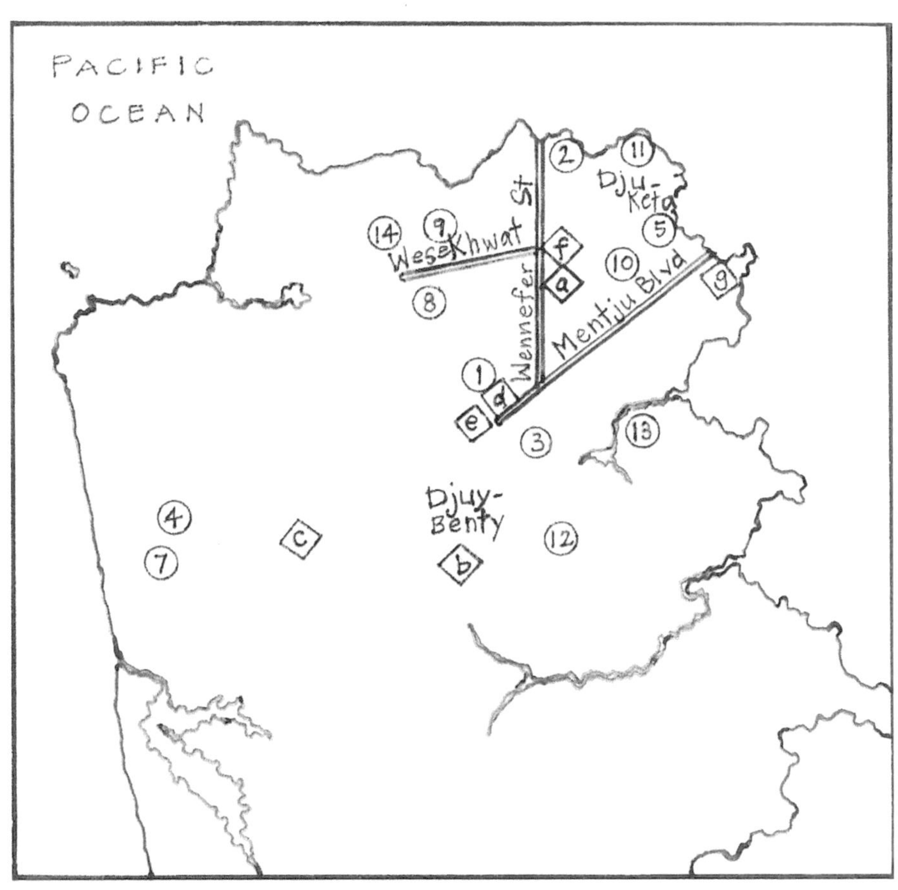

Menmenet

Key

	Temples		Locations		
a	Bastet	**1**	City Palace	**8**	Nesimen's House
b	Imen-R'a	**2**	Ferry Terminal	**9**	Palace of the Republic
c	Inpu	**3**	MacIntyre's Apartment	**10**	Per'ankh Restaurant
d	Ma'at	**4**	Necropolis	**11**	Shesmu's House
e	Mentju	**5**	Neferti Restaurant	**12**	U. S. Embassy
f	Sekhmet-Hut-Her	**6**	Nekhen's House	**13**	Wenmyt Restaurant
g	Seteh	**7**	Nekhen's Tomb	**14**	Yaotl's Palace

CHAPTER ONE
Shesmu Volunteers

"I don't like cats," said MacIntyre in my ear as we sat down at the small table in the Myu-Myu Club.

"It's just a couple of dances, then we can leave," I replied.

A social obligation. The head of the R'ames Society, Nesimen, was hosting us at a small after-event party. The Society, a nonprofit foundation, promoted talent in the culinary arts. Its annual award ceremony was the social event of the year in the culinary world. Menmenet was the capital and center of food culture in the Ta'an-Imenty Republic, and I was now the best chef in Menmenet. I was owner of the Neferti, my restaurant on the Bay waterfront that served New Remetjy cuisine.

But it was the Per'ankh restaurant that made me the best chef in Menmenet. I had the Best New Chef award certificate in my pocket, my girlfriend at my side, and a glass of an outstanding local white wine in front of me, and all was right with the world. My career was advancing by leaps and bounds since I'd taken over as executive chef of the Per'ankh, the restaurant where I'd apprenticed. It was the best restaurant in Menmenet. French fine dining, not Remetjy cuisine, but you couldn't have everything.

With Nesimen's happy approval, I invited some friends to celebrate with us. Nekhetsebek was my chef at the Neferti, and Henutsenu was the Neferti house manager. Sebek and Henutsenu were an item, which contributed to the roaring success of the Neferti—excellent communication between the front and back of the house.

MacIntyre whispered in my ear again. "It's not really the cats, it's the murders."

"OK, you'll have to expand on that for me," I said, sipping my wine. MacIntyre grinned and drank some of her glass of Hermitage, a big red Syrah from the

Rhône. She'd taken a liking to it when we passed some time there on a trip a few months back. She confined her knowledge of wine to telling the difference between red and white. I hadn't introduced her to Anjou so as not to confuse the issue with light rosé, but she was learning fast.

At any social event, Remetjy women compete with one another for the most alluring fashion, and Remetjy fashions tended toward extremes. But MacIntyre was not a Remetjet. She was a transplanted American. As a plainclothes medjat, she dressed halfway between the severe black American business style and the more conservative Remetjy, but tonight she had crossed over and adopted Remetjy party dress. The dress, what there was of it, was white with faint red and black designs at the edges, the edges shaped and folded to emphasize the attributes of the wearer. On one edge, she wore a gold feather pin, emblem of the goddess Ma'at whom she served as a w'abet, a working priestess. She'd explained to me early in our relationship that she wasn't religious, but you had to be a w'abet to get promoted on the force. That applied especially to promotion to semetyt on the Homicide Squad.

"Djehutymes—you remember my boss, don't you? Djehutymes assigned me to a new case today, a double murder at the Temple of Bastet, the powerful cat goddess. Now I'm seeing black cats everywhere." She sent her eyes toward the two statues of Bastet that adorned the sides of the elevated dance stage in front of us. Two huge, polished-basalt cats. "And meeting the Hem-Netjer-Tepy of Bastet tonight was a surprise, too."

Panekhet, the Hem-Netjer-Tepy of Bastet, was also the Chairman of the Board of the R'ames Society. Nesimen had introduced him to me along with another board member, R'aweben, a financier. I already knew R'aweben through my restaurant. I'd bought the Per'ankh with financing from a billionaire, Hernefer, who owed me a favor. He'd found it a pretty good deal over the last year. The restaurant went from success to success, and Hernefer wanted to expand, so he invited in R'aweben's finance company, the Henuttawy Group, and they invested serious debenu. I had a lot of capital at my disposal now, thanks to them.

Taneferet, Nesimen's wife, suggested recruiting me for a role with the Society, and Nesimen wanted to show me how influential it was. MacIntyre, being a hutyt-er-semetyu on the Homicide Squad of the Menmenet Medjau, had a cynical attitude toward the power those men represented. She had bowed nicely enough, though. She'd noted to me later that the two bigwigs didn't deign to come to the party with us working-class types.

The other members of our party were at tables to our left. Nesimen was a medium-height, 55-year-old man, a little plump, with a bald head and a cheerful smile on his round face. Taneferet was the same age, smaller than her husband and thin, with kind eyes and an amiable mouth. I'd known her most of my life, and I had a lot of affection for her.

I called Taneferet "Khenemset Neferet" because she had been my mother's best friend, right up to my mother's early death at 35, when I was 10. Remetjy extended families almost always have an "auntie" like Taneferet to add to the love showered on the children. But a khenemset is stronger than the usual informal auntie; she's more like a godmother in the Christian world. A khenemset's religious responsibilities relate to the goddess Ma'at. Khenemset Neferet had made sure I stayed on the path of Ma'at as I grew up, befriending me and helping my foster parents cope with a willful teenager. We'd lost touch after she married Nesimen and moved south. When Nesimen took the job at the R'ames Society and moved back to Menmenet, we'd gotten back in touch, seeing each other from time to time. It had been Khenemset Neferet who persuaded me to apply for Society membership. Then she talked her husband into putting me up for the chef's award. He needed only a little persuading, of course. I didn't know Nesimen all that well, as he often wasn't around when I visited Khenemset Neferet.

The Chief Financial Officer of the Society, Sennedjem, sat with his boyfriend, a man named Filip with some unpronounceable Polish last name. I'd taken against Sennedjem because he'd walked out of the room right in the middle of my acceptance speech earlier in the evening. And the man smirked; that's the only word for it. Both he and his boyfriend looked like eastern Europeans, but only Filip had the name to go with the look. Dark hair and beards, pale white faces, and thin, sneering lips on both of them. Filip looked like a bodybuilder, but Sennedjem looked like he could slither through anything. Fortunately, their table was on the other side of Nesimen's from us. I surveyed them—they'd ordered a bottle of vodka, everyone else had glasses of wine.

I advised MacIntyre, "Ask Henutsenu about Panekhet. She's a Bastet devotee. Maybe she has some insights into the Temple of Bastet hierarchy."

"Already have. Panekhet is a Great Man, according to her, but she doesn't know him personally. I didn't mention the temple murders." MacIntyre looked at the next table over to the right, where Henutsenu entertained Sebek. "And she also said this club was a great place. If you like cats, I suppose," she said. "Wonderful dancing entertainment. Which seems about to start." She took a fortifying swallow of wine.

The musicians were taking their seats in the small band area to the side of the stage, and the lights dimmed. Colored lights came up on the stage to produce a baleful, reddish background. The dancers, all female, appeared one by one from a door to the left of the stage as the musicians played a soft musical prologue. The Bastet statues were back lit, but the statues' eyes picked up reddish glints and glowed. Both music and dancers seemed a little random. The women glided in all directions, without purpose, and the music carried out that theme in sound, the clarinets predominating with low, soft, meandering notes.

I could hardly tell the dancers apart. Each dressed the same, had the same hair, even had the same features, though their skin tones varied from pale to deep black. The costumes they wore were light linen that covered everything but obscured nothing. As far as I could tell, they weren't wearing anything else. Their hair fell to their shoulders in black braids. I looked sideways at Henutsenu, who had the same hair but more richly decorated with gold beads. She smiled, cat-like, at home with the dancers.

The dancers wandered around the stage with their cat-like movements. Clarinets took charge, and the tempo increased. Their slow gestures coalescing into the same movement, the dancers flowed into a line. The Bastet statues framed them, one on each side of the stage, eyes glinting red, polished-basalt faces reflecting the dancers. The stoney cat faces grinned at me; just special lighting, but effective.

A noise intruded from my left. I realized I'd heard whispers for some time. I looked at Nesimen, whose head turned toward his wife, who looked at the pair beyond her, scandalized.

Sennedjem and Filip argued in loud whispers, the bodybuilder gesticulating. Sennedjem looked up at the ceiling, a smirk on his lips. Neither of them gave any attention to the dance or to the music, just to the vodka. Reaching a crescendo, the music led the dancers into faster and faster movements, their legs and arms waving in unison down the line, bodies undulating, their moves sensuous and suggestive.

Filip leaped up and pushed Sennedjem out of his seat. Sennedjem scrambled, then spun around, grabbed his glass of vodka, and tossed it into his boyfriend's face. The Pole roared and rushed at Sennedjem, carrying him forward toward the dancers. The rest of us sat dumbstruck. I rose, but not fast enough: the two men, struggling and lashing out at each other, crashed over the low edge of the stage into the dancers. The line disintegrated into a mass of arms, legs, and screaming mouths. The music stopped as the musicians froze, gaping.

MacIntyre beat me to it, rushing Filip, and tripped him from behind, then landed on his back with a knee and twisted one arm behind him. As she did this, I had reached Sennedjem, who showed signs of wear with blood on his face. He took his revenge on his incapacitated friend with a vicious kick to the side. I grabbed him around the middle, pinning his arms to his sides, then dragged him back off the stage, out of kicking range.

Nesimen approached with a stormy face, and Sebek was right behind him. Taneferet sat still, the same scandalized look on her face, making little, useless motions with her hands. Henutsenu had disappeared. Then two very large gentlemen charged into the room. They dressed as w'abu of Bastet, the sort of w'abu that dealt with unruly worshippers too drunk to behave themselves. These two would have been more at home at the Temple of Hepu than in the house of Bastet, except they were even larger than the Hepu bull. Henutsenu appeared right behind them, pointing out the problems.

The two w'abu split, one coming toward me and Sennedjem, the other approaching MacIntyre and her charge. Mine laid a hand on Sennedjem's shoulder with a squeeze that had Sennedjem gasping. I let loose and stepped back. The other w'ab stood back a little, admiring the tableaux with MacIntyre and Filip. MacIntyre got up, and Filip rolled over, out of breath and no longer interested in fighting. The w'ab smiled and bowed his head in appreciation to MacIntyre, who was smoothing out her dress. He leaned down and pulled up the Pole with one hand under his shoulder, lifting him off his feet.

Nesimen now approached Sennedjem, the storm breaking. With a pinched expression, he said in forceful tones, "I've warned you before. You're here to represent the society. You can't afford—*we* can't afford embarrassments like this!"

Sennedjem just scowled and said nothing, but at least that smirk had gone. The w'ab walked toward the door, moving Sennedjem along. His partner gripped the struggling Filip's arm and pulled him along. The four men disappeared through the door. Lights came up, and the two statues gazed at nothing with dull eyes. The party was over.

We'd all had our fill of the Myu-Myu Club, so we walked out into the alley behind the Hut-'Ankh-Tepyt hotel, where the Society had held the awards ceremony. Sebek and Henutsenu set off for her flat around the corner on Mentju Boulevard. I was still fizzing from my award and needed to put the melee behind me. MacIntyre said she was up for some one-on-one dancing, as long as there were no cats involved.

"Shesmu," said Nesimen, "I'd like to thank you and Hutyt MacIntyre for your help. I apologize profusely for the conduct of Sennedjem. He's not normally like that."

Khenemset Neferet spoke up from beside him. "He is, Nesimen. He is. You know he is. When are you going to do something about it? His drinking, his scandalous behavior. I've never been so embarrassed." She gave me a flustered look with her sad-looking eyes. It made my heart ache just to see the sadness in her face.

"No need for apologies. These things happen," I replied. "And Cheryl did all the rough work."

"No, that's yet to come," said MacIntyre, grinning. "The paperwork for off-duty incidents—you don't want to know. But, yes, no apologies needed."

Nesimen half smiled, but his mind was on something else. He turned the subject. "Shesmu, I'd like you to consider something."

Time to pay for our entertainment. I noticed Khenemset Neferet perk up; she must have put Nesimen up to whatever he was going to ask of me.

He went on, "I need—*we* need—help to get our message out, to get more members, to make ourselves better known in the culinary world. Our current membership in the restaurant world is aging fast, and we need to attract younger people to revitalize our efforts. Would you consider volunteering as a celebrity spokesperson for the Society?"

Khenemset Neferet smiled now, the sun coming out. I had some reservations, though.

I pointed out the obvious. "If your people all behave like Sennedjem, it's going to be a struggle."

He shook his head with dismay. "They don't. And we keep him out of the papers. Mostly." He smiled. "But with your help, we can neutralize any negatives. Your speech tonight was brilliant! You have a real talent for connecting with people in the industry." A good sales pitch. He'd rehearsed it. I didn't stutter my way through my speech, but it was little more than "thanks for the kudos and the money." But for all of Nesimen's humility about the Society, it was one of the more important institutions in Menmenet's culinary world. My career would only benefit from association with it. I already had two full plates, but one more wouldn't burden me that much.

The hopeful expression on Khenemset Neferet's face gave me no choice. I replied, "Yes, I'd like to help. Perhaps we could get together and review what's required? Tomorrow?" I noticed MacIntyre shivering, even with her coat on. Time to go.

"Yes, of course, sorry. You go on now and have a good time, you and Hutyt MacIntyre. Why don't you come to the Society offices tomorrow and pick up your award check, then drop by my office? I'll be in all day."

"Thanks, I'll do that." I hugged Khenemset Taneferet, bowed to Nesimen, and wrapped a warming arm around MacIntyre as we walked away.

It isn't so tough to take that step off the cliff. It's what comes afterward that's hard. Especially if you're not aware it's a cliff.

CHAPTER TWO
MacIntyre Visits a Cat House

CHERYL MACINTYRE WOKE UP THINKING about cats.

She didn't like cats. Oh, they were nice enough, but she wasn't the kind of housekeeper that enjoyed traipsing around after things that dropped fur all over the floor and lent you their fleas. She didn't much care for dogs, either. She was more of a people person.

But cats had their pluses and minuses. Thinking about cats led her to fantasizing about Henutsenu, who resembled a sleek, dark kitty with soft fur that you stroked to start that wonderful purr.

MacIntyre sighed at waking up alone. Henutsenu was nice, but the current love of her life was Shesmu. MacIntyre smiled at the recollection of the previous evening's club dancing and the later lovemaking. Even the frenetic medja activity with the smirking Sennedjem and his friend was thrilling. But those baleful black cat statues looking down on it all gave her the creeps. And Shesmu had to go home and rest after it all.

Shesmu. Cats. Medjau. The Temple of Bastet. Now, there. Work always came first. MacIntyre sighed again, threw off the covers, and dragged herself out of bed to make breakfast.

"Thank you, but no, I've eaten," said MacIntyre, eying with interest the plate of Remetjy delicacies on the conference table at the Temple of Bastet. Not that she was hungry, she took an interest in food now that she was sleeping with a chef. If she burrowed deep enough into her soul, she would discover the food interest was about intimacy and sharing and understanding others' interests. Right. More likely, she was curious. Didn't curiosity kill the cat?

Shesmu was always teasing her about her kitchen pantry, the empty shelves broadcasting her complete lack of interest and knowledge of food. She'd joked about eating out of cans, and the image had stuck with him. So she was in training, picking up everything she could about Remetjy food and French food and Italian food and Chinese food. Good Lord, no wonder so many people were obese.

Take this w'ab priest she was interviewing. Her powerful investigative mind and perceptions discovered right away that his main concern was the temple-provided snack tray placed on the table. Most of those snacks would contribute to another five pounds of jiggling flesh to join the 220 pounds already there. He had round cheeks, a round chin, a round face, a round neck, and round everything else that wasn't obscured by his voluminous priest's robes. She looked at the open page of her notebook: the Honorable W'ab of Bastet Tjay.

"Now then, Tjay," she started with a standard medja interview line. "Why don't you tell me what you saw and when you saw it."

The w'ab chewed and swallowed a small pastry shaped like a bird, the sugar coating crackling as he chewed. "It was awful, Hutyt. I got to work at the usual time, ready to open the offering hall and set up the offering tables for the morning rituals, and there they were. Two of our w'abu, right in the middle of the hall. Blood all over the floor. Made me want to throw up." He licked his lips and searched over the tray for some special pastry he had in mind. He found it and raised it to his lips.

"But you didn't throw up."

"Why, no. I suppose I have a strong stomach," he said, then ate the pastry. Crunch crunch crunch. The fake fur belt across his midriff rippled with pleasure, though that may have been MacIntyre's fanciful interpretation of the movement.

"And what did you do then, Tjay?"

"Why, called the Hem-Netjer. Hem-Netjer of Bastet Paneb," he hastened to specify as she opened her mouth to ask. She wrote down the title and name.

"But not the medjau," she said.

"Why, no," he responded. "It's a religious crime, killing someone in the offering hall." He shuddered. "The only thing worse would be to kill someone in the sanctuary, defiling the god. Bastet is not forgiving of desecrations, hutyt. Not at all forgiving."

Hutyt-er-semetyu MacIntyre had never been given a case in a temple, so much of this process was new to her. Idnu Djehutymes, her boss, had brought her up to speed the previous day.

"I'd come with you the first time, MacIntyre, but you can handle it. Remember, they stand on their dignity most of the time, and they guard their religious privileges as though their lives depended on it. They have primary jurisdiction for investigation of this. We're only involved in case it extends beyond the temple precincts. Just get the facts and report back. Right?" the Idnu had smiled and sent her on her way.

Right. Too bad the w'ab priests had already cleaned up all the desecrating blood and wiped the statue used to beat the two w'abu to death. Too bad they'd cleaned every single surface in the room to purify it for the cat goddess. Too bad the religious superiors here had already questioned every witness and told them what they could and could not say to the civil authorities who must be called in. This assiduity may or may not have thrilled Bastet, but MacIntyre found it aggravating.

She had at least inspected the bodies in the Temple of Hut-Her-Sekhmet morgue. Not much there, two dead bald guys with crushed skulls. Not pretty and not informative. The examining hem-netjer had informed her that his best estimate was that someone hit them forcefully with something hard. But the temple had cleaned the wounds in a purifying ritual before he got them. She had been firm enough with the examiner to extract a time of death, at least: about an hour before Tjay showed up and found them. The body temperatures were consistent with the w'ab's description of the stickiness of the blood pools. So all this had happened the morning of Shesmu's big award party. She was now picking up the tiny pieces left unwashed.

"Tjay, who else was in the temple at the time you came in?"

"It was early, not too many people about. I thought I saw a woman in the chapel praying as I went by, but nobody else."

"And you didn't know the woman?"

"I didn't see her all that well, just the impression of a dress and long black hair. It's quite dark in the chapel in the mornings." He selected another pastry. Crunch crunch crunch. "I called the Hem-Netjer at home, and he came in."

"Did you know the two w'abu at all?"

"Quite well. We worked together every day. They dealt with temple finance, collecting the offering money and so on."

"Did they usually come in so early?"

"No."

"Any idea why they were here?"

"No."

"Any reason you know of for anybody to kill them?"

"No; the most inoffensive men. Not an enemy in the world that I know of."

"Anything stolen?"

"Why, no, Hutyt. Who would dare?"

MacIntyre nodded, straining not to roll her eyes. Who indeed? She changed direction. "Other than the worshipper, there was nobody else in the temple?"

"Only the w'abu, and they were dead. But it's a big building, and it's not a secure facility. No guards or anything." He smirked. "Bastet herself takes care of security."

A guard cat. This was going to be a hard case to crack.

"Any CCTV?"

"What's that?"

"Never mind," said the exasperated MacIntyre. Security was not a priority at the Temple of Bastet. "Perhaps I should speak with the Hem-Netjer," she said.

Tjay levered himself up. "I'll fetch him at once. You're sure...?" He indicated the tray of goodies.

"No, thanks."

He picked up the tray and left the room. The room seemed larger for his absence.

Hem-Netjer of Bastet Paneb, unlike his subordinate, Tjay, was fully in control of everything. He said so. Twice. Before MacIntyre said anything at all. He was as skinny as a rail and as forceful as a locomotive that ran on one. Faced with such unbending authority, she used flattery and servility to get her way.

"Thank you so much for seeing me, Lord Paneb. This is my first visit to your temple, and it's a pleasure to have someone as authoritative as you to show me what I need to learn."

The hem-netjer smiled and nodded. "It is *my* pleasure and indeed my duty to do so, Hutyt MacIntyre." He looked her up and down. "You are European?"

"American, my lord, but transplanted here and now a Ta'an-Imenty Republic citizen."

"And a w'abet of Ma'at, I perceive." The feather on her right breast told him that.

"Yes, my lord, a conscientious one."

"And do you worship other gods?"

"I do, my lord, but I have not had the honor of worshipping the lady Bastet, I fear." Satisfying the goddess Ma'at took up all her time, that and sex. And now, food. Mustn't forget food. Shesmu wouldn't approve of forgetting food.

"Ah. Well, I shall explain things as I go as to a child. Will that do?"

"Certainly, my lord." God, how she would love to rip off his arm and beat him to death with it. But that wouldn't get her job done. "Perhaps you could start with the murders, my lord. The process for determining who the murderer is."

"A fine example, Hutyt. The identity of the murderer is, to us, less important than securing the sanctity and veneration of Bastet. The moment of my summoning by my subordinate, I understood that our first priority required the immediate cleaning of the offering room to get it open for service."

"You don't consider preserving the evidence at the crime scene as useful, then?"

The hem-netjer smiled a superior smile. "The religious crime of desecration of the goddess through killing in her precincts requires immediate religious rectification. Consequent justice applied to the miscreant must take a back seat to that."

"I see. Well, could you tell me how you intend to pursue your inquiry into that aspect of the offense?" MacIntyre tried deep breathing to control the surging resentment she felt, the resentment of a goddess who regarded justice as paramount. Which was to say, MacIntyre was pissed and didn't want to show it. The deep breathing slowed the anger and increased the oxygen to her brain, honing her wits to a knife's edge. Another fanciful metaphor wasted, as Paneb simply made her madder.

"I will turn to the goddess, of course, as any oracle must. Bastet's eyes see in the darkness of evil and pierce it to reveal her desires."

MacIntyre noted that "desires" did not necessarily equate to "truth," and that Paneb was careful in his choice of words, especially relating to the goddess.

"Will you question the priests of the temple or others that might have had a reason—"

"Should the goddess will it, Hutyt, and only then."

"I see. My superiors would beg you, my lord, to inform us should you find any way we might help the goddess in her search for—"

"That, too, awaits my interview with the goddess. Bastet knows her obligation to Ma'at, her aunt. Please be secure in the knowledge that Bastet's rage will fall upon the miscreant. There is no need for the civil authorities or the courts of Ma'at to involve themselves any further in the matter."

"Quite so, my lord, quite so. I will so inform my superiors." In very graphic terms, I will. What a disaster of a case. MacIntyre had seen every kind of corruption there was back in America, courtesy of her father and his lawyer friends. And she'd seen every kind of corruption in city government through her medjat work in Menmenet. Turning things over to a statue was new to her, and not welcome. But she had seen the stone wall of Bastet and didn't want to smash her nose against it, so she bid some toadying goodbyes to the hem-netjer and left.

CHAPTER THREE
Shesmu Comes Up Empty

MacIntyre had planned a day off for us for weeks, and today should have been the day. Then her boss assigned her to a murder at the Temple of Bastet, and she had to work. So, instead of a pleasant, relaxing day going somewhere with my girlfriend, I found myself at loose ends. I'd given my sous chef Qenna the reins at the Per'ankh for the day, and I couldn't take that joy away from him by showing up without warning.

I needed to pick up my award check at the R'ames Society. It would be a good opportunity to get familiar with the tasks required of a celebrity spokesman and with the people who managed those tasks. The Society's offices were at Dje-hutymes and Neferhetepu streets, in the heart of the shopping district, quite close to the Per'ankh, only two blocks away. The Society occupied an old palace that survived the Great Earthquake in 1906. Its grand facade was right out of Kemet: papyrus-shaped pillars supporting a two-story building with a well-landscaped interior courtyard that could hold 200 people for events.

The huge bronze doors between the pillars stood wide open. I walked in through the people standing and talking in small groups in the great columned hall framed by two stone stairways to the upper floors. By the stairway to the right, there was a sign: "Guests please register in the Main Office, second floor." I walked up the broad granite stairway and found myself in the Main Office. The receptionist sat at the reception desk, hands folded, with a glum look on her young face. She raised a wan smile for me.

"Hello," I said. "I'm Shesmu za-Akhen. I won the Best New Chef award last night, and I'm here to pick up my check."

"Oh." Her face did not give me confidence. "I'm afraid…."

I smiled. "Where is the finance office? I'll say hello to Sennedjem, too, while I'm there." I'll use whatever in I needed to get my money, which would solve a major refrigeration problem at the Per'ankh.

"Well, the office is down the hall, two doors on the right. But—"

"Thanks for your help." I dodged past her down the hall as she raised a hand in protest, but she didn't come after me.

The financial office had a lot more desks but not a lot more noise. A middle-aged Remetj man with reading glasses occupied one desk. An older woman stood next to the desk, looking worried. The man had all the drawers open and all the papers from the drawers heaped on the desk. He laid one paper down on a stack and took up another from a different stack. The man raised his eyes above his glasses and looked at me.

"I've come about a check," I said. "I'm Shesmu za-Akhen from the Per'ankh."

"How nice for you. You'll wait your turn with the rest of them. Downstairs." He pointed to the floor with his finger.

"I'm looking for Sennedjem."

"So am I. Again, you'll wait your turn. Downstairs, please."

I inspected him a little more closely. Sparse, graying hair; thick lips; a dark complexion with signs of not spending a lot of time outdoors; a twist to the mouth and eyes that told me he had a sense of humor. His body language was relaxed and unconcerned. His eyes met mine. Too much authority for just another Society volunteer. The man could be the Society's accountant, but those eyes weren't the eyes of a financial professional; they were the shark's eyes of a hunter. A hunter with a sense of humor. But humor wasn't on the top of his mind.

I asked, "Medja?"

He replied, "None of your business. Look, I don't have time for this."

Medja, definitely. Either somebody had died or there was something illegal going on at the R'ames Society.

"I might help," I said, thinking about Taneferet and her distress over Sennedjem.

The medja looked at the finance woman and asked her, "Do you know this honored individual?"

"Yes, he's an award-winning chef this year. We owe him an award check...." she trailed off with uncertainty in her voice.

I repeated, "I've come about the check. But I can tell you what I know about Sennedjem, if that will help."

"All right, let's go in the office for a chat, then." He took off his reading glasses and put them on the desk. He motioned for another man to watch the desk and its paper treasure trove, then showed me to a door in the back wall and led the way.

The luxurious carpets and overstuffed furniture suggested that this might be Sennedjem's private office. The medja led the way over to a pair of chairs near the courtyard window.

"First, may I see some identification?" I asked.

"You first."

I gave him my card and showed him my sepat ID card.

In return, he pulled out a small leather fold and flipped it open to reveal a badge and ID card. He held it up so that I could read it; it identified him as Rudj Baki of the Henet Baket Sepat. That was the sepat agency that handled taxes and other state revenue operations. It was a question of taxes, not death.

"Now," he said. "What's your story?"

"As the lady said, I won an award that came with a check. You've heard of my restaurant? The Per'ankh?"

"I don't get out much," he said. "And I live in the Valley. I want your information about Sennedjem, not a restaurant review."

I told him the tale of our intervention into Sennedjem's social life the night before, including Taneferet's concern and Nesimen's weak response to it. The eyes warmed a little as I described the fight, but he homed in on the main questions.

"Do you have any idea where Sennedjem is?"

"No."

"Do you have any insights into the finances of the R'ames Society?"

"No."

"Do you have any information about the Society other than what you've told me?"

"No."

"I sense a pattern." He smiled his most friendly smile.

"Have you spoken with Nesimen? Just what is the problem you're investigating?"

"That's none of your business."

"Nesimen's wife expressed a great deal of concern about Sennedjem last night. Nesimen waffled on his response, but if Sennedjem is the subject of your investigation, I'd like to help."

"I think at this point there's not a lot you can do for me. I appreciate your interest, but you need to leave this to us. Thanks for your information." He rose and guided me out the office door, his hand firm on my elbow. He pointed at the outer door, then down.

"What about my check?"

"You can file a claim form with the other creditors. But for now—" The finger pointed resolutely down.

"I know," I said. "Downstairs."

Creditors—and the Henet Baket involved—surely showed trouble with the Society's finances. I'd have to speak with Nesimen to find out more. It was time to locate Nesimen to find out what was going on.

I walked out into the reception area and up to the reception desk.

"Dark days, I'm afraid," I said, smiling. "No check. But can you tell me where to find Nesimen's office? He asked me to come see him today."

"Sorry about the check, lord. Erm…let me call over to his office and tell him you're here."

The woman busied herself with dialing and murmuring into her headset. Her eyes turned back to me, and she said, "Nesimen just arrived and wants to see you, Lord Shesmu. His office is down the stairs, across the hall, up the opposite stairs, and all the way in the back. Do you think you can find your way, or…." She looked undecided about showing me the way herself.

"Yes, I'll be fine, thanks. And cheer up, tomorrow will be better." She smiled, but her eyes told me she didn't believe it.

I got my exercise for the day on the two stairways, finally arriving in the opposite hall. It was silent as a tomb. I diagnosed heavy sound-proofing; if Baki's presence meant bad things for the Society's finances, bombs must be going off in these executive offices. I padded down the thick carpeting to the last door in the hallway.

I entered the plush outer office and saw through an open door an even plusher inner one. Nesimen stood in the doorway speaking to a carefully dressed and groomed Remetj sitting at a desk in the outer office. As I walked in, they both jerked around to look at me. Nesimen's hands came up in a defensive motion, while the other man's face was blank. Neimen recognized me and smiled, dropping his hands, but the other man rose and walked toward me, saying, "No statements. Please wait downstairs until we're ready for the press."

"I'm not the press," I said, gesturing at Nesimen.

He said, "No, this is Shesmu, the Best New Chef."

"I came for my check, as you suggested, Nesimen. But things seem to have developed."

His shoulders slumped and his voice sounded tired. "I can't understand what's happened. It's too much...."

The executive assistant gave me a long, cool look and walked back to his desk. He sat and stared at Nesimen.

I asked, "Can we speak in your office?"

He turned and walked into his office, and I followed. The assistant answered a softly ringing phone as I shut the door. I sat in a comfortable armchair across from a sofa, where Nesimen sat himself down, slumping with a pained expression.

"Can you fill me in on what's happened, Nesimen?" I asked. "The Henet Baket wasn't forthcoming."

"You talked with...?" He left the question unfinished, horror in his eyes.

"Yep, when I went for the check. No check. So, where's the money?"

"I don't know."

"You should know."

"I mean—it's all gone. All gone."

I spoke sharply to wake him up. "Nesimen. Snap out of it and tell me what's happened."

His head jerked up as he realized how far he'd slipped. He marshaled his defenses and said, "Don't talk to me like that."

"Sorry. But you needed it." And he did. The response of the head of an organization to a theft ought to be strong, and yet here was Nesimen, dissolving into a puddle of despair.

He sighed. "I suppose you are family, in a way. Yes, I guess I needed it. But, Shesmu...the shame of it all."

"Of what all? Tell me."

"Sennedjem, he's disappeared. Gone. Worse, so is all the money in our bank account."

"Your personal account?" Khenemset Neferet filled my horrified mind.

"No, no, of course not. The Society's account. That Sennedjem managed."

"I guess he managed it, all right."

"Yes. The shame." He shook his head, despairing.

A knock sounded on the door.

"Yes?" said Nesimen.

The door opened and the executive assistant stuck in his head. "My lord, the Board has called a special meeting tomorrow afternoon and wants you there to explain what's happened."

Nesimen stood up from the sofa as though electrified.

"The Board! How can I explain…justify…I know nothing…it's all gone! And I'll have to explain it to them."

The executive assistant ducked out, then came back into the office carrying a glass of amber liquid. Nesimen grabbed it with both hands and drank it down, then started coughing. I hoped I would not need to use my limited knowledge of air pathway clearing. I could smell the familiar aroma of good French cognac. A bracer.

The coughing fit passed, and the potent alcohol restored Nesimen to at least partial sentience.

I asked, "Can I help? Is there anything I can do?" I owed Khenemset Neferet all the help I could give her husband, however hapless he might be.

He stared at me as though I was a perfect stranger, then his eyes sharpened. "Yes, yes! The board…if you could—"

My phone rang. Qenna, calling from the restaurant. Qenna wouldn't call unless it was a dire emergency. "Hold on, Nesimen, I need to take this call."

"Shes? Where are you?" The stress level in Qenna's voice was way beyond anything I'd ever heard. The sounds I heard in the background of his call were not kitchen sounds, they were street sounds, men shouting, rumbling noises.

"Qenna, what's up? What's wrong?"

"Shes, you need to get back here! We've evacuated the restaurant!"

I spoke slowly to calm him down. "Qenna, slow down and tell me what's wrong." I was getting practiced at asking that question today.

"Shes, it's serious. Somebody called and said there was a bomb."

Nice. "Did you call the medjau?"

"Certainly I called the medjau, and the firemen too, then you. After I cleared the place."

"I'm at the R'ames Society. I can be there in five minutes. What do I need to know?"

"Inpu spits, how should I know what you need to know?" It had rattled him, Qenna never swore.

"All right. I'll be there right away. Keep your eye on things." As if he wouldn't. My heart screamed at me to get a move on.

I told Nesimen, "Got to go, problem at my restaurant. Let me know about the board meeting, all right?"

He nodded, and I hurried away to rescue my restaurant.

CHAPTER FOUR
MacIntyre Finds a Stray Cat

AFTER MACINTYRE FINISHED HER UNPRODUCTIVE interviews at the temple, she called her best friend Henutsenu. Henutsenu was the sexiest woman MacIntyre knew, and the attraction was mutual, but they both had their boyfriends to think of. Just friends, for now. But Henutsenu had one other quality that MacIntyre wanted to explore: she worshipped Bastet. Her friend picked up, and they exchanged warm greetings.

"Want to have lunch?" asked MacIntyre. "I'm suddenly free today."

Her friend laughed. "It will be so exciting to see you, Cheryl! I haven't seen you since last night! Yes, if we do it here at the Neferti, I'm on duty part of the day—sick employee." Henutsenu managed the Neferti restaurant for Shesmu, who owned both it and his main restaurant, the Per'ankh. But she occasionally filled in at her old job as hostess.

"That will be fine. Comped?" MacIntyre couldn't afford the Neferti prices on her salary, but as her boyfriend was owner along with Sebek, the chef…it was all in the family.

"Of course, standing orders of the owner." MacIntyre heard the smile in her friend's voice.

"Every time I come here the food's different," complained MacIntyre as she faced up to Sebek's special of the day. "I just get used to something and whish, something new is in front of me."

"You poor, suffering girl," commiserated Henutsenu, tasting her Green Sea Bream with green tomato and chile sauce.

"Fortunately, it's all edible, thanks to your boyfriend," said MacIntyre. The chef, Sebek, had brought the dishes out himself, causing a small stir among the VIPs sitting in the window seats.

"He's mastered the fish," commented Henutsenu. "Perfect."

"You approach each dish like I approach a corpse," noted MacIntyre, tasting her Roast Breast of Chicken with Forest Mushrooms.

"Eww."

"I was talking earlier with a w'ab who said he had a strong stomach; given the size of it, I wasn't that surprised."

"Your latest case?"

MacIntyre looked at her friend in a judging way. It was OK to tell her. "The Temple of Bastet. Two murdered w'abu in the offering hall."

Henutsenu put down her fork and knife and looked a little ill. Bad judgment on MacIntyre's part, or maybe it was the corpse remark. MacIntyre kicked herself and swore to do better.

"Let's talk about something else, like sex."

"No, sorry, it's just…I worship there, you know. Two w'abu? Who were they?"

MacIntyre gave her the names, and Henutsenu shed a few tears. "I knew them both, gentle men. Who would want to kill them?"

"The w'ab I was questioning, Tjay—"

"Oh, Tjay—he's the one with the stomach!"

MacIntyre grinned. "Yep. So, he said the same as you, no one. It was agony for me to question him and Hem-Netjer Paneb. They both regarded the murders as a religious offense against the goddess. They cleaned away all the crime scene evidence, and they won't let us investigate."

Henutsenu nodded. "I sympathize, I suppose, but you must understand. Bastet is not a forgiving goddess. She rages and tears at evildoers and those who desecrate her temples. The priests keep things very regular and clean at all times. So you have no hope of catching whoever did it?"

"Technically, I'm not investigating. The Temple is. But if I were investigating, it would be hopeless, yes. Tjay did mention one lead I would follow up. He said he saw a woman worshipping in the chapel as he walked by, just before discovering the bodies. He—what's wrong?"

Henutsenu had again put down her knife and fork, but this time she covered her mouth with both hands and her eyes grew large. "Cheryl—that was me! I was there worshipping early this morning, trying to clear the things that happened last night from my mind. The chapel is right down the main passage from the offering hall!"

"You—" MacIntyre's thoughts crashed around inside her head.

Henutsenu reached out and gripped MacIntyre's hand. The two women looked at each other in silence.

Henutsenu said, "I suppose I'd better go to the temple and tell them. Or should I go to the medjau? It's so confusing!"

The crashing trains of thought got back on their tracks in MacIntyre's brain. She could clearly visualize the train wreck. She couldn't let it happen.

"Henutsenu, you should keep quiet for now. Let me poke around a bit, figure out what's what. When I'm sure I understand what's going on, we can talk about it and decide what to do."

"But—"

"No; the situation is crazy! I don't want you involved until I understand what's going on. Please?" She gripped her friend's hand more tightly.

Her friend's face took on a determined look. "I'm not naïve, Cheryl, but I did nothing wrong, and Bastet knows that. The goddess would never let harm come to one of her worshippers unjustly."

"She let a lot of harm come to her w'ab priests! Henutsenu, the gods can only do so much against the evil men do." MacIntyre didn't believe in the gods. She did believe in evil. She had a lot of experience with evil, and she was sure she would do a better job of protecting her friend from it than the goddess Bastet.

"Promise me," she said.

Henutsenu let the emotional argument overwhelm her religious fervor. "All right, Cheryl. But if you don't come up with anything soon, I'll need to talk to the hem-netjer."

"Give me some time, a few days. All right?"

"All right, but I can't wait long, Cheryl."

MacIntyre shook her brain back into working order. "Did you see anyone, hear anything unusual at the temple this morning?"

"Let me think back. I walked straight to the chapel. No one was around, no one in the chapel. I prayed to Bastet, then left. The offering hall is a little further along the passage from the chapel, so I didn't see what was in it. I heard nothing." A thought washed over her face. "Those poor men were lying there dead the whole time. Bastet must have been furious. And yet she let me pray on about my own little problems, regardless. She is a kind goddess."

When she's not raging and avenging her priests. Religion is not rational. MacIntyre asked Henutsenu some questions designed to make her remember anything she saw or heard, but her friend appeared to have been oblivious to anything beyond her own prayers.

"There must have been someone there before you. Anything, any object, out of place, or unusual?"

"Not that I can remember."

MacIntyre sighed. "Not much to go on, but I'll have to work with it. You were my only lead!" She gave her friend a wry smile. "All right, I'm through with the questions."

"Now, finish your chicken. I have to work!" Henutsenu gave MacIntyre's hand a final squeeze and resumed eating her fish.

CHAPTER FIVE
Shesmu Gets Bombed

THE UNIFORMED MEDJA WEARING BODY armor and holding an assault weapon pushed it at me to bring me to a halt. "Whoa, whoa! Sorry, lord, street's closed, you'll have to move on." Beyond him, the clusters of Per'ankh employees and medjau faced the restaurant. A large, red fire extinguisher propped open the front door.

I said, gasping from my run from the R'ames Society, "I'm the owner of the restaurant, my sous-chef called me."

"Identification?"

I extracted a business card and my driver's license. The medja inspected them, both sides, and gave them back to me, and stepped back. I asked, "Who should I talk to? Who's in charge?" He pointed to another medja in full uniform, talking into a phone.

I walked over to him. He finished his call and turned to me. I said, "I'm Shesmu za-Akhen, I'm the owner."

"Ah, good. Imy-er-medjau Menna," he said, and the world collapsed on me without warning. The next thing I remember is opening my eyes and looking up at the sky. I lay on my back on the street, and I couldn't hear anything but a loud ringing.

I rolled over and levered myself up to my knees and took stock. Nothing felt broken, but I hurt all over. I saw various people in various states, flat out, or on their feet and helping others. My eyes focused beyond the people to what remained of the Per'ankh. The door had disappeared, along with the fire extinguisher, most of the windows, and a good deal of the facade.

Menna picked himself up off the pavement much as I had, shaking his head, a scrape across his broad cheek. His uniform cap lay on the ground several feet away. He walked over and picked it up and stared at it for a minute, then put it on, slowly. He turned and looked at the restaurant, then at me, still kneeling. We stared at each other for several seconds. He walked over, offered me a hand, and pulled me to my feet.

His mouth moved, and I heard, as from far off, a thin voice saying, "Are you hurt? Anything broken? Do you need medical help?" I said no, then said, loudly, "I can't hear anything!" He touched his own ear and nodded. He turned away and walked toward a group of medjau in uniform and started issuing commands. Qenna stood across the street gesticulating to a group of white-clad restaurant workers. Through the ruined facade of my restaurant, there came the flickering light of flame. Firemen rushed into the Per'ankh to save the building. That wouldn't take much time, but I could see that the ensuing investigation and its consequences would occupy me for months.

CHAPTER SIX
MacIntyre Takes Charge

MACINTYRE TOOK A CALL FROM her boss as she stood outside the Neferti after her lunch with Henutsenu. She tore her mind off her friend's troubles to deal with Djehutymes.

"Hi, Mes. Just finished lunch, getting cracking—"

"Shut up, MacIntyre."

"Right."

"Get over to your boyfriend's restaurant."

"Which restaurant? He's got two."

"The fancy French one."

"What's up?"

"The whole place."

"Sorry?"

"Bomb went off. Blew the whole place to pieces."

MacIntyre mouth opened and nothing came out. Her heart was not in her boots, it had exited to the street and was trying to dive into the bay. Finally, she found her tongue enough to ask, "And…Shes?"

"Don't know, but I think he's OK. Go and check it out. See the super, Imy-er-Medjau Menna. Tell him I sent you. See if anybody's dead." He hung up.

MacIntyre ran for her car. The next few hours flew by. MacIntyre found Shesmu between insurance and newspaper interviews, sitting on the curb just staring at the ruins. He looked up at her with a dazed expression, then his face lit up and he moved to get up, but she sat down next to him and enfolded him in her arms. The badge pinned to her blouse pressed against his cheek, and he shifted to a softer position. She let go and wiped dirt and blood off his face.

She asked, "Was there any call before the blast? Menna said two people went to the hospital, no one dead so far."

"What?"

She repeated the question more loudly to break through the ringing bells in his ears and the cotton fluff in his brain.

"Qenna said he'd gotten a call." He waved a dispirited hand.

She stood up and looked around, found Qenna standing with a group of cooks from the restaurant, and walked over to him.

"Qenna," she greeted him.

"Cheryl." They were on a first-name basis because she was one of the people who ate free in his restaurant. He never seemed very happy about it when she did.

"I'm collecting information about what happened, helping out," she said.

"And?"

"Shes said you got a call before the bombing."

"Yes, fortunately in good time to get everybody out." He regarded his demolished domain with a sour expression.

"Can you tell me exactly what the caller said?"

"Exactly, burned into my heart. 'There's a bomb going off in a few minutes, get everyone out or they're dead. Tell Shesmu to cough it up.'" I have no idea what 'it' is, but Shes needs to deal with 'it.' Now." His voice dripped with all kinds of negative emotions: blame, worry, anger, urgency. A very expressive voice. "The caller spoke Renkemet with some kind of foreign accent, I don't know what kind."

"Thanks, that's very helpful. Have you told the imy-er-medjau?"

"I have told every single person I could find who I thought might want to do something about it. Now I've told you. Are you going to do something about it?"

"Right away. But I don't think I'll be having dinner with you tonight," she joked, trying to cheer the angry man up.

Qenna just shook his head and stared at the ruins. No sense of humor.

She walked back to Shes and filled him in, repeating everything in louder and louder tones until she got tired of it.

Shes said, "What the hell did they mean by 'it'? The only thing I cough up is bomb dust." Shes's phone rang, and he didn't notice. MacIntyre pointed at the phone, and he looked at it and answered.

"Sebek, thanks for calling, but I can't really hear and I'll talk to you later. I'm in the middle of things here. The bombers said this was a warning, I need to work on this."

He listened, pressing the phone hard against his ear.

"I'll take you up on that, the restaurant is going to need a lot of help and work, but not today."

MacIntyre, looking at the ruins, knew that no cook would set foot in that restaurant for months.

"Let me talk to him," she said.

"What?"

"Gimme!" She neatly grabbed the phone out of his hand.

"Sebek? Cheryl. You've heard about the Per'ankh? Good. Listen, we're into something we don't understand, and bombs are going off. It's not out of the question that the bomber would go after other parts of Shes's life," she said, looking at her boyfriend, "I think you ought to close the Neferti, or at least post a couple of guards trained in counter-terror methods."

With some shouting and prodding, Shes finally understood and nodded. It was obvious: he couldn't afford to lose both restaurants and his best friend.

She continued, "Shes agrees. Here's a number to call, these guys are really good at stopping these kinds of things from happening." She read off a number from her own phone. "Call them now, Sebek, don't wait. Give them my name. I'd even close the place for a day until you get protection in place." The number was for an Aztec crime lord of her acquaintance; he was very good at protection. His services came with various kinds of prices but were usually worth the cost.

"Give me that thing." Shesmu snatched the phone. "Sebek? Me again. Look, get the guards, I'll cover it somehow. But closing the place.... I don't know if we can afford to do that. What do you think?" He listened to Sebek. "Say that again. Well, if it's a warning, I'm hoping they think the big one is enough. Will you stick? Good. I've got a bunch of temporarily unemployed cooks standing right in front of me. I'll send them over." He hung up, then went over to talk with Qenna. MacIntyre trailed along after him.

"Listen, I thought it would be a good idea to get the staff back to work. The Per'ankh is going to be out of commission for at least a few days. How about taking the crew, those that want to go, to the Neferti?"

Qenna's eyes changed from angry to thoughtful. "I could take the opportunity to cross train them, get them out of their usual way of doing things."

"What?"

"OK," shouted the sous chef.

"Good, Sebek will appreciate the help."

Qenna looked at the ruins and pursed his lips. "A few days? Months." MacIntyre agreed; Qenna was a realist.

"The insurance will help."

He looked at Shes, smiling a very small smile. He asked, loudly, "And you're going to be supervising every detail?" He was ironic.

"No, I don't think so. You can do that. I'm going to be finding out why somebody wants to bomb us and how to make them stop."

"With Cheryl helping, I hope." His eyes left Shes and went to MacIntyre. She revised her opinion of him upward.

"Well, she'll be working on it. Helping is a strong word."

MacIntyre kicked him lightly on the ankle, then said, "Let's go talk to the imy-er-medjau."

"What?"

Swallowing a word that wouldn't help, MacIntyre grabbed Shes's arm and pulled, and he and Qenna followed her over to where Menna stood supervising the investigation.

Menna said, "We should have some results by tomorrow, but it looks like the bomb went off in a little room toward the front." He spoke loudly, having as much of a hearing problem as Shesmu, who appeared to make out his words.

"The coat check room," Qenna said.

"Likely." Menna nodded.

"Any deaths so far?" asked MacIntyre, mindful of her boss's main concern.

"Two hospitalizations in serious condition, no deaths," said Menna.

"I hope their lunch had salmonella in it," said Shes. Qenna rolled his eyes; he didn't like food poisoning humor. MacIntyre smiled, but the imy-er-medjau didn't. He didn't look like he smiled much, if at all, and he probably didn't like bomb humor. Every profession has its quirks.

CHAPTER SEVEN
Shesmu Makes a New Friend

THE PREPOSTEROUS EVENTS THAT ACCUMULATED in my life wouldn't let me alone. MacIntyre helped, but my sleep was not restful. The top of my list was my emotional reaction to losing my restaurant: joy.

I'm not a contemplative person, but that one called for it. Working my body was where I did my best thinking, made up my best recipes, resolved my thorniest business decisions. I couldn't work it out in the restaurant anymore, so I had to find another way to solve the puzzle of why I felt joy looking at a bombed-out ruin. I hadn't raised these emotions with MacIntyre, as intimate as we were, because I wanted to look it over first.

The stick-fighting club? No, I'd just visited two days before. I added up the days since I'd last picked up my bow: a month.

I opened the locked cabinet in the garage that held my equipment and took out the acacia-wood recurve bow. The past attracted me today more than the more accurate, high-tech present: the fiberglass compound marvel with its cams, weights, and sighting doodads.

The acacia bow was all I had left of my father. He'd handed it to me on my fifth birthday, then he was gone, vanished, leaving my mother and me to grieve and wonder. Then my mother died, five years later, and only the bow remained. When I first held it, I couldn't even pull the string back. But I kept at it, and by my teen years I was a respectable sport archer representing my school, though not with the acacia bow. I kept that bow in good shape over the years, my way of remembering my absent parents.

I put the bow into a case that already held ten arrows, ten for the ten fingers on the mummified hands of Wesir, Lord of the Dead. The bow was a thing of the past, but I didn't go that far with the arrows, which were made of aluminum, god-fingers or no. Wooden arrows warped far too easily and flew off in unexpected directions with the least change in humidity. Aluminum didn't warp, and it didn't break when you missed the target, though that didn't happen very often these days.

The trouble with archery as a sport is that it's difficult to find a place to do it. Bows are old technology, and there are many more gun ranges than archery ranges. During a brief fad about twenty years ago, the city had created a public archery range in one of the few municipal parks. Most parks were temple parks, open only to worshippers of the temple's god. The Didiresy Open Space allowed in anyone. Over the years, the archery range degraded, but the city still replaced the targets. What they didn't do was eradicate the rodents that dug beautiful underground palaces below the field. You took your life in your hands walking to the targets; you had to watch where you put your feet.

Aside from stray rodents, I was alone on the field for most of my practice session. Endurance training is simple: you stand and fire arrows at the target for as long as you can pull the bow back. Well, not that simple; you also have to keep your form correct and integrate all the other aspects of aiming, releasing, and follow-through so you don't pick up bad habits.

Once I got into the rhythm, I let my mind range over my problem: why joy? Why not sorrow, anger, pain, or any of the other destructive results of loss that might have afflicted me? Pull, release. Adjust. Pull, release. Adjust. Joy?

I let my mind stray to my history with the Per'ankh. Nekhen, its founding chef, took me on as an apprentice. I moved up to sous chef when I left to start my own place, the Neferti. Then Neferaset happened. Neferaset was Nekhen's beautiful young wife. She was also my lover. I betrayed my mentor and friend with her all the way to his murder last year. That pain and joy was over, and it ended badly for Neferaset. She had to leave Menmenet under a cloud, but I managed to buy the Per'ankh with financing from Hernefer. I had things to prove, to myself and to others. I proved them when the R'ames Society awarded me the Best New Chef award. That award made me happy! Why would the destruction of the restaurant that made the award possible make me joyful? And now the Henuttawy Group had validated everything by investing even more debenu in me.

Contemplation is a fine thing when it works. But the best thinking in the world can't make sense of an irrational feeling. I finished the latest flight of ten, then took a break to let my arms relax. I was stretching them out, pulling one way and then the other, when an old, blue Ford with the finish peeling off pulled up beside the field. A man emerged from the car and walked over to me.

"How's the field?" he asked. His Renkemet was good but subtly accented.

"Watch your toes. The gophers are biting today."

As always, the man's stoney face expressed nothing. I'd seen this man on the field, on and off, for ten years, and we had the same short conversation every time we met. He'd never introduced himself, and he'd asked no questions about anything but my acacia bow, which fascinated him. His own bow was a modern compound bow, a hunting bow, and I assumed he was a hunter practicing for his next outing. His face was local, the local that goes way back: Ramaytush or Miwuk most likely. From the speed and impact of his arrows, his bow was powerful; he probably hunted bear and elk up in the mountains. He could hunt elephants with that bow, had there been any elephants up there.

The man looked at the ten arrows in my target and asked, "Target not cooperating?"

"My heart isn't in it today."

He said, "You're running with the wrong crowd, Shesmu. It shows."

I didn't know who this man was, didn't know his name, and he shouldn't know mine.

"I'm sure you're right," I said, "but I'd like to know how that's your business?"

He pointed at his car. "Let's talk. Cold."

My new pal unlocked his car in two steps: buttons on his phone followed by unlocking the passenger door for me manually once he'd seated himself. It surprised me only in that his car looked as though it was older than locks.

The door creaked as I opened it. I had to push aside plastic bags and empty coffee containers to sit. The seat was a bench seat; this car was *old*. He'd retrofitted it with fancy security. I saw a GPS device stuck to the dashboard. Papers, electronic equipment, and clothes rose in piles on the back seat. I deduced he didn't live in his car; there wasn't room unless he slept in the trunk, and the smell wasn't right. The car was warm from use and its heater. I waited. He settled himself behind the steering wheel.

After a minute of silence, I asked, "What's this about?"

He reached into his pocket and took out a small leather folder, opened it, and showed it to me. Another medja. An unusual one, though; he was a member of a force I'd never heard of—the SecInterPol. His name was Karkin, a Ramaytush name. The identity card gave his authority in English, French, Russian, and Renkemet, but not Ramaytush.

"International security police," he said. He clarified this with "Genève. HQ."

I said, "SecInterPol. International. No local jurisdiction?"

"True. Behind the scenes, watch things in Menmenet."

"I've never heard of SecInterPol."

"We prefer that."

"So I'll ask again, what's this all about?"

He paused. His hands rested in his lap, motionless. The odor of the car became more annoying. I waited.

He stirred, rubbed his nose, and said, "R'ames Society. Sennedjem. Money. Things like that."

"Money?"

"Money. Lots. How much do you know about Sennedjem?"

"Pretty much everything the medjau know."

"Your girlfriend. So, not much."

Depressingly correct. I stared at him. How did he know about my girlfriend?

He said, "Other people know more. That's important."

"What other people? Do I need to drag this out of you?"

"Bombing. All connected."

"Connected how?" I asked, and my phone buzzed. I looked at the display; MacIntyre. "I'd better take this. It's my girlfriend."

His eyes never left mine. I answered the call. MacIntyre sounded tired.

"Hi, Shes. Checking in, taking a break from investigating cats."

"Well, things have moved on again. I'm here in a car with a local guy I've seen around for 10 years who turns out to be an international medja."

"International? What do you mean?"

"SecInterPol; a man named Karkin."

"What kind of local?"

"He hasn't said. He hasn't said much at all."

She used an unladylike word. "What have you gotten us into now? I thought dating a chef would make a change, but give me a break."

I laughed. Karkin gazed at me. The car was foggy with the two of us breathing, the old-car odor stronger.

I told MacIntyre, "We're connecting the R'ames Society, Sennedjem, money, and the bomb. That's all he's said so far."

She was silent.

"Are you there?"

"Yes, I'm thinking; shut up for a minute."

I shut. I smiled at Karkin. Why not?

"Shes?"

"Still here."

"We'd better get together. Bring that Karkin. To my office."

I told Karkin, "Cheryl wants to see us at her office." He was already moving his head no before I finished the sentence. I said into the phone, "He says no."

"Let me talk to him."

Karkin's eyes never left mine, and his mouth made very little movement as he said things like "Yes" and "Maybe" and "No." Sometimes he was silent for a while, motionless; other times, he would nod or make the negative motion with his hands. After a while he just gave the phone back to me, MacIntyre still talking at him.

I said again, "He says no."

"Kidnap him." I think she was joking.

"I don't think that's practical."

"Why, is he bigger than you?"

I looked him over. "Yes, and he's better armed." Karkin's eyes were still on me, his hands motionless in his lap.

"Huh." Silence. "OK, we'll talk it over tonight."

"Fine."

I disconnected and looked at Karkin. "So, connected how?"

"Russians."

I stared. Russians? Sennedjem looked Russian, though he had a Remetjy name.

"What Russians?"

He shook his head.

"My intuition tells me I've learned all I'm going to learn from you."

"I'd run with that."

I didn't tell him I'd kept my nose straight and my fingers the same length all these years by not running through dark kitchens full of knives. "Is there anything at all that you can tell me?"

"Not right now."

"Ever?"

"Might." His hand slipped into his pocket and brought out a small wallet. He extracted a business card. The card had two things on it: "Karkin" and a local phone number. Wonderful.

I nodded to him and got out of the car. I collected my bow and equipment from the field. The center of the center of the target was safe today. When I looked up, Karkin's Ford was gone.

CHAPTER EIGHT
MacIntyre Discovers Cats Don't Like Her

"FOR CRYING OUT LOUD, MES, there must be some way to do it!" said MacIntyre, clutching her phone in frustration. At the other end of the phone, an obstructive Idnu Djehutymes reiterated the religious and civil legalities involved in the murders at the Temple of Bastet with her until her eyes crossed.

She sat in her little red sports car, parked across the street from the Temple of Bastet. It was the day after her boyfriend's restaurant had gone to its afterlife. As no one had died, Imy-er-Medjau Menna had requested her to take herself off to find something else to do, as he did not need her services on that case.

She had explained to her boss that the Pussycat Murders—her dynamic way of summarizing the killings at the Temple of Bastet—demanded her attention. After rejecting her nomenclature, he then rejected her proposals to work on the case. So she tried to find a way in that would work for him. It wasn't going well.

"MacIntyre, take the fluff out of your ears. Or does it go deeper? There is no way that we can interfere with the temple's investigation. It's a religious offense against the goddess, nothing to do with us."

"Two people murdered, Mes!"

"Two w'abu murdered. Ma'at is blind to their being people."

"So am I, but—"

"No buts, MacIntyre. Do not—I repeat, *do not*—investigate this case. It's not our case." He disconnected.

Her grip on the phone would be perfect for firing the thing at the temple across the street, but it wouldn't help. She put the phone away and glared at the big temple. She hadn't dared to bring up her best friend Henutsenu's presence at the crime scene. According to Djehutymes's logic, it would be an even bigger reason for her to leave it alone.

She had to find out more about what was going on in the temple if she was to help her friend. Her options weren't great. She was not a good candidate for undercover operations, being a blonde, blue-eyed American. Besides, she'd already exposed herself to all the people involved. And using an informant wouldn't work. The people she'd met so far weren't likely to tell her their secrets, and her one friendly connection was Henutsenu. Her using a "suspect" as an informant, however innocent, would impress no one at the Temple of Ma'at.

That left the direct method: talk to the hem-netjer and ask him to approve her participation in the investigation, right up front. All legitimate. Mes wouldn't like it, but once Paneb let her in, he'd have to go along. Sure he would.

MacIntyre hopped out of her car and crossed the street to the big temple doors. She pulled one door open enough to squeeze in, then shut it again.

A lower-level w'ab greeted her and asked her purpose in visiting the Lady Bastet. She asked to see Tjay. Going through him would be better than just asking for Paneb. The w'ab asked her to wait. She had other plans.

MacIntyre found the chapel where Henutsenu had spent the early morning of the murder praying to the goddess. It was a quiet room in a hall off to the side of the main hallway, two doors down from the offering room where the w'abu had died. There was an offering prayer ceremony going on in the offering room. MacIntyre stepped into the chapel and heard nothing. The room must be soundproofed, giving credence to Henutsenu's claim of hearing nothing.

On the way back to the main hall, she stepped into the offering room behind the small crowd of supplicants. She cast a semetyu's eye over the place. Not a trace of blood, no disarranged furniture, nothing that might show two men had died there. Just a huge, black statue of a goddess with a cat's head. She felt its forbidding stone eyes boring into her. As she turned to leave, she saw the door opposite had a sign, "Feline Veterinary Clinic." Clearly the Temple of Bastet was equipped for all things cat-related.

She arrived back in the main hall as the corpulent w'ab approached.

"Why, Hutyt MacIntyre, how pleasant to see you. Have you come to offer something to Bastet? I believe a ceremony is underway—"

"In a way, Tjay. I need to speak with Hem-Netjer Paneb."

"May I ask what your business is with the hem-netjer? He'll want to know."

"I need to speak with him about the murders. My superiors have all kinds of questions." Which was true, most of them like "Why are you doing this, MacIn-tyre?"

"Oh." Tjay's thick lips folded downward in disapproval. "A sad business. The hem-netjer won't like it."

"I'd also like to make an offering to Bastet." She fished out a 10-debenu note and gave it to the w'ab. "I'm sure you can find the best way to put that to use for the temple."

"Why, thank you, Hutyt. I'll put it into our kitty. Let me see if the hem-netjer has a few moments for you."

The fat man waddled off into the depths of the temple. She sat on a short bench to wait. The hall contained several statues of the goddess Bastet. It also contained the occasional black cat wandering through in search of whatever cats looked for. One cat jumped up on the bench and stared at her with yellow eyes. Funny, growing up in Boston, black cats were something to avoid, especially on Halloween, and God help you if one crossed your path. Here, they were everywhere, the sacred animals of the goddess Bastet. Hard to get used to. She wasn't superstitious; and she wasn't allergic to cats, or she'd be disabled by now. She checked whether anyone was looking and pushed the cat off the bench. It stalked off, tail whipping back and forth.

MacIntyre understood little about the intricacies of Remetjy religious practices or the politics of the temples. She was a w'abet of Ma'at, but in name only; she'd taken the test and gone through the initiation purely to make sure that she could advance beyond the bottom rungs at the Temple of Ma'at. Back in Boston, her family was Congregationalist, and that religion looked nothing like anything she'd ever seen here in Menmenet.

The government temples, like Ma'at, Imen-R'a, and Mentju, were most familiar; they resembled the government offices in America, just with fancier titles and odd little rooms here and there devoted to things that she didn't regard as government functions.

MacIntyre did not know what a hem-netjer did in a temple devoted to religious worship like the Temple of Bastet. The middle of the priestly hierarchy did most of the work of the temple, but she had no clue what that work entailed. She'd have to ask Henutsenu about it. Her bet, having had a lot of experience with American evangelical churches in her youth, was that it involved money. Which was why she'd parted with the 10-debenu note to Tjay, correctly figuring it would persuade him to agree to her wish to talk with Paneb. No way Djehutymes was going to reimburse that little contribution.

"What's this about murders, Hutyt?" Hem-Netjer Paneb stood before her, a questioning look of disapproval on his face, his hands folded in front of his robe.

"Could we find somewhere more private to talk, my lord?" asked MacIntyre.

"I suppose so. Come to my office. You may have ten minutes, no more."

"Have a seat, Hutyt," said Paneb, taking his own seat in a chair arranged across from another chair. His office was on the small side, with little decoration other than a small offering hetep with a foot-high black cat statue in a niche in the wall. She deduced from this that he worshipped Bastet, which she already knew. The office offered few other clues to the man or his job. She sat.

"Now, what's this about the murders? I thought I'd made the situation clear yesterday." Paneb had the same air of inner certainty that he'd exhibited the day before. His frown implied he had only grown more impatient at her persistence in contradicting that certainty. More flattery might help.

"It struck me yesterday, my lord, how diligently you and the other priests care for your temple. The goddess must appreciate your efforts. A friend of mine worships here and has nothing but praise for you and the temple."

"Thank you, Hutyt; we do our best for our goddess." Paneb smiled with superiority and brevity. "But I cannot see—"

"It's just that seeing that care, and being a homicide semetyt, there must be something I can do to help with your investigation. I talked to my superiors." She would not tell him what they had said, but a little backup might help her convince him. "I could help in several ways. For example, I examined the bodies at the morgue in the Temple of Hut-Her-Sekhmet, my lord, and—"

"You *what?*"

"Examined the bodies. I am well known at that temple, my lord, having investigated many murders over the last two years, and they were happy to show me—"

"Who gave you permission to do that?" Paneb was, not to put it finely, steamed.

"I'm very sorry, my lord. I just felt—"

"No one gave you permission. No one asked you to do that."

"No, my lord, but—"

"Did your superiors tell you to come here today?"

"No, my lord, but—"

"Did I not make clear that the goddess Bastet controls everything in her dominion? That the Lady does not appreciate outsiders sticking their nose in?" Now he was getting insulting.

"Now, just a minute, my lord—"

"I am sorry, Hutyt, but I must end this interview. You will remove yourself from the temple; you are not welcome here." He paused; his voice and face softened. "You mentioned a friend, a worshipper in our temple. Perhaps your friend can help you better understand the Lady Bastet and how we all honor her here in the temple. But for now, I must insist you leave."

The hem-netjer arose and shepherded her all the way out to the main door of the temple, which he closed firmly after pushing her out.

MacIntyre drove a little faster than usual through the streets of Menmenet down to the waterfront. Paneb may have acted rashly in banning her from the Temple of Bastet, but he had one good suggestion: talk to her friend about it. Henutsenu was the only way she would get anywhere now, suspect or not.

She parked her car in the back lot at the Neferti and went in through the kitchen door in the back. It was the middle of the afternoon, so the lunch crush had died down, and the line cooks were cleaning and prepping for dinner. She saw Sebek talking with a cook.

"Hi, Sebek."

"Cheryl, good to see you! Too late for lunch, though. Might be a quail left over somewhere."

She smiled. "I've come to talk with Henutsenu, not to sponge a lunch. Where is she?"

"Oh, you just missed her. She left fifteen minutes ago. She decided she wanted to go to her temple for a little prayer session." He clucked. "After the club fight a couple of days ago, she's spending a little too much time with the cats."

"Ah, OK." A tiny shiver of apprehension frizzed up MacIntyre's spine. Better call her friend before she says anything wrong. Or, worse, before she decides it's time to inform the hem-netjer about her presence in the temple during the murder. MacIntyre walked into the empty dining room and called her friend. Voicemail. Maybe she was still driving. Maybe she was praying and had her phone silenced. Maybe, maybe. The shiver transformed into a sinking feeling in her gut. She left a voicemail.

"Henutsenu, this is Cheryl. Call me right away. As soon as you can, OK? It's important."

CHAPTER NINE
Shesmu Takes the Heat

I PULLED MY CAR INTO my driveway, and as I got out, I saw two medjau emerge from a black car parked across the street. I knew they were medjau because I'd met one: Rudj Baki of the Henet Baket Sepat.

"Shesmu," said Baki.

"Rudj Baki."

"This is my associate, Huty Seba." Huty Seba could easily get a job as a bouncer in a very rough bar. That Baki felt it necessary to bring along support made me a touch apprehensive.

"Huty. To what do I owe the pleasure, Baki?"

"There are a few questions we'd like to ask you. May we step inside?"

"Um. Do I need to get my sehy here?"

"You have that right under the Rule of Heru."

Heru. Not Ma'at. That meant it was about taxes, not more mundane criminal activity. I relaxed, as I had paid my taxes in full. My restaurants were private businesses that paid only local taxes and fees, nothing to the Henet Baket. Still, letting medjau into your house gave them permission to do all kinds of things that might not prove in one's best interest.

"Why all the mystery, Baki? I explained my situation, did I not? At the R'ames Society?"

He didn't smile. Huty Seba cracked a knuckle. Then another one.

Baki said, "What you explained appears to be only a small part of the complicated goings-on at the R'ames Society. The more we looked into the books, the more we suspected that the Society has some serious issues with illegal money flows."

"What's that got to do with me? I'm only interested in the flow of money from their Best New Chef award."

"Not according to the executive director, Nesimen. He said you're attending a board meeting this afternoon. We're interviewing all the board members, tracing the tentacles of corruption throughout the organization. Nesimen says he puts his complete faith in your knowledge of the Society's operations. He says you'll vindicate him. That's why he's invited you to the board meeting."

That's what you get for volunteering. "Nesimen exaggerates. I knew nothing about the Society two days ago other than that it might help my professional career. Now I know where Nesimen's office is, and that's all I know. I'm going to the board meeting to offer moral support as a friend."

"Not according to Nesimen."

"He's riding a horse of hope, trying to escape the oncoming legions of medjau. You, in fact."

Baki smiled an amiable smile. Seba cracked another knuckle. "I've been doing this work for quite a while now, Shesmu. I've found that following bees leads you to honey. The queen bee seems to be this fellow Sennedjem. We're going to pester anyone associated with Sennedjem and the R'ames Society until we find him and the honey."

"I wish you the best of luck. I've got my own problems."

Baki smiled again. "So I've heard. Another interesting phenomenon I've observed. When large amounts of money are involved, looking under the surface, one finds currents that link apparently unrelated events. Explosions in businesses may represent several events related to money flows. I'm not accusing anyone of anything. Yet. But I have to investigate, and events like that come in bunches."

"You're stretching."

"And the Russians?"

Russians again. Karkin had been right, it appeared.

"What about the Russians?"

"Rumors, stories, informants. Currents under the surface, Shesmu. Your name has come up. Russian mafias seem to know all about you."

What Russians? Mafias? What links Sennedjem with my restaurant blowing up? This man Baki liked his metaphors; I didn't. The waters closed over my head and the currents took hold of me. I had to stop talking to Baki. Every word I spoke pushed me deeper into his rip currents. Time to swim sideways.

"I'm sorry, Baki, I have to go. And I have nothing more to say."

"I'm putting you on notice, Shesmu. If you're involved in this business, we'll find out and detain you indefinitely until we find our honey. If you decide to talk, here's my card; call me." He handed me an official card with his contact information. Seba cracked another knuckle, and the two medjau left me in no kind of peace.

CHAPTER TEN
MacIntyre Reaches Bottom

"MacIntyre, in my office, now!"

MacIntyre had not even reached her desk when she heard this command from Idnu Djehutymes's office. She stepped into the office to find her boss's face matched his tone: grumpy. Familiar territory.

He pointed at the door. "Close it." She did.

"Sit." He pointed at the chair with a jabbing finger. She sat. Definitely grumpy, but maybe a little more than that. Maybe pissed off would better describe his attitude.

"What the hell are you doing, MacIntyre?"

Trying to pretend she didn't know what he was talking about wouldn't work. Mes wasn't stupid, and he understood perfectly well what she had wanted to do.

"I couldn't just sit there and let it go, Mes. I had my own reasons, but the main one is that I can't let murders go unpunished. That's what we are here for."

"MacIntyre. Meddling with a temple's prerogatives is not wise. Not wise at all. Why do you imagine you can get away with that?"

"I suppose I don't, but I bet I might find out enough to justify the intervention."

"But you didn't, did you?"

"Well—"

"And you pissed off a hem-netjer, didn't you?"

"Well—"

"And that hem-netjer pissed me off, didn't he?"

"Apparently."

"None of which seems to affect your attitude."

"Well—"

"Who is Henutsenu?"

That stopped her cold. She had not brought Henutsenu into any conversations with Mes about this affair. Once he got hold of the end of a string, he'd unravel the whole carpet with a stunning lack of concern for her needs.

"I—she's a friend."

"How close a friend?"

"A good friend."

"Good enough to lie for?"

This calumny incensed her. "What do you mean?"

"I have all your reports on this murder right here." He jabbed a finger down onto a folder. "I've read it all. Twice. Did you just forget to file a report when she told you about her role in the murder? Or did you just decide not to report it?"

"I haven't had a chance," replied MacIntyre, wincing.

"And guess what? The Temple of Bastet has arrested her."

"What!" She'd waited and waited for Henutsenu's callback, to no avail. "Why did they arrest her?"

"She confessed to a crime."

"What crime?"

"Murder."

"She did not."

"That's what the temple says. They also said she told them you knew she was there. And you haven't reported that."

"She was there, but she saw nothing. Henutsenu has no motive. She's kind and caring. Bashing two men's heads in with a statue is not her style at all. She didn't murder anyone. She wouldn't!"

He rolled his eyes. "How many times have we listened to that line coming from witnesses? The last three times, you kept saying things like 'Golly gee, Mes, anybody can murder anyone.' Do you recollect that?"

"Sure, but—"

"But Henutsenu is your friend, so you believe she wouldn't murder anyone. MacIntyre, I believe *you* would murder just about anybody that got in your way. I just haven't seen the bodies. If the Temple of Bastet says she's a murderer, that's up to them to deal with. It's a religious offense, murdering w'abu in the offering room."

"But—"

"Shut up, MacIntyre, before you get in any deeper. You're already over your head," he said. "No report here means you suppressed evidence of a religious offense. Under your oath as a w'abet of Ma'at, suppressing evidence is itself a religious offense, obstructing the goddess through suppressing ma'at. I'm explaining this, even though you know it, because I am required to do that before I take your badge and gun. Which I will now do. And, under the Rule of Ma'at, we will use anything you say against you in the court of Ma'at. Do you understand?"

"Yes, but—"

"Gun and badge, MacIntyre. You're suspended. Without pay."

MacIntyre sat in her car parked across the street from the Temple of Bastet. She obsessed over her friend Henutsenu, imprisoned somewhere inside. MacIntyre, having failed at just about everything else, had to see her. She was certain that asking would just prompt the temple to eject her. What to do? She saw worshippers going in and out, some carrying cats, some not. An idea wormed its way into her brain.

She remembered her walk down the hallway in the temple to the chapel where Henutsenu had not been murdering the w'ab priests. "Feline Veterinary Clinic." She had paid little attention. She didn't own a cat and had no intention of ever needing such a clinic. And she had no notion that a clinic was in any way involved in the murders. But one of the many benefits of being a worshipper of Bastet was access to what she assumed was high quality, caring, and effective veterinary care for one's kitties. And, so, access to the temple.

She needed a cat. Temporarily.

She made a mental list of all of her friends—the ones that wouldn't care that some foolish medjau higher-ups thought she was corrupt. She started calling. The first five she reached were not cat people. Two had dogs, two had nothing, and one had a pet snake. The sixth was an ex-lover, a woman she'd spent six months dating, trying to decide whether it was worth it and coming down on the side of a regretful no. They were better friends than lovers. And she had a cat.

An hour later, MacIntyre walked back to her car holding a cat carrier containing one outraged specimen of the feline persuasion named Tikhet, which translated to "Little Sweet Pea" in English. Tikhet was a tabby cat, orange and white, male, and in good condition for his age, according to its owner. Certainly his voice was in good condition. Little or sweet-pea-like, he was not. Asked for symptoms MacIntyre could mention to a vet, the woman had laughed and said that cats were a mass of symptoms. You just had to pick one. How about not eating his dried food, she said. The cat would only eat the most expensive canned cat food available in the store. When a new flavor came out, the cat somehow knew it. Tikhet then refused to eat the old food stored in the pantry. At any rate, her friend said, just tell the vet that the cat was refusing to eat his dried food and go from there.

"Is the kitty in pain or anything?" asked the vet nurse after MacIntyre described Tikhet's problems to her.

"No, just his usual whining," said MacIntyre. The nurse looked at her appointment book.

"The first appointment we have is in an hour and a half. Do you want to wait, or will you come back then?"

"Oh, I'll wait." She looked around the room. Every chair was filled. "Can I leave Tikhet here, next to the window, and go pray in the chapel for a few minutes? There's nowhere to sit here."

"Certainly, my lady. I'll keep an eye on Tikhet." Tikhet, despite the caring tone of the nurse and the hope of fixing whatever problems he had, continued to express his outrage. A curious tomcat came over to investigate the noise and nosed at the door of the cat carrier, further inflaming the captive Tikhet. Tikhet's opinion of other toms was audibly even lower than his opinion of MacIntyre.

MacIntyre smiled at the nurse, placed the carrier near the window. Tikhet's new friend jumped up on top of the carrier and prowled around, driving Tikhet into a frenzy. MacIntyre left them to it.

The temple was a one-story affair with a maze of hallways and rooms off the main hall. Henutsenu could be anywhere, but dungeons were usually in basements, so MacIntyre started her search there. She spent a few minutes locating a stairwell, finding it hidden away behind a large statue of the goddess. A sign on the stairway door warned of no exit, suggesting she was on the right track. She descended to the basement and through a door, then through another door. MacIntyre found herself in a long corridor that stretched away to the back of the building. She saw a man sitting in a chair, presumably guarding the prisoner. She hadn't given too much attention to tactics; the level of effort would depend on the man's credulity and diligence. Given the level of security she'd encountered at the Temple of Bastet, she wasn't worried.

As she approached, she saw that the guard was a young w'ab. He stared at her in dismay.

"You can't be down here, lady. This is a restricted area." Diligence rating up one point. Try talking him down.

"Oh, that's all right. Hem-Netjer Paneb sent me down. I'm to speak with the prisoner for only ten minutes to let her know her trial date and details. I won't need the whole ten minutes. Could you open the door, please?"

"I suppose it's all right." Credulity rating up ten points. No brute force necessary. The w'ab found a key on a large key ring. The door swung open, and MacIntyre entered. Henutsenu, sitting on a bunk bed, looked up. MacIntyre made a face at her, and her friend instantly blanked her expression.

"OK," said the w'ab. "I'll be outside if you need anything. I'll knock when the ten minutes are up. You knock if you want out."

"Thanks awfully, that's very helpful," said MacIntyre, smiling at him and acknowledging both his diligence and his credulity. The young w'ab blushed, and the door closed behind him.

"Cheryl, what are you doing here?" asked Henutsenu in a whisper, after the two women had hugged and kissed each other. They sat next to each other on the bunk.

"Seeing if you're all right," replied MacIntyre. "What have you said to them?"

"I told them everything I told you. They didn't believe me, and the hem-netjer had me brought down here. They keep coming down and questioning me, the same questions over and over. I've told them and told them I didn't kill anyone. Why would I?"

"How are you holding up? I can help you escape if you want to."

"Oh, I'm fine. The Lady Bastet has some purpose in mind in keeping me here, but she knows I didn't kill anyone. No need to escape. She'll protect me."

"Sure she will. Great." MacIntyre patted her friend's hand while she marveled that such a worldly woman would be so religious. "I should have brought a cake with a file in it. I wanted to make sure you were all right and to let you know that we're all doing everything we can to help you." She hugged and kissed her friend again, a longer kiss this time.

"How did you get in here?" asked Henutsenu, stroking her friend's hair.

"Borrowed a cat," said MacIntyre. "Then lied a lot. I wanted to ask you, have you heard anything that might help us?"

"They won't tell me anything."

"Who is questioning you?"

"Mostly that awful man Paneb. I don't know how he's risen so high in the temple with his attitude toward worshippers. Once by Hem-Netjer-Tepy Panekhet, he's been very nice about everything but says there's nothing he can do until the trial in two weeks." She paused. "I did get a funny feeling he was worried about something. His questions about the murders were perfunctory, like he didn't care that much. Paneb was furious about the deaths. Those two w'abu reported directly to him and he's taken it personally. He thinks I did it."

"What do you think Panekhet might be worried about?"

"He'd heard about the fight at the Myu-Myu Club. He wanted to know if I thought there was any connection between that and the murders, and he asked a lot of questions about Sennedjem."

The guard knocked on the door. MacIntyre said, "Be right there," and hugged and kissed her friend. "Don't worry, we'll fix this and get you out of here."

She rose and knocked on the door. "OK, ready." The credulous w'ab let her out. She thanked him again and walked away.

Back in the vet's clinic, Tikhet had worn out his welcome. The nurse said, "We looked in the chapel, but you weren't there."

"Had to go to the restroom," replied MacIntyre. "Is kitty all right?"

"He's…quite a cat. Anyway, the vet will see you now." Tikhet continued to object to the proceedings. The vet was very helpful in explaining how to train a cat to eat different food after palpating the animal to check for whatever vets check for. He didn't blame MacIntyre for the scratches at all. "Occupational hazard," he laughed. He stuffed Tikhet back in his carrier without further ado, and MacIntyre thanked him and left.

MacIntyre took the cat back to her friend and left the carrier unopened while she took a hurried leave. She said she was late for an appointment and promised a fancy lunch soon. She had no wish to see what Tikhet would do when released from confinement.

CHAPTER ELEVEN
Shesmu and MacIntyre Take a Holiday

I TOOK THE CALL FROM MacIntyre sitting in my kitchen, contemplating my encounter with the Henet Baket.

"Shes, I need a holiday."

"Who is this, really?" I asked. MacIntyre had never taken a holiday since I'd known her.

She laughed. Then, her voice serious, she said, "It's this Temple of Bastet thing. Mes just suspended me without pay. For obstruction of Ma'at. And…."

"And?"

"Tell you later. Anyway, I need a break to think and plot my comeback. Let's drop everything and go somewhere else."

I found this suggestion attractive; I was ready to get out of town myself. Russians were on my brain, and the restaurant, and I remembered MacIntyre had expressed an interest, so I said: "Oysters."

"What?"

"Oysters. You remember we were talking about my oysters, the last time you ate at the Per'ankh?"

"Oh. Yeah. The Russian."

"Besides his oyster farm, he runs a little bar up in Milaya, and he's been trying to get a bed-and-breakfast going. We could eat oysters, then retire to see whether they really do increase libido."

"Yes! Let's do it. I'm ready for lots of oysters fresh from the bay. Meet you at the ferry at five. I'll bring my car. I so love those roads up north!"

By the time I arrived at the North Bay ferry terminal on foot, there was still no rain, and the wind had died down. MacIntyre had just arrived in her small red convertible.

We bought tickets and found our way into the belly of the ferry. MacIntyre zipped the little red car into the line and killed the engine. She had chosen American holiday clothes, loose jeans and a white tank top covered with a denim jacket. She extracted a huge parka from her trunk and covered it all up. We climbed up three levels to the viewing deck to wave goodbye to the city. The ferry roared into life and drew away from its dock on schedule, and the city receded, the white houses brightening the gray day.

The parka was necessary equipment for the ferry trip. I wore my normal winter jacket, a heavy linen affair, and once the boat was moving into the wind, it wasn't quite enough. MacIntyre noticed my expression, smiled warmly, and didn't offer to share.

"I didn't think it would need expedition clothes," I explained. "Can we go inside?" We walked back down one flight into the main deck cabin with its welcoming bar and heaters. I felt the usual sense of claustrophobia, but it didn't win out over the arctic temperatures outside. "Drink?"

"Red wine," MacIntyre said to the woman behind the bar. I requested beer. We took our drinks over to a small table by a forward window. MacIntyre sipped wine and said, "Crappy day on all fronts. How about yours?"

"Crappy describes it. My hearing's better, my archery's worse, my life is a mess of dangerous problems, and the Henet Baket says I'm on their list of deadbeats."

She eyed me to see if I was being facetious and decided I wasn't. "Do tell."

I related Karkin's attempt to link all my problems and Baki's attempt at intimidating me into confessing to even more problems.

She sipped her wine and grinned. "Well, if you've got all that money, we should have a pretty good time tonight."

"Right. All my money just got blasted into pieces. At least until the insurance payments roll in."

"And the Russian?"

"I doubt he's responsible for blowing up my restaurant, but he knows everybody in the local Russian community, and he's a good place to start."

She sipped her red wine, staring out the window at the passing shore lights, preoccupied with unknowable thoughts about unknowable people. The ferry moved up the bay, passing the little towns and tourist hotels that dotted the landscape. She sighed.

"What's up, Cheryl?" I asked.

She looked at me. "It's Henutsenu."

"What has she done now?" Henutsenu and MacIntyre had grown thick as thieves. There was an attraction there that would have made me jealous; but I loved them both. Two powerful women could generate an awful lot of disturbance if they put their minds to it.

"Confessed to murder. Or so the Temple of Bastet claims."

"Um." Very unwelcome news.

"They've arrested her."

"The temple? Not the medjau?"

"The temple. It's a religious crime, not civil. That's why Mes suspended me. I knew she was there at the crime scene, but I didn't report it. I wanted to wait until I could figure out how to keep her out of it."

"She's the heart of the Neferti, she and Sebek. Arrested? It might as well be a bomb there, too."

"The hardest thing for me to get over, moving here, was how much your religion is a part of everything, such as government. Everything is a temple. Everyone is a priest. Hell, even I am a priestess, a w'abet of Ma'at, and I don't believe a word of it. The temples can even override the civil authorities and laws. It would be whimsical if it didn't have consequences. Now Henutsenu is a victim of it all. At least she's OK. She's so religious she thinks Bastet will bail her out."

"How do you know she's OK?"

MacIntyre smiled. "Snuck into the Temple of Bastet and talked to her. She's OK. Oh—one thing we might check out. The hem-netjer-tepy, a guy named Panekhet, seems interested in Sennedjem and the fight at the Myu-Myu Club. Could be a clue."

"A clue to what? Why is that name familiar? Ah, yes. The R'ames Society board member we met after the awards ceremony."

"Anything about Sennedjem is a clue. What Sennedjem has to do with Bastet, I do not know."

I said, "We can work all this out, together. Later tonight. After the oysters."

"One more thing. I called a friend at the Temple of Ma'at to run a check on Sennedjem. You'll never guess what we found."

"He's a slave trader from Central Asia?"

"Nope."

"A secret agent of the Shetasen?" The Shetasen was the police organization that handled secret political affairs, secretive about the identities of their medjau.

"I'd guess not, though that might be the case."

"You're kidding, right?"

"He goes back about five years, then nothing at all. No birth records, no tickets for speeding, nothing. Five years ago he applied for a tax license for the R'ames Society, and that was the first we'd heard of him."

"How did he get the license with no background?"

She smiled again. "I daresay his virtue was obvious to all who met him."

"He bribed somebody."

"Even multiple somebodies. I don't think he's a Shetasen agent, though. The records aren't flagged as secret, which they would be if the bureaucracy needed to cover him up. This is definitely a clue that we have to investigate."

I looked out the window. "We're arriving."

The ferry pulled into the terminal at the top of the Bay, and we moved the little car out of the hold along with a string of slow-moving commuters. MacIntyre was impatient, pulling out and passing a couple of lumbering utility trucks with a suppressed roar from the sports car's engine. She whirled around a curve, then passed a slow-moving pickup truck, our headlights sliding over the dense trees, the light lost in the darkness.

I opened my mouth but closed it again at her look. "They say," I said after a pause, "that fear builds appetite. I've never believed that."

She nodded and said, "I wouldn't know." The ride ahead was going to be fun, shooting around the snaky one-and-a-half-lane road that wound its way up to the little bay that held our destination.

Her eyes darted my way as we went around another curve, and she smiled.

We drove up the long peninsula that formed the western side of the long bay into the small town of Milaya. We were close to the border of Russkaya Amerika, the Russian country to the north of the Republic. The oyster bar had started as a nameless Russian roadhouse up the coast on the other side of the border. My Russian friend figured out that oysters would do well in a bay near Milaya, a tiny town of ranch hands that worked on the ranches further out along the peninsula. Now, the oyster wranglers lived there too.

The lights of the town—all two of them—illuminated the storefronts on the west side of the road. The east side had only a set of docks stretching out into the bay. MacIntyre swung her car into the little parking lot by the side of the stores, and we emerged into the damp night. The tiny bar next to the parking lot was just a one-room board shack brightened up with a coat of white paint. It had no sign.

MacIntyre surveyed the place, then looked at me reproachfully. "This is it?" The parka fur pushed up her blonde hair to frame her face with a halo of hair and fur, making her look soft and fluffy. Misleading; the nameless bar was in for a surprise.

I pushed through the beat-up, full-length swinging door, letting out a flood of noise, heat, and light. I thought we'd hit a town meeting. The noise resolved itself into a group of five men and the bartender talking at the top of their lungs. The heat was a huge Russian stove against the side of a wall. There was a pile of unshucked oysters on the bar, and three piles of oyster shells on towels, with a few oyster knives scattered around the scene of the crime. A plate had a pile of smallish piroshki, and three unlabeled bottles of a clear liquid that I assumed were vodka. The bar had become a zakuski table, a table of small plates, side dishes for the vodka. Here, the oysters had a special status, being the business of the place. But the vodka was still the main event.

The bartender looked over, saw me, and grinned and waved. Then he saw MacIntyre, framed in her parka hood, and the grin got wider. He was seven feet tall, massively muscled, and the grin appeared out of the middle of a wild black beard. The noise paused as the little crowd assessed the newcomers. We must have passed the test, as they made room and motioned us to join them.

"Cheryl," I said, "meet Pyotr Semionovich Podgoronov, who runs this place and the oyster farm. Pyotr Semionovich, this is Cheryl MacIntyre, my friend with an avid interest in oysters."

He engulfed her hand in a European-style two-handed handshake. "Very pleased to meet you, Cheryl. MacIntyre—that's a Scots name, nyet?"

MacIntyre took off her parka and put it on a side table. She generated a lot of appreciation from the men at the bar as they took in her blond hair and tank top. "Yes," she said, "but many generations back; I'm an American from Boston."

The bartender's sharp eye picked out the feather pin that showed she was a w'abet of Ma'at. "Bozhe moi, a medjat! We'd better be on our best behavior." He grinned. "What will you have?"

"What goes with oysters?" asked MacIntyre.

"Vodka."

I said, "It's not a fair question. Pyotr Semionovich thinks vodka goes with everything. In large amounts."

Pyotr Semionovich reached down below the bar and pulled up a clear bottle with some green strands in it.

"Zubrovka!" he shouted above the din. "The best. Polish, but you can't have everything."

"What's zubrovka?" asked MacIntyre.

"That," I said, pointing at the pickled herb. "It's a kind of grass, nice flavor if you like that sort of thing. It's good vodka, I'm sure. No diesel fuel." Pyotr Semionovich poured two small glasses of the wonderful zubrovka.

"Na zdarov'ye!" he shouted, tossing off his glass. He reached for an oyster with one hand and grabbed a knife with the other. With a fluid movement, he popped open the shell, cut loose the oyster, and tossed it off as well.

"I'll drink the vodka if you'll open the oyster for me," said MacIntyre.

"A pact!" said Pyotr Semionovich.

MacIntyre examined the glass of vodka, sniffed it with an air of medjat suspicion, smiled, and tossed it off. Cheers arose from the crowd. Another oyster, another quick flip of the knife, and MacIntyre downed it. An expression of delight settled on her face, mirrored in the faces of the men surrounding her. Pyotr Semionovich's hand smacked down on the bar, sealing his approval of the operation along with his roar. I reached for the knife. My glass of zubrovka went down well, followed by an oyster I shucked even faster than Pyotr Semionovich had. More roars erupted from the crowd.

"Rossiya has no oysters, but zakuski are zakuski," he said, referring to the spread on the bar. "I'd serve caviar, but I haven't got any. The mother-beset Remetjy government has made it illegal to import the stuff, the poor sturgeon are an endangered species." He looked as though if he had a sturgeon at hand, its days would be numbered and childless. "And I can grow oysters in the bay, but not sturgeon. They're not *native*. As if European flats were native to the Ta'an-Imenty." Russians had a cynical attitude toward government, even if it wasn't Russian.

MacIntyre asked, "How did you get into oysters?"

Downing another zubrovka and an oyster, Pyotr Semionovich shrugged and said, "They were here when I came. I bought in, and I made it work."

"And how did you wind up here? It's pretty far out of the way."

"Ask a lot of questions, don't you?"

"Sorry, occupational disease for a medjat. Just ignore me."

"Never, you're far too beautiful." Catcalls from the audience.

Pyotr Semionovich leaned on the bar, his forearm massive, the diminutive vodka glass tiny in his huge hand. He looked for a while at MacIntyre in the impassive way Russians have. He said, "I worked my way down the coast from Novoarchangelsk about five years ago, helping on fishing boats, working the docks, anything around water. I grew up in Petropavlosk. Docks and boats were my playground. I've been around the sea all my life. Russkaya Amerika, Sibir' too. Lovely. But I can't go back." He left the reason for that unspoken, but when someone couldn't go back to some place they loved, it was because it didn't love them.

"Ta'an-Imenty doesn't have an extradition treaty with Russkaya Amerika," observed MacIntyre. Pyotr Semionovich nodded, but his eyes narrowed. He shot a warning glance at two of the oyster wranglers, who were chortling and whispering to each other.

I asked, "Do you know anyone named Sennedjem? Despite the name, he looks Russian. Tallish, but not as tall as you, black hair and small beard, thin, shifty looking."

"That could describe half the inhabitants of Moskva. The male half. And they all look shifty." There was humor in his voice, but his eyes didn't smile. "Never heard of him. Why do you ask?"

I said, "He's the financial officer of the R'ames Society down in Menmenet. We're trying to find him."

The noise level from the men sitting next to us had risen a notch. MacIntyre watched them as they played a game involving numbers of oysters and drinks, all expressed in loud Russian. They had a small coin on the bar and five oyster shells. The game involved buying a round of drinks if you didn't guess which oyster shell covered the coin.

None of them were any good at it, so there was a lot of drinking being done. Pyotr Semionovich reached out one arm across the bar to grab the wrist of the man moving the oyster shells. He squeezed. Silence again fell over the room. The hand opened, not of its owner's volition, and the coin dropped out. A roar burst from the rest of the men. A small con, but the reaction was fierce, an anger fueled by heat, vodka, and Russian emotion.

MacIntyre and I moved away from the bar. The too-skillful Russian expostulated with his friends, still in Russian, but the rest were intent. They grabbed various appendages, lifted, and threw the miscreant out of the bar into the road through the swinging door.

"Well, " said MacIntyre. "Not a lot of call for community policing up here, I'd guess."

"Not much," agreed Pyotr Semionovich, with an equanimity that I couldn't quite match.

"What will happen to him?" I asked.

"Depends how he landed. With luck, he'll be out at the oyster beds in six hours, along with the rest of us." Another oyster, another glass of vodka. But there was nothing at all in the clear blue eyes that gazed at me over the bar. I couldn't quite figure him out. I'd spent some time with him, setting up the deal for supplying oysters to the Per'ankh, and he'd been nothing but cheerful.

MacIntyre made desultory efforts to question the Russians about Sennedjem. They all played dumb. They either didn't speak Renkemet or English, or they were too drunk to understand the question, according to Pyotr Semionovich. MacIntyre shrugged and continued her intake of grass-fed alcohol accompanied by shellfish.

She leaned over and whispered in my ear, "These guys know more, but they're a stone wall. We won't get anything out of them. Na zdarov'ye!" She drank a shot of vodka and smiled as Pyotr Semionovich shucked another oyster for her.

The liquid consumption next to us slowed as time passed, and the oysters over the coin moved slower and slower. It was a relativistic effect; the more vodka you consumed, the slower time moved. Soon it would be the next work day for the oyster wranglers and time for us to sleep.

"We'd better get back to Menmenet," I suggested, fishing for an invitation. I knew the Russian wouldn't disappoint.

"Stay here," said Pyotr Semionovich. "It's too far and too late to go back, and you're not Russian."

"What's not being Russian got to do with it?" asked MacIntyre.

"Remetjet and Americans can't hold their vodka," replied Pyotr Semionovich.

MacIntyre looked at him scornfully.

"I have a nice guest house. I put a lot of money into it. Somebody ought to use it," said Pyotr Semionovich.

"All right, lead on," she replied, downing her last shot of vodka and the last oyster.

The giant put away the remnants of the zubrovka. He admonished the oyster wranglers to watch themselves and not burn the place down and took off his apron. We followed him through the back door, which was a series of wood slats with uneven gaps as wide as a thumb. After the heat of the big stove, the cold, damp air cleared our minds. In the darkness, we could only see the white blur of Pyotr Semionovich's shirt just ahead of us. MacIntyre put her parka back on; I relied on the alcohol that had replaced half my blood.

The walk wasn't long. The air smelled of pine trees, wood smoke, and damp earth. We walked up the crude driveway to the guest house up the hill from the bar. Done in a fanciful Russian style, with turrets and onion dome and ornate wood trim, looming out through fog and darkness, it seemed like a huge Russian cathedral.

We followed Pyotr Semionovich up the porch steps and through the door he unlocked and held open. The grand stairway curved up to the second and third floors above us, the great dome looming above. MacIntyre looked around in astonishment.

"If this is the guest house, what does his main house look like?"

"It's much more reasonable, right down the road. He built this thing on spec as an inn, but so far the area hasn't broken into the Remetjy tourist market. We prefer the valley and the rivers."

She walked over to an open door and looked in at the sitting room that doubled as a breakfast room. The light from the hall glinted off the shining kitchen appliances at the far end. She turned back toward Pyotr Semionovich.

"How much is this going to cost us? I'm unemployed."

Pyotr Semionovich grinned his best black-bearded grin and said, "Free of charge, I'll write it off as a marketing expense. You just pay for the things you break. And I sell more oysters."

At the top of the stairs, there was a double door facing us. Pyotr Semionovich walked over and pulled open both doors. The huge plate-glass window opposite us dominated the room, though there wasn't much to see at the moment.

I said, "It's a bit public, isn't it?"

"Only if you're worried about people on the other side of the bay with telescopes. Will it do?"

The room was full of comfortable furnishings, and the bed looked inviting. I glanced at MacIntyre, who grinned and nodded.

I said, "Yes, this will do fine. We'll register any complaints with the management tomorrow morning."

"The management will be dead to the world," he replied. "I'm off to supervise the oyster wrangling. Spakoinoi nochi, druz'ya." He smiled again, engulfed MacIntyre in a Russian hug, parka and all, then gave me one too. He closed the door as he left.

The dim, early morning light illuminated the room through the big windows. My mouth felt like it was full of cotton, and my head was like a hot-air balloon that had crashed to earth and collapsed. I lay on my back. MacIntyre's arm rested over my chest.

I moved sideways from under her arm. She opened one eye under the mass of blonde hair spread across the pillow. The eye regarded me with suspicion. Then her memory caught up. She closed the eye and groaned. "My God," she said in English. "Oysters."

"I don't think it was the oysters." I sat on the edge of the bed, rubbing my eyes.

"What time is it?"

"Seven o'clock. If you can believe that clock over there." She groaned again, eyes closed, not with pleasure.

I got out of bed and tried my mobile phone, but there was no service. There was a phone on a table over by the door, so I punched in the kitchen number for the Neferti. Khay answered.

"Shesmu! Where are you? Henutsenu has disappeared, Sebek has gone crazy, and I have sixteen French chefs looking for carrots to peel!"

Khay was the sous chef at the Neferti and my first line of defense for problems that eluded Sebek and Henutsenu. He supervised things and made sure deliveries came in and food went out. When Sebek took a day off, he'd substitute for him. Both Sebek and Henutsenu being gone was a challenge beyond his skill set, though.

"Where's Sebek?" I asked.

"Fuck knows. I've tried his mobile, got nothing," said Khay. "I'm more worried about Henutsenu."

"Yeah." I closed my eyes. "Well, she's in jail."

"Jail? What do you mean, jail?"

"The Temple of Bastet has arrested her for murder, according to my sources."

MacIntyre, my source, struggled out of bed and groped her way into the bathroom, naked. The clock moved around to 7:30, then 7:45, while MacIntyre showered and I dealt with the crisis. I gave some instructions to Khay, during which Qenna arrived, and I left them to it. I left a voicemail for Sebek asking him to get back to the Neferti to get things organized as soon as he could.

MacIntyre emerged from the bathroom, still naked. She looked more like her usual self, though with a grim set of mouth. On seeing me without clothes, her mouth relaxed, and she walked over and hugged me, then turned to find her clothes.

We had a quick breakfast in the magnificent, empty dining room downstairs. There was a large samovar and Russian tea, along with a pot of American coffee. The warming tray had dishes of sirniki, a kind of cheese pancake, accompanied by pitchers of raspberry kissel and smetana, a soured cream. Alongside these rested slices of Doktarskaya kielbasa sausage, black bread, and a bowl of buckwheat kasha. Largesse. MacIntyre and I stared at the table, looked at each other, and groaned. I tried a little of each. One has a professional obligation, after all. But my stomach drew the line at Russian tea. MacIntyre ate a pancake with kissel and drank three cups of coffee.

We emerged into the brightening day with the fog still swirling over the narrow bay. We walked down the rough driveway to MacIntyre's car. The bar was closed tight, no sign of Pyotr Semionovich. She unlocked the car, we got in, and she prepared to drive.

I was fastening my seat belt when I realized MacIntyre had stopped moving. She held her sunglasses in her right hand, looking at them.

"What's up, Cheryl?" I asked.

"Shut up a minute."

I shut. She was still for thirty seconds, then shook her head and put on her sunglasses. She stared out the front window at the bar, then said, "Somebody's searched my car. I keep my sunglasses in the compartment between the seats so they don't get sat on by large medjau or cooks like you. They were on the dashboard."

"You could have left them there yesterday."

"No, I didn't. I put them away before I got to the ferry terminal. I remember thinking I wouldn't need them because the day was overcast. And I didn't want you to sit on them."

"Why would anybody search your car?"

"Looking for oysters to harvest, I guess." She popped the trunk, got out, and walked around to check it. She rummaged a bit, then closed the trunk and got back in the car. "Searched, definitely, but nothing's missing. Shotgun, flares, laptop, fighting sticks, all there. Theft wasn't the object."

"What do you want to do about it?"

"My head hurts. I want to drive, not think. Let's talk on the ferry." She started the engine, and we drove off. The road felt even more curvy to my distressed stomach.

On the ferry, we walked up to the upper viewing deck and looked at the Bay and the approaching city skyline. This was more my kind of speed, slow and steady. It was chilly, but neither of us wanted a drink in the lounge.

MacIntyre asked, "How well are you acquainted with Pyotr Semionovich? Or his people?"

"I don't know. His eyes when you asked about his background were different than I've seen before. Emptier. And he was quick with that vodka to distract us. Worked, too. I've met him five or six times to negotiate the oyster contract, and I've drunk a fair amount of his vodka. I've seen his people off and on, never gave them a thought. But after last night, I'm not sure anymore. At least, after what I remember of last night. They could be Russian gangsters, I guess."

MacIntyre stared at the bay passing by. "If they are, their business isn't very lucrative. That bar was the most ramshackle place I've ever gotten drunk in. That's not a dive bar, it's a bottom-of-the-ocean bar. And nobody's staying in the guest house."

"Maybe somebody was looking for cash to buy more vodka. What do you want to do about it?"

"I'll get a friend to run a check on Pyotr Semionovich to see if he's gang-connected. Of course, I shouldn't be running checks, since I'm suspended; it's against regulations. Most things are."

"How do you keep your job when you break the rules so much?" I asked.

"I don't break the ones that count in court. I've figured out the system well enough to know how not to get caught. You hang out with criminals, it's catching. Entertaining, too." She grimaced. "Until Mes gets wise to it. Like now."

There was a gleam in her eye I interpreted as her plan to break more rules. I didn't want to discourage that, so I turned my attention back to the approaching city. "I've got a busy day ahead. I have to check on the Per'ankh and the insurance. I've got to find Sebek. And Nesimen's told the Henet Baket things that aren't so. I've got to start there first. Could you drop me at the R'ames Society building on Djehutymes Street?"

"Sure. After that, I'll talk to Mes to get reinstated, then see what happens. I'll check on Henutsenu, try to find out what's happening at the Temple of Bastet. I'll call you."

CHAPTER TWELVE
Shesmu Goes Shopping

THERE WAS A SMALL PAPER sign taped to the door of the R'ames Society palace: "Closed for Normal Business Until Further Notice," with a phone number. I called the number and got put through to Nesimen. He said, "Shesmu, great to hear from you! Look, I've got some errands to do nearby. Can we walk and talk?"

"Sure," I said. I waited at the door about five minutes, then the portly Nesimen emerged. We exchanged bows, and he gave me an apprehensive look.

"I heard about the bombing, Shesmu. It's awful. What a terrible loss for the cuisine of the city and for the Society."

I agreed to this, thinking privately that it was a bigger loss for me personally, but to each their own value system. He waved a hand in the general direction of the shopping district, and we walked.

"The Henet Baket—"

He interrupted, raising a hand. "I know, I know. That man Baki is impossible. He as much as told me I was personally responsible for losing all the money. Personally! I ask you. That man Sennedjem has a lot to answer for."

"I agree, but now they're coming after me."

Nesimen grimaced. "I was afraid of that. Yes. Guilt by association. I'm so sorry. Oh—and I suppose you'd better not come to the board meeting after all. It wouldn't help much now."

"I want to help. I need to clear my name. It won't help in the rebuilding of the Per'ankh if my reputation gets damaged. How can I help?"

"I'm afraid I don't know, Shesmu. We'll have to wait and see what happens with the Board and with the Henet Baket."

We ambled along the street with other shoppers intent on acquisitions. This part of the shopping district was for the very well-to-do, comprising jewelers, couturiers, and art galleries. People came to this part of the city to spend large amounts of money for small amounts of solid goods. You could buy high Remetjy fashion, tomb goods, fancy European shoes, and very pricey lunches. I didn't know it very well. Nesimen was right at home.

We didn't go far. We turned into the Maupassant et fils jewelry store. Or at least we turned. The door was locked, and Nesimen pushed the buzzer. I saw a well-dressed European inside check us over, then hurry over and unlock the door. He said, in accented Renkemet, "Honored Nesimen, alive, sound, and healthy! Welcome to our house. What can we help you with today?"

"Today I want a couple of things, Jean. The dj'amu necklace?"

"That's ready. I'll have Paul bring it right out." Jean signaled with his hand to another European behind a counter. Paul acknowledged the wave and went through a door in the back. "And what else, Honored Nesimen?"

Nesimen turned and looked me up and down. "I think..." he said, "Yes, a watch. How about the Swiss Lateque Louis, Jean?"

"Certainly, monsieur. This way, please." Jean led the way over to a small counter. He stooped behind it, opened a drawer, and pulled out a small jewelry box. He laid the watch it contained carefully on the counter. Nesimen reached out and stroked the watch. There was no other way to describe it. Then he turned again to me and said, "So, Shesmu, what do you think?"

I said, putting as good a note of appreciation into my voice as I could, "Beautiful. Way out of my personal price range." Jewelry made me nervous; I preferred to put my money into fabulous ingredients, ephemeral as they were.

Nesimen grinned and said, "Put it on."

I demurred, but he insisted. Jean helped me adjust the leather band. I looked at the time; it was wrong. "Nice," I said, without meaning it much. I didn't wear a watch. My sense of time was so acute from working in a restaurant kitchen that I didn't need to.

"It's yours." Nesimen smiled again. "My treat."

"Sorry?"

"I can't do anything about the Society award money, so I want to make it up to you personally. Enjoy the watch."

Nesimen clearly thought that a bribe would allay any concerns or suspicions I might have about his behavior. I carefully undid the watchband and, handing the watch back to Jean, I smiled at Nesimen. "Thanks very much for the thought, but in the circumstances, I shouldn't accept it; it would make Rudj Baki very nervous. Let me help you figure out your issues with Sennedjem instead."

Nesimen looked a little taken aback by my refusal of his bribe. "I'm not sure..." he began, then stopped. Jean gave me a French half smile and, with a wistful expression, carefully replaced the watch in its case. At that point, Paul emerged from the back room with a flat black case in his hand. He walked over and handed it to Jean, who put it down on the counter and opened it.

Nesimen, his attention diverted from the perplexing conundrum I'd set for him, lifted the dj'amu necklace out of the case. It was a modern interpretation of an ancient Remetjy style. Dj'amu was an alloy of gold and silver that had a particularly nice sheen when made into jewelry. Nesimen held the necklace up in front of himself, at once inspecting and admiring the art. Seeing me eyeing him, he said, "For Taneferet, you know. Her birthday."

Nesimen had crossed the line from bribery to outright lying. Khenemset Neferet was not a dj'amu-necklace sort of person. On a formal evening at an awards ceremony where everyone was dressed to impress whatever gods might have been taking an interest, she had worn a simple linen gown with very little jewelry and just the makeup appropriate to a fifty-plus lady. A conservative fifty-plus lady, at that. She had no interest in impressing the men around her or even the watchful gods of fashion, just in dressing appropriately for the occasion. Whoever was the intended recipient of the spectacular necklace, it wasn't Khenemset Neferet.

I decided the air in the shop was too rich for me. "Why don't you finish up with Jean? I'll wait outside." Nodding to Jean, who seemed philosophical about losing a customer, I walked out to the sidewalk.

Nesimen emerged from the shop a few minutes later and told me he had one more stop to make.

I asked, "Sennedjem doesn't appear to have much Remetjy blood in him. What were his origins?" MacIntyre had told me he didn't go back more than five years in government records; perhaps Nesimen could fill in the blanks.

"Do you know, I never thought to ask him. I assumed he was European, but I never asked. One doesn't, you know."

"Yes. How about his resume?"

"I never saw that. The Board hired him without consulting me. I've had nothing but trouble with him since."

"Is that usual? To hire someone high in the organization without consulting the chief?"

"Oh, yes. With nonprofits, boards do whatever they want."

Stymied by his lack of knowledge, I got more direct. "Did you ever encounter any Russian connections in his interactions with the outside world?"

"Russian? No, I don't think so. We've made overtures to the folks up north, but they've never been interested. No. And Sennedjem was always quite secretive in his financial dealings. He told me secrecy was required as part of his fiduciary responsibility." He raised a hand to stop me as I opened my mouth. "I know, I know. Obviously false. But the board supported him."

"It had to be his need to conceal his thievery."

"Yes," said Nesimen. "Sadly true. Well, here we are." He stopped in front of an upscale men's clothing store. "I'll say goodbye here, Shesmu. It's been great talking with you. With luck, you can restart the Per'ankh soon. Best wishes and so on for that!" He bowed and dashed into the shop before I could even respond with more than a bow.

I walked off toward the Per'ankh to check on how things were progressing, thinking about what I'd just learned. Or, at least, what I hadn't learned. Nesimen professed to so little knowledge about events that it made me question his professional competence as the head of a major nonprofit. And it helped me with Baki's suspicions and Karkin's dark insinuations about Russians not at all.

CHAPTER THIRTEEN
MacIntyre and Shesmu Confront The Medjau

"I'M *WHAT?*"

MacIntyre, standing in front of Idnu Djehutymes's desk, couldn't believe what she heard. She'd asked her boss to reinstate her, but the idnu responded by confronting her with charges filed against her for corruption.

"Dirty, MacIntyre. I don't give it any credit, but the official charges mean we've got to—"

"Who? Who's charging me?" MacIntyre tried to keep her voice down, and the effort hurt her throat.

"Here's the report." Mes handed her a single sheet of paper. The heading was InterSecPol, the International Security Police. Of course, it was that idiot Ramaytush, Karkin—his organization. But no—the origin was Genève, Suisse, not local. So, the head office. In very direct terms, the report accused her of being in the pocket of the Russian mafias operating out of the southern part of Russkaya Amerika. Information received, it said. She closed her eyes. Got to stay away from that vodka. Her head was still bulging with the pain of excess. Russians, again. What did it all mean? It didn't matter what it meant, it was just wrong.

"There's no real source here," grated MacIntyre, waving the paper in Mes's face. He snatched it back.

"I don't care, MacIntyre. I have bosses too. When they hand me a report like this about a medjat I've already suspended for suppressing evidence and exceeding her authority, I don't have a choice. Regulations. When a police organization sends us a report like this, we file charges and investigate. The hearing is in two weeks, couldn't make it happen any earlier. The investigation—"

"Hearing for what?"

"Dismissal."

"Fuck you, Mes." MacIntyre felt her eyes burning.

"Regulations, Cheryl. It's not personal—I don't believe it for a minute. But, no, I'm not reinstating you. Request denied. And I ought to arrest you and put you in jail according to the regs, but why waste my time with it?"

"Mes, you know me. I'm not dirty, I'm not corrupt, I'm not in anybody's pocket! I live like a nun."

Djehutymes smiled.

"OK, bad simile. Still."

"I expect you to cooperate fully with Rudj Chen of the organized crime squad. He'll be in charge of the investigation. He's the one who sent me this report. Cheryl—I really do hope that he finds you innocent. You're a good homicide semetyt, one of the best, and I'd hate to lose you."

I took MacIntyre's call while standing in the street in front of the ruins of the Per'ankh. In the middle of the ruins of my life. What a disaster. Nothing salvageable. The phone call with my insurance agent was the latest disaster. The insurance company had decided the bomb represented arson and fraud. I asked why, and the agent wouldn't give me any specifics, but he hinted at my involvement with criminals. I may have gone too far in the ensuing exchange of views. He said I'd have to sue them to get the money and their reasons for not giving it to me. I hung up on him.

The phone rang; MacIntyre.

"What?" I said into the phone.

"Is that any way to answer your girlfriend's call for help?"

"Sorry, just got some bad news about the restaurant."

"Can't be worse than my bad news."

We caught up and agreed that our news was equally bad. We both swore off vodka for life. MacIntyre wanted to swear off oysters too, but I convinced her that such a thing was irrational and unnecessary. No point in going overboard.

MacIntyre said she was going to see Rudj Chen, the medja in charge of investigating the charges against her.

"I want to come," I said.

"I can handle this, Shes."

"Of course you can handle it. I want information. This guy knows all about Russian mafias, right?"

"I guess. My confidence in medja intelligence is low today."

"He might tell us something about why everybody is talking about Russian mafias. And my involvement with them."

"OK, meet me at the Temple of Ma'at. Third floor, Organized Crime Squad."

I took a bus west through the crazy quilt of streets over to the Temple of Ma'at, where the medjau roosted when they weren't out catching murderers and thieves. Ma'at being a severe goddess, the building loomed. I found MacIntyre at the door of the organized crime squad. She'd changed from her American clothes to Remetjy business attire, a conservative linen skirt and shirt, tan with gold highlights. Dressed for saving her professional life. Her mood was foul. I could tell by the set of her shoulders and the clenched fists. Plus, she said it right out loud.

The head of the Organized Crime Squad, Rudj Chen Ju-long, was at his desk. He was a small man in his mid-forties. He wore a snappy light blue linen suit.

"Hi, Cheryl," he said, using the English greeting. "Who's your friend?"

MacIntyre had fire in her eye and ignored his question. "Mes tells me you're the one in charge of firing me."

"Investigating the charges, not firing. That comes later."

"Made any progress? Should I clean out my desk?"

"Don't make this harder for me than it already is, Cheryl. For instance, by bringing your boyfriend along. All it means is I'll investigate him, too." He smiled at me. "Your name is—?"

"Shesmu, Shesmu za-Akhen." I said. "Maybe you can tell us what's going on?"

"I'm asking the questions, not supplying answers." He stared at me. "Shesmu. The restaurant bombing, right? Of course."

MacIntyre sat without being invited. I sat in a chair next to her. "We were up in Milaya last night," she said.

"Podgoronov's place, right?"

"Yes. And when we left this morning, I found that somebody had searched my car."

"Anything taken?"

"No, just disarranged. We went there because yesterday, Shesmu had a visit from a guy named Karkin, who told him he's of interest to the Russian criminal element."

"Karkin." Chen compressed his lips. "InterSecPol."

MacIntyre asked, "What have you heard, Ju-Long? Why is InterSecPol butting in with reports on me? Why is Karkin interested in Shesmu? What is all the talk about the Russians? What's going on with Sennedjem and the R'ames Society? And why does this InterSecPol think I'm in some gangster's pocket?"

Chen rocked in his chair. "Imagine my surprise when I learned that Hutyt-er-Semetyu MacIntyre accessed Sennedjem's file by proxy. Fast work, MacIntyre. Also against the rules; it's not your case. It's just what you might do if you were in the Russians' pocket, along with Shesmu here."

MacIntyre was unrepentant. "What about my questions?"

Chen said, ignoring her, "And what about this restaurant bombing? Imy-er-medjau Menna tells me he suspects Russian mafia involvement there too. You got a gang war going? What did you do to make them use bombs? Or did you use your own bomb?"

I didn't like the direction things were taking. "I don't know what you're talking about."

Chen sat back in his chair and stared at us. After a minute of silence, he said, "A lot goes on below the river surface. It's like a nice, peaceful stretch of river, reeds waving in the wind. You step in and you're up to your ankles in crocodiles. For example, Cheryl, we've noted your ongoing relationship to the Aztec crime lord Yaotl."

MacIntyre, surprised, said, "How'd you find out about that?"

"Information received."

"Fuck you."

"That's not very helpful. What about Yaotl?"

"He's…an informant."

"Yaotl? A snitch?" Chen cast an unbelieving eye on MacIntyre. "He's at the center of organized crime in Menmenet. We'd know if he was a snitch."

"No! Not a snitch. He…keeps me in mind when things happen. That's all."

"Keeps you in mind how?"

"You don't need to know."

"If you want to keep your job, yes, I do."

"He helps me out occasionally, when I need it. He lets me hear about… developments. In other gangs."

"You're getting information about organized crime that you're keeping to yourself?" Chen's tone was nasty. "This is my turf." Chen wrote a note on his legal pad, the strokes firm and sharp. He looked like he would not smile for a long time.

"About this metaphorical river," said MacIntyre. "What's going on, then? Below the surface?"

"I can't tell you."

"Can't or won't?"

"Won't." He pursed his lips, then said, "The squad has very specific rules about sharing sensitive information. On a need-to-know basis only. Not only do you not need to know, we don't need that information flowing right to Yaotl. And we don't need it bandied about Russkaya Amerika, either." Chen stared at me to make sure I got his message.

MacIntyre smiled the little smile that meant she was getting hot. Her cheeks had a nice, rosy glow to them. I shifted my seat to get out of the range of the volcano about to blow.

Chen, not picking up the obvious signals, or not caring, said, "OK, that's enough for now. I need to look into the Sennedjem-Russian connection, get onto the liaison with InterSecPol, get deeper into what you've been screwing around with. What you two need to do is go home and stay there until I tell you it's OK to come out again. No Yaotl, no Podgoronov, no bombs. Right?"

"Sorry," I said, "I can't do that. It's my livelihood."

Chen stared at me, his eyes taking on a reptilian look. "You'll have to do what you have to do, Shesmu. Be careful. That's all."

MacIntyre still had the small smile, but the flush had gone from her cheeks, replaced by a dangerous, mottled pallor.

She said, "I can't do that either. Different reasons, but I can't. There's face, medjat face."

Chen shook his head. "I'll have to insist. And dirty medjaut don't have any face to save."

Then I saved Chen's life. MacIntyre stood up out of her chair, fists curled tae-kwon-do style. I grabbed her arm and pulled her out of the room.

CHAPTER FOURTEEN
MacIntyre Consults an Expert

MacINTYRE WAS LUCKY TO HAVE a boyfriend like Shes. Used to situations conducted under pressure, he grew calmer rather than enraged when confronted with official idiocy.

He'd once explained it to her. "You can blow up in the kitchen and throw pots at people, especially in French kitchens. Doing it to health inspectors showing you the rat they've just found dead in a closet or to a planning official looking at the plans for your new restaurant: that doesn't work so well."

The pair left the Temple of Ma'at, and Shes guided the furious MacIntyre into the park near the city temples.

"We'll walk it off, Cheryl. A walk is a great way to let off steam," he told her, holding her hand as they ambled around the park. "Lets you reflect, gets your heart moving, makes you pay attention to your body."

"When does it kick in? I'm still ready to kill the son-of-a-bitch."

"Different people have different rates of cooling. It's a physical constant embedded in your genes."

"I'm not wearing jeans."

He laughed. "If you can joke, you're cooling down."

MacIntyre knew what she had to do, but she knew Shes wouldn't approve. Tough.

She said, "I have to make a call. You can listen, but don't interrupt."

"That's ominous, but OK. Let's turn on this path. It's empty. Nobody will intrude."

"OK."

She looked up the right man in her contacts and called him. He answered after three rings.

"Hutyt MacIntyre, a pleasure to hear from you. How may I be of service?"

"Hello, Yaotl. Something's come up that I need to consult with you about."

"I suspect this need may involve discussion of the unfortunate destruction of your friend's restaurant."

"It does. I need information."

Silence. Then Yaotl said, "Come ahead. On balance, we are all paid up at the moment, but information does not come without cost in my business."

"I realize that, but lives are at stake. Money doesn't matter." MacIntyre at once thought better of this negotiating tactic and added a qualification. "Much."

"I will check your bank account and make adjustments to my expectations."

"An hour from now?"

"That will do. I will be at my house."

She hung up.

Shes said, "You're not serious."

"When you need information, go to the primary source."

"But Chen—"

"Ju-Long is a good cop. He knows his business, but he thinks I'm dirty. He's making a mistake, and I need to rectify it. Since you won't let me kill him, the only thing left is to bring in a consultant."

"To kill him?"

She smiled. "No, Yaotl doesn't kill medjau. He's assured me of that repeatedly. Too much heat, he says, even though he likes chili peppers in his food. No, I just want his take on what the Russians might be up to. And on why InterSecPol reports I'm dirty."

"But Yaotl—Cheryl, you're taking on too much risk."

"I don't want to depend on you for a dishwashing job, Shes. I need my career back. And I need to help Henutsenu. That's the risk, the risk of doing nothing and winding up taking you up on your offer of washing dishes at your restaurant. And losing my best friend. I hate washing dishes."

"Right. Well, I'm going to worry no matter what. I'd better find Sebek and talk to him about Henutsenu. I need to look into Nesimen. And I'll consult, too. Karkin. He can tell us what's happening at InterSecPol, if I can get him to say more than one or two words."

"Fine. I'll make sure I let you know what's happening with Yaotl and the Russians, and you do the same with Karkin and InterSecPol. If you don't hear from me in, say, two days, start looking for my body."

"I'd rather hold on to it right here."

A short interval passed while MacIntyre allowed his attentions. Then she left him to his walk.

Yaotl had the biggest palace on the Tjesut, the ridge along the northern edge of the city that sloped down a steep hill to the bay. The Tjesut, with its spectacular views of the bay and the north, was where the Menmenet elite built their mansions. Yaotl had brought in an Aztec architect from the Modernist school who produced a wonder of technology. The palace was a pyramidal building that joined glass and concrete into layers, a bold statement among the classical papyrus-columned mansions of his neighbors. MacIntyre would bet they loved the palace no more than the man, an interloper in their midst.

The Aztec butler was a tall man who kept his thoughts to himself behind a calm demeanor. He guided MacIntyre through the house to the back door, telling her that his boss was gardening. Yaotl preferred to meet with her there, she knew, because of his fear of bugging devices inside his house. The butler guided her to a glass greenhouse that housed Yaotl's desert garden. It contained cacti and other rare plants from his homeland, which was a lot sunnier and drier and hotter than Menmenet. As the butler opened the door, the room greeted her with a blast of dry heat.

The small, hawk-faced man said, "Thank you, Etzli," and dismissed the butler to his other duties. Yaotl nodded to her, then pointed at a large barrel cactus. "Mildew," he said. "No matter what I do, no matter what I try, no matter how much money I spend. Mildew."

"Sorry to hear that. Can we talk Russians?" You had to get to the point with Yaotl or he would talk you to death about nothing. Maybe that was his preferred method of executing medjau—boring them to death.

"Russians, Russians. Everybody wants to talk about Russians. I would cheerfully inhabit a world in which there were no such people."

"Yet here we are. What can you tell me?"

"What can you offer me in exchange? Remember our agreement. You give me information about my competitors, and I give you information in exchange. Now that your colleagues have suspended you and brought you up on charges, you cannot deliver on that agreement."

"You talk too much, Yaotl."

"It is a personal failing, I admit." He smiled. "But I get the job done."

"You may talk too much about me."

"Is that an accusation, Hutyt?" Yaotl was still smiling, but somehow his teeth appeared sharper.

"An inference. One of our detectives thinks I'm dirty because of our relationship."

"Unfortunate, but I am not the source of that information. Perhaps you should look in a mirror."

MacIntyre ruefully reflected on all the people she'd told about her adventures with Yaotl. Too many. And Chen was a pretty good semetyt with excellent insight into criminal organizations.

"All right, I'll accept that. But the situation is fraught. Whatever is happening to Shes is spilling over on me, and I need to fix that."

Yaotl smiled. "Thank you for your business, supplying guards to the Neferti restaurant. It was a wise move for you. The individuals responsible for the incident at the Per'ankh restaurant will think twice when confronting my men. There may be a solid business model in this sort of work, protective services, having dipped my sandals into the water." MacIntyre, having had some experience with criminal organizations, and in particular Yaotl's, guessed that such a business would involve making the threats, then guarding against them. To each business its own approach. Should she ask for a fee as compensation for providing him with the idea? She should not.

"What about the Russians?" she asked, dragging the conversation back to the main point.

Yaotl walked over to inspect a smaller cactus, studying it. "Mildew. Hutyt, how much do you know about buying explosives?"

"You can't just order them up over the Internet?"

Yaotl smiled. "Fortunately not."

"How so?"

"I devote a small part of my sales operations to such materials."

"How small?"

"Minuscule. But I have a monopoly on such things in Menmenet."

MacIntyre's mind stretched. "So whoever blew up the Per'ankh bought the materials from you or brought them in from somewhere else."

"Importing would be too dangerous—if I discovered the practice. No one has done that."

"Wouldn't it be as dangerous to you if the medjau traced the explosives back to you?"

He smiled. "I have a monopoly. No tracing necessary. And I do have certain ways to avoid exciting the attention of your colleagues."

He's paying somebody off. Menna? Somebody on the organized crime squad? Somebody in the Court of Ma'at? She filed all this away on her mental to-do list, in case she ever got her job back. If there was dirt in the medjau to clean up, she wanted to be the one scrubbing.

"So, who bought the explosives?" she asked.

Yaotl walked over to a third cactus. "Mildew. No matter what I do."

"Fine. All right. What can I offer? Money."

"10,000 debenu."

"For a name? Not a chance. Anyway, I don't have that much, and I'm out of a job. 1,000."

"For such a man as your boyfriend, Hutyt, I judge you would pay more. You might get some funding from your boyfriend."

"1,500."

"And since the problems seem to have migrated from him to you…"

"All right. 2,000. I can't afford more. And you know damn well that getting me out from under this will help you in the long run."

Yaotl was unmoved. "2,500."

There was no chance Shesmu would fund this. He was too honest and law abiding. She'd dip into her retirement. No more caviar lunches, and she'd cut back on her bar bill. Good thing she was sleeping with a chef. At least she wouldn't starve to death.

Reluctantly, she said, "All right. 2,500."

"Done. I will get someone on the job this afternoon. We will find the purchaser and see what we can find out about the motivation for such a bad review of your boyfriend's restaurant. I will also see if I can determine why anyone would believe that you are involved in my business. So unlikely! One thing I can tell you: Russians have expressed an interest in expanding their business dealings beyond the border of Russkaya Amerika. I have been in negotiations with them off and on, here and in Gorni." He sighed. "Russians. A people of very little subtlety."

"What kind of negotiations?"

"I will leave that to your capable imagination, Hutyt. It would be bad business for me to reveal such things to you or to anyone else. Let us just call it mergers-and-acquisitions work."

"Fine. Call me."

She was claustrophobic in this room, surrounded by all these large, prickly killer plants from the desert. With or without mildew. She preferred the safety of wandering around in the fog of Menmenet.

Etzli the butler showed her out.

CHAPTER FIFTEEN
Shesmu Uncovers an Imposter

Sebek wasn't hard to find.

I walked into the Neferti, and there he was in the bar, fortifying himself, dressed in his chef's uniform. Fortunately, it was between lunch and dinner, and the bar was mostly empty. A pair of well-dressed ladies taking a late lunch at the bar sent surreptitious glances of concern at the distressed chef.

"Sebek," I said, as I sat down on a stool next to my best friend.

"Shes, I 'm lost," he said. Red eyes, pronounced bags—he was in bad shape. "Henutsenu's somewhere in the Temple of Bastet, arrested for sacrilege and defiling the precincts of the goddess by murdering two w'abu."

"Cheryl told me."

"I can't…they won't let me see her. Threw me out of the temple. Now I can't even get through the door."

"Cheryl has seen her, and she's OK."

He stared at me in shock. "How?"

"How does Cheryl do anything?"

"Right. Sorry, stupid question." He smiled for the first time.

"You should be in the kitchen, Sebek."

"What? No. Can't face it."

"It's your job to face it." I made this a gentle reminder, not a criticism.

"Shes…" His voice trailed off, the hopelessness clear in his drawn face.

"You need to be in the kitchen, Sebek. It's chaos in there without you, Khay and Qenna and too many French cooks that don't get how to cook Remetjy food. Look, I need to deal with bombs and revenue agents and the R'ames Society and Russian gangsters and the gods know what else. I can't dive in to help, Sebek. You've got to do this for me. Get a grip!"

Sebek sat up on his stool. "Yeah, OK. Sorry. It's just that Henutsenu…."

I cut into the potential downward spiral. "Here's what I'll do. If you get it together and go in there and take charge, I'll work with Cheryl to find and help Henutsenu. Cheryl is desperate to help her. I'll work together with her on it. Leave it to us, Sebek, and do what you do best. We'll handle Bastet." If I couldn't convince him, I'd have to fire him, and I didn't want to do that.

I saw his face set in determination. "Yes, all right. I'll do what I can."

"As soon as I find anything, I'll tell you. Now get in there." I slapped him on the back. He hugged me and left for the kitchen.

"Great work, chef!" exclaimed the bartender, admiring my management skills.

"Thanks. Pour me some of the aquavit there, will you?"

He did, and I felt the strong liquor course down my throat and warm my heart. Now it was time to deal with Nesimen and the R'ames Society, and Karkin, and the Russians, and MacIntyre. Much easier than keeping a first-rate kitchen running like a Swiss watch.

On the bus ride to the Tjesut, I thought up five different approaches to getting Khenemset Neferet to tell me everything she knew. In the event, I didn't use any of them; she told me everything she knew in the first five minutes.

Nesimen's house was on the wrong side of Tjesut, the heights rising out of the Bay in the north central quarter of the city. It was the wrong side because it looked out on lower Menmenet rather than on the Bay. All the great houses were on the north side; cut-rate millionaires lived on the south side to save money.

The house was not ornate; it didn't make a statement, and it didn't contribute to the architectural tone of the city, and it didn't signal any kind of magnate. It was just a house. The usual white, blank wall rose right from the sidewalk, just like the rest of the houses on the block. It was the kind of house I would expect Khenemset Neferet to live in. I rang the doorbell next to the painted wooden door and waited.

A little window in the middle of the door opened, and behind the grill I saw Khenemset Neferet's eyes inspecting me. "Shesmu?"

"That's right."

She opened the door. "It's so nice to see you, Shes." She hugged me, and I hugged her back. Her face was stressed and tired, the lines more pronounced than I remembered. She looked old and worried.

"I want to help," I said, "and events are catching up with us."

"Nesimen had a call. They needed him at the office."

"He's in for a long day."

Her mouth was set. "Sennedjem?"

"I'm afraid so."

We walked across the little hall behind the front door and into the house. Khenemset Neferet led me into the comfortable sitting room and offered me tea, which I accepted. She was back with a pot in a minute. She told me she'd already made some for herself. Even under stress, she was well dressed in an understated way, a long Remetjy dress with only a little decoration on the sleeves, very suitable for a middle-aged, well-to-do Remetjet. No jewelry to speak of; certainly no expensive dj'amu necklace. All the years I'd known her, she never worn expensive jewelry.

I asked, "Can you tell me anything more about Sennedjem or what Nesimen thinks about it all?"

She considered for a minute. "Nesimen is frightened, but he won't tell me what he's frightened about. He complains off and on about Sennedjem's behavior, but he gets this look on his face, angry, afraid, and does nothing. Nothing!"

I asked, "Has he said anything about money troubles at the Society?"

"No, he comes home and says everything is wonderful. Until Sennedjem does something, and he complains about that, but never about money."

"Khenemset Neferet, is Nesimen the sole source of income for the family?"

She said, "We live on his salary and his inheritance. He takes care of all the bills."

Better to tell her now rather than her finding out later on her own. "Khenemset Neferet. Ask him about money. You need to do that."

She looked down at her lap, then up at me. "It's that bad?"

"Does Nesimen often bring home gifts for you?"

"Gifts?"

"Yes, jewelry, expensive clothes, that sort of thing."

She looked down at her simple dress and up again at me in bewilderment, then said again, "It's that bad?"

"It could be. The Henet Baket have taken over the Society offices."

She looked up. "Did they catch that Sennedjem?"

"Catch?"

"I mean, did they arrest him or question him?"

"No, he wasn't there."

She looked blank. "Not there?"

"It would seem that Sennedjem had other things to do and didn't show up for work. And he took all the money the Society had with him."

A tear appeared, running down the side of Khenemset Neferet's nose. She shivered. What I'd told her was not welcome, and it also raised powerful emotions in her. That raised emotions in me. But I had to continue in the role of investigator, not family friend.

I asked, "Can you tell me anything more about Sennedjem or the problems you noticed at the Society?"

Embarrassed, she wiped away the tear, but she still quivered. "Not really. I never knew that much. Nesimen only talks about the people he's met and the places he goes, never about the business."

"The other night in the Myu-Myu club, why did you mention the problems with Sennedjem to us after the fight? Nesimen didn't want to talk about it."

"Oh, he's infuriating! Nesimen, I mean. Why can't he do something about it? We'd been out with Sennedjem several times, and the last two times, the man was out of control. When he drinks, he drinks too much. He gets really rude. I've never understood him. He can't be a Remetj. Just look at him." She exhibited all the disdain of the middle-class Remetjet for the foreigner.

I said, "He looks Russian, not Remetjy." Russians everywhere.

"Yes, I'm sure you're right."

I brought her back to the point at hand. "But why the other night? Why tell us about the problem? Why get us involved?"

She looked away from me. "The time before, at the Wadjwer Club, it was a woman he had with him. They drank vodka, glass after glass. She was European, dressed..." She seemed at a loss for words. I saw her throat move as she swallowed what she wanted to say.

"Provocatively?" I asked.

"Like a whore." The word sounded dirty coming from Khenemset Neferet, and she meant it to sound dirty. She had to force it out. She'd had a nice, middle-class Menmenet upbringing. One didn't mention things like whores with such an upbringing. One tended not to think about things like fraud or tax medjau or whores. But one rarely needed to; Khenemset Neferet suddenly did. And she didn't like that.

"What happened?"

"He started taking her dress off, right there." She stopped, speechless with the memory.

"And got thrown out?"

"Yes. Nesimen was beside himself. We were with some important people from New York, visiting to see how the Society works."

"And they saw."

She closed her eyes and looked down at her lap again.

I continued, "And Nesimen? Why didn't he fire Sennedjem?" I would have.

"I don't *know*," she said, emphasizing the last word, still shaking. "He said he couldn't do anything about it, that it wouldn't be good for the Society to drag everything out into the light of day. He said the Board wouldn't let him do anything. We don't argue; but that night we argued. Then, the other night, with you and your medjat friend there, I thought I'd make him confront it. It was too much for me. And you've always been there for me, for us."

I responded, "Well, it's out now. But I can't say he's confronting it yet. And the Board isn't any better."

"Nesimen hasn't even mentioned my telling you about the problem. He acts like it doesn't exist. I don't understand it. And what you're telling me is frightening me." She put a hand over mine, mutely asking for reassurance.

She was right, in a way; I brought a world through her door that she'd barely touched in her sheltered life, and there would be a lot of pain for a long time. I didn't think there was much more information in her; Nesimen seemed to have kept her clueless. She'd have to tell it all to the Henet Baket. I didn't know how I could reassure her.

"Do you have anyone you can talk to for support?" I asked.

"I'll go to the Temple of Hut-Her and ask the goddess for protection."

"You do that," I said, but I wasn't very hopeful that Hut-Her would help. She was a strong goddess, one that cared deeply for and protected women, but relying on goddesses for help was hit or miss, in my experience.

My need was for truth, ma'at. The Henet Baket or the medjau could help but probably wouldn't because they thought I was in the pocket of Russian gangsters, along with my dirty medjat girlfriend. I'd have to tease out a little truth on my own.

I walked home and made myself a pot of Remetjy tea. I settled into a comfortable position and worked the phone.

My first call connected me to Nesimen's executive assistant. I reminded him who I was, then requested the resumes of Nesimen and Panekhet, the Chairman of the Board of Directors. I had prepared a little speech about my interest in the

R'ames Society and wanting to learn more about its leadership to promote it. The assistant didn't ask, he just said, "Email OK?"

"Sure. I appreciate your helpfulness."

"You're very welcome."

And the resumes appeared in my inbox. I looked them over. I consdered what it told me about Nesimen, realizing I hadn't spent much time with him in the two years he and Khenemset Neferet had been in Menmenet. All I knew was the little that Taneferet had told me about him at various times, and what I'd observed in the last few days. Generous—to a fault, and corrupt. Independently wealthy, from an inheritance. Not as clued in to his Society's workings as one might expect given his position. An avoider—somebody who wanted unpalatable situations and people to disappear.

On impulse, I called Panekhet using the contact information on his resume. I hoped he could tell me more about Nesimen, as he had worked closely with the man. Talking to Panekhet would kill two quail with one stone, as I'd gather background on both of the men. And I could follow up with him about Sennedjem and Henutsenu.

Panekhet's resume wasn't long. He'd spent most of his working life at the Temple of Bastet, working his way up the hierarchy to his current position as the Hem-Netjer-Tepy of the temple. He managed its multi-million-debenu budget, successfully according to the self reporting on his resume.

I got through to Panekhet after talking my way past a couple of gatekeepers. After I greeted him and reminded him of our meeting at the award ceremony, he said, "Congratulations, Shesmu, on your award. I was very sorry to hear about the Per'ankh, it's a great loss to the city. I've eaten there many times, under both Nekhen and you, a lot of great memories."

"Thanks very much," I said. "I appreciate the award. I'm also interested in the Board of Directors of the Society, how it all works."

His voice was dubious. "You're rather young, aren't you? Do you have any money? I mean, are you wealthy? Because that's what you need to join the board."

I laughed. "Oh no, my interest is in the Sennedjem situation."

He was silent for a minute, then said, "Sennedjem? What's your angle on that? That's a Henet Baket investigation, isn't it?"

"I just don't want the Society to get too much of a black eye. And the Henet Baket may believe I am involved. I'm also trying to help Nesimen because his wife is an old family friend. Sennedjem has caused them and the Society a lot of trouble."

He put two and two together. "You were involved in that fracas at the Myu-Myu Club, weren't you? Right after Nesimen introduced us."

"Yes. The latest is that the Henet Baket decided I'm involved with Sennedjem in the financial goings-on at the Society."

"Oh, I see."

"So, can you tell me a little about how the Board went about hiring Sennedjem?"

"We didn't hire him, Nesimen did." His voice conveyed his distaste. I didn't warm to him.

"Ah. Yes. But you hired Nesimen?"

"Yes." A terse response, impossible to interpret.

"How did that happen?"

"Sorry?"

I rephrased. "How did you identify Nesimen as a candidate for the head position of the Society?"

"Oh. Well, we'd met him at earlier charity events. When the previous head retired, the board formed a committee to search for a new one. Nesimen's name came up."

"Came up? Who suggested it?"

He was silent for a minute. "I did."

"Because you'd known him from before?"

"Slightly. We'd talked over dinner twice. He'd done some executive management for charities and so on. He's independently wealthy from his marriage, and he was so friendly and outgoing, he'd make a great head. And he has. And he was into food."

"Yes, I've been on the receiving end of his charm, too. His resume shows his management credentials, very impressive. By the way, why do you think he's wealthy?" Khenemset Neferet had said it was Nesimen's inheritance that was putting food on the table for the family. Her family didn't have a grain of millet in the cupboard.

There was a moment of silence on the line. "Just, I guess, the way he talked, the way he spent money, the things he referred to in stories, and so on." There was a faint note of question in his voice, which I ignored.

I pushed a little harder. I looked down the resume and randomly picked an item.

"It says on his resume that Nesimen was head of the Ta'an-Imenty Bone Cancer Society. Did any of the references you checked come from there?"

Another moment of silence. "I don't believe we checked any references. We felt we understood him well enough."

No reference checks.

"And did you check his degree at the University of Niutimywer?"

"No. Not that important to us."

"No, I see that." I wondered what would have been important to the directors and decided that Nesimen's golf game would exhaust the limit of their patience. Why not ask? "Did you play golf with him?"

Panekhet was exasperated. "What's that got to do with anything?"

"Nothing, not a thing. I was just wondering if he was a large-stakes gambler or not. Most rich golfers bet on their golf games."

"Oh. Well, no, we didn't play for money, just for fun and as a good place to talk. It was a foursome, three directors and Nesimen."

Thought so. Ah well. My mind skipped. "OK, thanks. Oh, and by the way, I'm sorry about your troubles, too."

"Troubles?"

"The murders of the two w'abu. I read about it in the paper this morning. The arrest." I cleared my throat. "Henutsenu, you may recall, works for me in my Neferti restaurant. I'd like to know—"

His voice was abrupt. "I'm not much involved in that, and we don't like to talk about internal temple affairs with outsiders. Look, Shesmu, I have to go. I'm late already." I was alone on the phone. So much for Henutsenu.

I was sure that Baki would investigate Nesimen along with every other aspect of the R'ames Society. Everyone knew that the Henet Baket insisted no taxpayer should cheat the state out of a single deben. But he thought I was involved, and that might bias his investigation. After my talk with Panekhet, I felt I knew less about Nesimen than before. Time for some facts.

I picked up the phone and in quick succession got through to the registrar at the University of Niutimywer. Then I spoke with the personnel people at three of the organizations on Nesimen's resume. None had heard of him. The entire resume was a lie; not just a tiny lie, a big lie. My hunch was that the R'ames Society's values reflected that of its head: a shell with nothing inside except corruption and falsehood. Poor Khenemset Neferet! With a sinking heart, I verified Panekhet's divinity degree; at least he was who he said he was.

My phone rang.

I answered, "Hello?"

"Karkin. Let's talk."

* * *

Karkin's car still smelled musty. A glimpse at the back seat showed the same mess of equipment scattered in piles. On top was his bow, with a quiver full of arrows.

He guided the car away from the curb in front of my house and turned the corner to the north.

I said, "I'm always happy to see you, but you could tell me where we're going and why you're kidnapping me."

He negotiated a double-parked car and headed across Mentju Boulevard, saying nothing. After two or three blocks, he reached toward a mess of papers next to him on the bench seat and extracted the top one. He handed me the paper.

In English, it had the fuzzy quality of a cheap fax machine. The logo at the top sat next to the SecInterPol header. The paper itself was all in capitals, making it even harder to read.

"SA TO ALL FIELD OPS MNMNT. RECENT BOMBING INCDNT RELATED TO INCREASED CO ACTV IN VLDK AND NVAR. ML PRP SENNEDJEM HAD CONTACTS WITH RANUKHOVA CO GORNI. ACTIVE CONTACT WITH PRNC PRP SHESMU MNMNT. POSS CO PREJ ACTION. POSS ASSOCIATE TO COR MNMNT POL PRP. TAKE NO ACTION RPT TAKE NO ACTION TO INTERFERE WITH ACTIVE INV RUSSIA."

After going through this missive twice, I looked up. "I thought fax was a thing of the past. Your secret organization is right on top of things, isn't it? I hope this means more to you than it does to me. What the hell is this supposed to say?"

Karkin said, "Bombing is gang war between you and Russians in Vladivostok, Novoarchangelsk, and Gorni. You're a principal perpetrator. Sennedjem working with gang in Gorni and with you in Menmenet. You're associating with corrupt police in Menmenet."

"Oh, I see." I was a little hot. "So I'm fighting an international gang war with all kinds of Russians. Corrupt police?" My heart sank. "MacIntyre?"

"Told 'em they're wrong. No response." He kept his eyes on the road, going through a yellow light. "No action."

I closed my eyes and contemplated the situation. MacIntyre would love this. At least I didn't have to worry about conversation topics at our next meal.

I opened my eyes and asked, "Why are you associating with associates of known principle perpetrators? When your on-top-of-things organization commanded no action?"

He squinted his eyes, the closest I'd seen to an emotion in him. "Limits of intelligence."

"I can safely say there's an enormous amount of limited intelligence at play here."

"Gonna have to deal with it. Sennedjem. North. Gorni."

The car went down the hill toward the ferry terminal on Mehetet Street. My phone rang. The caller id told me it was MacIntyre.

"We have problems," she said when I answered.

"You said that before."

"They're worse."

"No kidding. I'm in a car with Karkin at the moment, avoiding Russian gangsters who want to start a gang war with me. Oh, and did I ever tell you I'm a master criminal running a gang in Menmenet? How about you?"

"Master criminal? I've drained my bank account to get information from a master criminal. A real one."

"Yaotl? Is that legal?"

"Sure, as long as he doesn't have to kill anyone to get it. A coin toss. We need to get together and talk."

"Karkin thinks we're heading north on the ferry." I turned to Karkin. "Do you —"

The windshield exploded. Glass pieces rained in on us. Karkin stamped on the accelerator and swerved. The car belied its antique appearance, roaring and tearing forward. We barreled west toward Tjesut along the bay front.

I looked around the car. There was a bullet hole in the back seat. The bullet must have come through the windshield and passed right between us. I became aware that the phone that I still held open in my hand was squawking. I put it to my ear. "—going on? Talk to me!"

"Sorry," I said. "The windshield just exploded. It looks like we were less successful at avoiding the gangsters than we thought. I guess we'd better meet up somewhere in the West part of the city, since that's where we're heading, fast."

"Shes! Where?"

"How about Nekhen's chapel in the necropolis?" Maybe I could get Nekhen's ka on my side. I'd visited his chapel several times while I investigated Nekhen's murder, and it had become a familiar and welcoming place for me. I could only hope the Russians didn't know that; no reason they should. If we could evade them.

MacIntyre said, "All right, I'll meet you there."

Karkin's car raced up the steep Tjesut hill, leaping upwards at cross streets, crashing down and bouncing on all wheels. The wind coming through the hole where the windshield used to be buffeted my face. Karkin squinted against it, but his expression was otherwise unchanged. I looked back for pursuers; there was a red car two blocks back that sped after us. I told Karkin, and he nodded.

I said, "I need to meet MacIntyre at the necropolis. Can you get us there unobserved?"

Without answering, he turned west, tires screeching, and headed out into the Asian quarter of the city. The streets got narrower and the housing denser as we moved from the rich enclave on the Tjesut into the Setetiu district. Karkin started turning right and left along the twisty streets; I quickly lost any sense of where I was. Karkin reached down and picked up a black device and pushed a button with his thumb. We careened into an alley and into an open door. He pushed the button again, and the door closed behind us. We were in a barely lit parking garage.

Karkin pulled his car up against a wall and motioned for me to get out. The door creaked with metal fatigue as I opened it and climbed out. I knew what it felt like. Glass fragments scattered everywhere off my clothes. The garage floor was rough concrete, deeper pits here and there showing as shadows in the dim light. Without bothering to lock the car or even close the doors, Karkin walked across to the other side of the garage, and I followed. He carried his bow and quiver, the only thing he took from the car.

A tiny car, black and shiny, nestled in a space against the wall between two palettes of boxes. Karkin pushed a button on his key ring and the lights flashed and the doors unlocked, and we crammed ourselves into the little car. He stowed his bow and quiver in the small space in back of the seats. He pushed another button, and a second garage door on the other side of the garage opened. We drove out into a different alley and heading south toward the necropolis, unaccompanied by any unwanted followers. I was in the hands of a professional.

CHAPTER SIXTEEN
MacIntyre Makes Progress Backwards

MACINTYRE TURNED HER LITTLE RED car into the necropolis parking lot and parked near the Temple of Inpu. The day was bright with sun, the air fresh, and the sea sparkling in the distance. She walked down the paths to the mid-levels, passing by the large and elegant tombs of the rich and famous.

Half way down the hill, her phone rang. Yaotl.

"I have some good news and some bad news, Hutyt MacIntyre."

"Give me the good news. I need some."

"They are the same news, I fear. We have traced the explosives and identified the person who ordered the bombing. How much do you know about the Russian mafias in Russkaya Amerika?"

"Nothing."

"We will not pursue a tutorial today. Suffice it to say, there is a small group of Russians in a town called Gorni. That is located inland and to the north, just over the border."

"I've heard the name. What about this group of Russians?"

"They are the remnants of a once-powerful mafia in Novoarchangelsk. They lost an argument with another mafia there. What was left of them fled to the south, to Gorni. Now they are trying to regrow their operations. Gorni harbors little in the way of opportunity for crime, being dirt poor. Hence, Menmenet."

"And this group bombed the Per'ankh?"

"Yes."

"Were you able to find out why they did it?"

"They believe your friend Shesmu is the person they most need to kill in Menmenet. Our sources are very clear on that."

"But that begs the question of why."

"It does. We simply do not know. It is difficult to underestimate the level of intelligence these Russians exhibit. But sheer stupidity is not enough to explain their beliefs. Also, our sources report Sennedjem has ties to this group and its leader."

"Do you have a name?"

"Marya Semionevna Ranukhova."

MacIntyre got out her notebook, asked him to spell it, and wrote it down.

"Hutyt. I must warn you that this Ranukhova gang is quite dangerous despite their intellectual incapacity."

"Thank you, Yaotl. I'd say I owe you one, but I'm all paid up."

"You are."

"I remember you said you were negotiating with the people in Gorni. I would imagine that, should our efforts be successful, this group will no longer be a negotiating problem for you."

"Very true, and we appreciate your efforts on our behalf."

MacIntyre, about to respond to this sardonic witticism, heard the crime lord chuckle as he hung up.

MacIntyre waited at the door of Nekhen's chapel. Her medjat senses were aflame with a desire for action. She watched Shes and a small First Nations man with a stone face approach at the pace of two desert tortoises.

Shes stopped in front of the chapel. He suggested, waving a hand at it, "Why don't we go in and get a little privacy?"

MacIntyre looked around: no person was in sight as far as the eye could see. It was a slow day in the necropolis. Muttering under her breath, she opened the door to the chapel and entered. Lights went on, revealing the decorations on the walls. Nekhen, Shes's mentor, appeared in all the panels, working in his kitchen, visiting tables in his restaurant, and shopping in a market. Various gods filled the roles of cooks, customers, and vendors.

The floor was clean, and the walls glowed in the light. The hetep altar was clear; no one had been by with an offering since the last time the w'abu of Inpu had cleaned the place. She shivered; it gave her the creeps, a cold shudder as though someone was stomping on her grave.

Shes approached the hetep. "We'll have to leave some money as an offering."

MacIntyre said, "I'm suspended without pay, and my boss says he'll fire me and put me in jail. Why don't you contribute something for me, and I'll pay you back once I get out of prison and find a new line of work."

Shes put a 50-debenu note on the hetep. That ought to keep Nekhen's ka in groceries for at least a week. At the least, it should bring a smile to the face of the next w'ab who happened by.

MacIntyre said, "Where is *your* tomb going to be, Shes? I'd better know now. You'll be needing it soon." Karkin responded to this sardonic sally with a small clucking sound without changing his expression in the least. Shes ignored it and said, "Karkin tells me we need to go north, to Gorni."

This incensed the already fed up MacIntyre. She faced Karkin. "Do you mean to tell me, you rotten son of a bitch, that you knew all along who was responsible? Do you mean to tell me I just gave up five years of retirement income to have a master criminal tell me what I already should have been told? Do you—"

Karkin sighed, pulled out a piece of paper and gave it to MacIntyre. She held it up to the light. A bad fax from Karkin's headquarters in Genève, in full caps and barely readable. She read.

"Shit," she said in a flat tone, in English.

Shes said, "Is that a general ejaculation or a scathing commentary on the quality of international medjau intelligence work?"

"Shit!" MacIntyre said again, with more force, thrusting the paper back at Karkin. "Son of a goddamn bitch." She took her notebook out of her pocket and held up a page for her friends' inspection. There were five words on it: "Gorni Marya Semionevna Ranukhova Sennedjem."

Karkin stuffed his paper back into his pocket without comment. Son of a bitch. MacIntyre glared at him as she put away her notebook.

Shes said, "We can't keep running and hiding, so the first thing we need to do is to make a deal with the Russians somehow."

"Let's go," said MacIntyre.

Karkin considered things for a minute, then said, "Suspended?"

"That's right."

"Won't help much."

MacIntyre interpreted this laconic assessment as a warning. Pursuing Russian gangsters would likely push Chen over the edge and get her fired. She didn't care. She needed things to happen.

She asked, "What about that last part about TAKE NO ACTION? Is that your real concern?"

Karkin grunted, "No. Wrong."

"So, let's go," she repeated.

"Dangerous. Crazy Russians."

MacIntyre just stared at him with as much contempt as she could muster in a scornful smile.

"Car," said Karkin. A pragmatist. Shes smiled and said nothing.

Fifteen minutes later, the three of them walked across to a small, black car in the temple parking lot. MacIntyre walked all the way around it (six steps) and said, "What the hell is this?"

Karkin said nothing.

"Does it at least fire rockets from the back or something?"

Shes said, "I don't think there's room in the back for a rocket. Or for you."

"I'll follow you to the ferry." She got in her car, started it, and gunned the engine to show her frustration. Karkin pulled away and picked up speed, and she threw her car into gear and followed.

CHAPTER SEVENTEEN
Shesmu Makes a Deal

Karkin zipped his car down the hill of the Tjesut and onto the car ferry. MacIntyre pulled onto the ferry right behind us. I put on a jacket Karkin unearthed from the back of his little car. MacIntyre donned her large parka and again looked like an Inuit. Karkin wore a green military jacket that looked as though it had seen service in at least three different centuries of armed conflict. We sat up near the front of the ferry looking at the bay and squinting into the wind coming over the scratched plastic windbreak in front of us.

MacIntyre's voice emerged from the hood of her parka. "OK, Karkin. Talk to me. Tell me why I'm heading north to see a Russian mafiosa."

Karkin shifted in his seat. "Complicated history."

"Humor me."

"Russkaya Amerika, colonized by Russia in the nineteenth century. Down to Slavyanka Reka, the Russian River."

"Right."

"Novoarchangelsk set up as the capital, up north. The Gulag stretched all across Sibir' and into Alyeska."

"Right."

"Vori."

"What's a vori?"

"Vor. Thief. Not political prisoners, convicts. Formed into gangs and developed businesses, criminal businesses. Top dogs."

"Right."

"50s, Stalin dies, Gulag empties, vori set up shop across Soviet Union. 90s, Soviet Union breaks apart, Russkaya Amerika becomes a country. Apparatchiki and KGB men take over, but vori still there. Oligarchs take over the West, vori take over the East: Petropavlosk and Novoarchangelsk."

"Got it. And Ranukhova is one of them?"

"Ranukhov was a minor vor, set up in Novoarchangelsk. Stupid. Made enemies in the apparatchiki. Gang war, Ranukhov killed. Widow fled south, set up her own vori gang in Gorni. Nothing going on there. Couldn't expand north —so looked south. Menmenet." Karkin fell silent.

The hood nodded and MacIntyre's voice came. "Where do you come in?"

"My station is Menmenet," Karkin replied. "InterSecPro's mission is to find out what's going on in crime everywhere. So I keep track of things in Menmenet."

"Didn't these guys try to shoot you today? And we're going right to the head woman?"

Karkin nodded. "I am. You don't have to."

I said, "I do. I need to know why she bombed my restaurant and tried to shoot me. I need to put a stop to that."

MacIntyre said, "I have to see her to find out why InterSecPro and the medjau think I'm working with them."

Karkin grunted and said, "Better inform your next of kin."

We watched the brown hills of the North Bay loom larger and larger, sharing a depressed silence.

Leaving the north ferry terminal, Karkin led us on a long, twisting ride further north along the Bay. We passed through rolling coastal hills that gradually turned into forested foothills and came to the border of Russkaya Amerika at the Slavyanka Reka. You don't need a passport to go to Russkaya Amerika from the Ta'an-Imenty Republic. They just check you over for drugs and fruit. They care more about the fruit.

We crossed the river and drove into the little town of Gorni, what there was of it. Evening was coming on, and there were few streetlights. The standard white-washed stucco Remetjy houses and buildings in the South gave way to Russian-style wooden houses painted dark colors.

Karkin pulled to a stop at a 4-meter-high chain-link fence with razor wire twisted in circles along the top. All it lacked was a guard tower. Several floodlights lit up the area inside the fence. They illuminated a uniformed guard with a dog.

This was not just a dog. It was a primal force. The dog had massive jaws and shoulders and paws the size of small hams. Its small eyes blazed with ferocity. The only good thing about this dog was that it was on the other side of the fence. Karkin, of course, had other ideas about that.

I huddled with MacIntyre while Karkin walked over to the fence. I expected the dog to erupt, but he didn't. He only glared and wrinkled his lips, exposing large yellow teeth. My guess was he didn't brush often enough after the raw meat meals he ate. Karkin spoke in Russian. The guard imitated the dog, sneering with not much better dental hygiene. Karkin spoke again. The Russian stopped sneering, made a small ducking movement with his head, and spoke into a microphone on his shoulder. After a minute's silence, the receiver crackled, and the guard opened the gate.

With Karkin leading the way, we carefully stepped past the guard and the dog. The yard was devoid of life, bare dirt with an asphalt path leading straight up to the weathered, unpainted door. The house was larger than the surrounding ones, but it was nowhere near as well kept. It looked like an abandoned house repaired just enough to be lived in. The paint peeling off the siding was pinkish and had perhaps been red long in the past. Weathered gray wood showed through the flakes of paint.

We walked up creaking wooden steps to the porch. Karkin knocked, and the door opened. Two guards and a man wearing a black suit appeared in the short hallway. The man in black spoke in Russian. Karkin replied in the same language and translated.

"He wants to pat us down."

The guards shifted their automatic weapons to emphasize their intent. The man in black moved around and between us, never getting in between us and the guards. He patted us all down with quick and efficient hands. He spent a little longer on MacIntyre's parka and removed a small pistol from a pocket. MacIntyre shrugged and grinned.

The inspection done, the man in black motioned us forward to a door at the end of the hall. We walked into a sitting room with two sofas and several chairs scattered around. It was a long room, twice as long as it was wide, with a stove in the Russian style against a wall. The room was a little cool; the stove was not lit.

A blonde woman with the large bones and heavy features of north Russia sat in a large chair facing the sofas. She wore a shapeless black dress and heavy black shoes that did nothing to improve her looks. The dress didn't conceal her massively muscled arms, either. Her angry eyes speared us, and her face proclaimed that now that we were here, her day had not improved.

MacIntyre and I sat on a sofa. Karkin stayed on his feet and spoke in Russian, and the woman replied. They traded words for a while, with Karkin translating for us every so often.

"This is Marya Semionevna Ranukhova. She's the person we were discussing earlier. This is her territory now. She is asking why we're here and who you are."

I asked, "What do you think? Should we explain ourselves?"

"Yes. She's listening." He added a warning. "I don't know how much Renkemet she understands."

Marya Semionevna's eyes narrowed to slits and moved from me to MacIntyre and back again. She spit a short question at Karkin. He responded with our names. Marya Semionevna grimaced and spoke.

"She said Hutyt MacIntyre is a corrupt medjat protecting you and your gang, Shesmu."

"Let's try to clear up some of these delusional beliefs." I paused and thought. "First, tell her I'm a cook, and only a cook. I'm not a criminal mastermind. I'm not interested in taking over her territory. I don't even cheat on my business taxes. Much. And MacIntyre is not corrupt. She's protecting me, but it's because we're in love."

He spoke for a long time, all in sliding z's and tch's, emphasizing a word here and there with a motion of his head or a hand. When he finished, Marya Semi-onevna sat saying nothing for a minute, eyes narrow, then said, "Dyer'mo."

Karkin said, "Bullshit."

"What would it take to convince her?" I asked.

"Of what?" asked Karkin.

"That I'm not a threat to her or her operation."

"Your head on a plate."

"I like my head, and I don't plate such things in my restaurants." I pressed my lips together, then said, "You convince her."

More Russian from Karkin. He seemed willing to use more words in that language than in Renkemet. After a few minutes, her eyes became less suspicious, and she pursed her lips in wary acceptance.

"Can we push our luck by asking about Sennedjem?" I asked. Even the mention of his name, which she recognized, sent Marya Semionevna back into tight-lipped, narrow-eyed suspicion.

"All right, then not."

Karkin shot me a glance that told me to shut up. He talked for a few minutes in his soft monotone, the sibilants flowing. Whatever he told Marya Semionevna, she again lost the suspicion.

"Told her about you and Sennedjem," said Karkin to me. "Explained about Nesimen. Told her medjau are looking for him too. She says Sennedjem and other sources told her about you. And Hutyt MacIntyre."

Marya Semionevna interrupted him, a little impatiently, and rolled out several short sentences. Decisive.

"She says she wants to recoup her losses. She wants you to pay. You got 20,000 debenu?"

"Well, I might have until she bombed my restaurant. No, I don't have 20,000 debenu. What does that represent?"

"Money Sennedjem was supposed to launder but instead stole."

"Ouch."

"She's unhappy with Sennedjem."

"I can see why. But we have nothing to do with that."

Karkin explained this in some detail to Marya Semionevna, but her eyes did not warm up. She made another decisive declaration.

"She says she could have us killed right here and buried under the floor. She says she could feed us to her dogs."

"You know, if she keeps harassing us, I could get riled up," said MacIntyre. She tapped her foot with impatience. I felt like a guy observing a train wreck from inside the train. MacIntyre brushed her hair back over her ear. "Tell her she's missed her chance for that, and now she's got medjau from five separate organizations looking for her. On that scale, we're not a threat. Her dogs eat too much of the wrong food, anyway. Tell her that."

Karkin spoke again in Russian, without taking his eyes off MacIntyre. His expression was unchanged, but there were certain muscles in his face that had subtly shifted. His eyes were grim.

Marya Semionevna listened with her eyes closed. Her face muscles had sagged a bit, lengthening the shape of her face and making her appear older. Karkin stopped, and Marya Semionevna just sat, absorbing the situation. Finally, she opened her eyes and looked at Karkin, then at MacIntyre, then at me. She asked a question.

Karkin turned to me and asked, "What about your restaurant?"

"What about it?"

Karkin answered without asking Marya Semionevna. "She wants to know if you want compensation for the restaurant." His eyes, locked on mine, told me I was obtuse.

"Tell her I don't need compensation, the restaurant was well insured, but that I'd like her assurance that there would be no more bombs."

Karkin spoke, Marya Semionevna replied, "Da."

MacIntyre said, "What about Sennedjem?"

Marya Semionevna's reaction was anger again, with a short sentence. Karkin said, "She uttered an impolite suggestion about fornicating with his mother." He blinked. "It's a common Russian suggestion." I took his word for it.

Marya Semionevna spoke again, with less heat. Karkin said, "She's giving him to us."

"What?" asked MacIntyre.

"She's giving him to us. Sennedjem." He waited for another long stream of Russian. "He's over on the coast at her brother's house." His eyes got bigger as she said what sounded like "Eta mayu brat'."

Karkin said, "I didn't know this. Pyotr Semionovich Podgoronov is her brother. Sennedjem is staying with him in Milaya."

A long, electric silence followed this revelation. Marya Semionevna stared at us with flat, dead eyes. I didn't see any resemblance, mental or physical or spiritual, with Pyotr Semionovich. If she had a ba at all, it was black, twisted, and deformed. For the first time in my life, I realized it was a good thing that bas were invisible.

Karkin said, "Same patronymic. Should have guessed."

I asked, "Why is she telling us this?"

Karkin asked. She answered. He said, "She wants to get rid of Sennedjem. She thinks he deserves to die, but she says her dogs wouldn't touch him out of disgust. And she wants her money."

Marya Semionevna smiled. It was not pretty. Having finished her analysis of Sennedjem's character, she paused, stared at us for a minute, then asked a question.

Karkin translated, "She asks, would you consider taking a 10% commission for collecting the debt owed her? Say no. She's suggesting you kill him." That last remark was Karkin's, not from Marya Semionevna. She still smiled, applying butter to get me to agree. A tempting prospect, to do away with that smirking thief. So many problems solved. And I could use the money.

I sighed. "No. I'm a cook, not a butcher."

MacIntyre smiled; after all, my namesake god, Shesmu, is the Butcher of Souls. Not the best image at the moment.

"Very good choice. Nyet," Karkin said to Marya Semionevna. She stopped smiling and shrugged. She said something else, looking at MacIntyre.

"Perhaps for a similar amount of money, Hutyt MacIntyre would consider…?"

MacIntyre, smiling again, shook her head no.

Before we got any more unacceptable propositions, I suggested, "Get her to call Pyotr Semionovich, to tell him to help us. I'll make sure she gets her money." That outcome would be unlikely, but it was worth a try.

Karkin spoke, and Marya Semionevna replied. "She said they don't speak, but she'll write a note."

Marya Semionevna walked over to a small table and wrote on a pad, ripped off the note and handed it to Karkin. He read it and handed it to me. Black ink, Cyrillic characters. Karkin said, "A note to Petya. Sennedjem lied about you being a gangster. Give you Sennedjem so you can get back her money. Give you any help you need to do that. Signed love, Masha."

Affecting. The note was in Cyrillic script, which I can't read. I handed it to MacIntyre, who glanced over it and handed it back.

"I'd take it out in oysters for the rest of the bastard's life," I said, "if I had a restaurant. Don't translate that, please."

I rose and, acting on the general principle of not aggravating people who would kill you on the spot, bowed deeply. The same man that let us in, let us out after giving MacIntyre her gun back. The dog growled deep in his throat as we passed. The guard drooled.

We made it to the ferry terminal just in time for the last ferry back to Menmenet. Karkin went off to see about his other car. It was late by the time MacIntyre's red car pulled up outside my house on Dju Keta.

"I'm too tired to drive home. How about a bed for the night?" she asked. "And I'm hungry."

"I have some leftovers that I can whip together. Come on in."

The leftovers proved satisfactory. We fell into bed after midnight, looked at each other, kissed, and fell asleep before we did anything more about it.

CHAPTER EIGHTEEN
MacIntyre Hits Bottom Again

ALL THE PEOPLE MACINTYRE NEEDED to talk to wouldn't be around until at least 9 a.m, so she relaxed into a leisurely Shesmu breakfast after a sunrise-drenched lovemaking session. Spiced fava bean puree on fresh-baked flatbread, cured olives from the Neferti kitchen, 10 different varieties of date, and a large pot of Remetjy tea. Way better than her usual corn flakes. But her mind was on Henutsenu, who still languished in the dungeons of the Temple of Bastet.

She popped another olive into her mouth, chewed, and ejected the pit into a small pit urn.

"Something occurred to me last night," said Shesmu.

"Me too. Too tired, though. And it was good, this morning."

"I meant, about our adventure yesterday." He smiled and reached for her hand, and they sat in mutually aware silence for a minute. "Do you remember what Marya Semionevna said about who told her I was a competitor?"

MacIntyre thought back. "She said Sennedjem told her." Her eyes widened. "And…she said other sources confirmed it. Damn! We should have followed up right there. I wasn't paying enough attention, too mad."

Shesmu took out his phone and made a call.

"Hi, Karkin. Look, Cheryl and I remembered Marya Semionevna told us about some other sources that verified Sennedjem's lies about us. Did she say anything you didn't translate that might give us an idea about—"

Shesmu listened for a few seconds and disconnected.

"He said no?" asked MacIntyre.

"He said medjau."

"What?"

"He said the sources were medjau. There is somebody on the city payroll taking money from Marya Semionevna. It has to be a medja. Karkin doesn't want you looking into it."

"He said all that?"

"Well, no. But it's what he meant."

"Fuck. Why in the hell didn't he tell me?"

"Wouldn't say. My guess is he judged you or I would throw a fit, too dangerous."

"What were his exact words?"

"Let's see. 'Medja. Paid off by Masha. Telling you too risky. Looking into it. Don't tell her.' I interpreted that last 'her' to mean 'you.'"

MacIntyre contemplated her lover with smiling eyes. "Thank God for a man who doesn't pay attention to his male friends."

"Yeah, but it's just that I think your investigation is going to fix my problems. Go to it."

MacIntyre pushed her chair back from the table.

"See you later. Got a little songbird to find and a tattered reputation to stitch back together."

MacIntyre stood at the door of Yaotl's palace on the Tjesut, the morning sun lighting up the pyramid of glass into a spectacular blaze. Her thinking was that, if you want to find a corrupt medja, the easiest way is to talk to a corrupter.

The door opened, and she confronted the calm-faced Aztec butler, Etzli.

"Hutyt MacIntyre."

"Eztli. I need to see Lord Yaotl."

"You did not call ahead," said Etzli.

"No, something has come up, no time."

"Lord Yaotl is not at his best, mornings," warned the tall Aztec.

"I'll risk it," she replied.

The butler admitted her and gave her a seat in the entry atrium. The space rose through the multiple floors to reach the apex of the pyramid, flooding the area with morning light. The palace was so quiet, it reminded MacIntyre of a tomb. A shiver ran through her; premonition of her own tomb?

Eztli was gone for what seemed an eternity, but she had lost all sense of time. Ten minutes passed in the real world, while she obsessed on the crazy one she'd entered, with Russian mobsters and bombs and crooked medjau and temple murders and imprisoned friends. This was not your ordinary fucked-up homicide investigation. This was serious.

Etzli returned, padding on soft sandals so that what little sound his approach made was lost in the huge space above her. She watched the big man approach and strove to interpret his face. She got nowhere; Etzli had honed his granite facial expression over many years of service to a man who held many secrets.

"Hutyt MacIntyre. It would please Lord Yaotl to see you in the breakfast room. Please follow me."

Etzli led her through shining glass halls, some covered with tapestries or curtains, others exposing rooms full of Aztec furniture and art. They emerged into a sunlit room facing east. Through two walls of the corner room, she could see Yaotl's garden waking to the day. The dew glistened on the waving grasses and glittered in the sun, an organic counterpoint to the pellucid building.

Ordinarily, Yaotl's face varied from austere to grim, his sharp Aztec features and wrinkled visage giving him a forbidding expression. This morning, as he looked up from his breakfast, his face expressed sourness and an obstinate quality that did not bode well for MacIntyre's mission. She barreled ahead anyway. As she opened her mouth to speak, Yaotl jumped in first.

"Please sit down, Hutyt, and join me. Would you care for some tlaxcalli and beans? A sweet corn cake?"

"No, thank you, Yaotl, I've had breakfast."

"Then a beaker of xocolatl? Freshly made by my cook."

MacIntyre broke down at the notion of some chocolate; somehow the idea of ingesting that substance fitted her mood. She sat and said, "Yes, all right. Thank you." Etzli placed a ceramic beaker in front of her and ceremoniously poured the hot drink from a jug waiting on a sideboard. The dark, rich liquid released a complex aroma of spices and dark fruit. She sipped; bitter and spicy with cinnamon and a hint of chile and a round, robust flavor that stayed with her.

Yaotl eyed her. "Now, what is so urgent that you must interrupt my breakfast? I dislike working out of business hours, Hutyt."

"I understand, and I'm sorry to intrude on your meal, Yaotl, but it's urgent."

"There is nothing urgent occurring in the city that involves me or my operations."

"It's not you, it's me. You may remember that I told you my colleagues think I'm corrupt, and that got me suspended."

"I have a vague recollection of this matter," admitted the crime lord, but his eyes were sharp and penetrating.

"And you may remember your hint about the Russians," she said.

"Yes. I understand you paid a visit to Madame Ranukhova. May I say, Hutyt, that action was ill advised?"

"It wasn't my idea."

"Even so. I believe your religion has a story involving lions and angels. While your god may shower fortune on you for your good works, I wouldn't push it too far, Hutyt. Angels are rare in my business, I have found."

"And in mine, Yaotl. I'm not much into angels, anyway. Why I'm here—the Russian told us she had verified her information about us through a corrupt medja on her payroll. Maybe not in those words, but it fits."

"Corruption in the medjau? Could such a thing be possible?" Yaotl smiled a sour smile. "Why, our relationship is pure and blameless, Hutyt. One could hardly call it corrupt."

Which was to say, as he had said before, "Look in the mirror." MacIntyre didn't want to stare too hard in any mirrors right now.

"I need to know who, Yaotl. I have my suspicions, but surely you have enough connections in the medjau to know who might be corrupt."

Yaotl took a sip of xocolatl and made a face. "Hutyt, you are putting me in a false position. It is not in my best interest to tell you anything about my operations. I will help you with peripheral matters that do not concern me in return for your help in identifying threats to my operations. But that is as far as it goes. Why would you even think I might tell you such things?"

The dour expression on Yaotl's face intensified. "Let me propose a hypothetical situation for you, Hutyt. Say there was a medja high in the organization that a businessman such as myself could persuade to take certain actions in return for generous payments to offshore bank accounts. Say that such a medja, being overly greedy, took such payments from other businessmen, possibly involving conflicts of interest. Under what circumstances would it help that businessman to reveal such a relationship to someone such as yourself? Someone who, in pursuing blameless justice and good citizenship, might reveal that relationship and bring all the parties into the pitiless light of the goddess Ma'at. What am I to suppose from such a thing, Hutyt?"

"You talk too much, Yaotl." MacIntyre sipped the last of her beaker of xocolatl. Did she have enough leverage over the man to threaten him? No, she did not. All her threats would be empty.

"You ask too much, Hutyt," rejoined the crime lord. "Now, as much as I am warmed by your presence, I must ask you to excuse me. Business awaits." The tall butler removed the empty beaker and hovered behind her chair.

MacIntyre sighed. "It was worth a try." She got up.

"Hutyt," said the Aztec. "I regret that I cannot help you with your problems. I am moved to suggest, though it is certainly not in my interest, that in your further investigations, you look toward the Temple of Bastet. It is not precisely a den of lions, but cats are notoriously corrupt creatures that can be dangerous. You may find there that for which you search. Farewell, Hutyt." The crime lord nodded a dismissal, and Etzli escorted MacIntyre out.

Having tried one side of the war on crime and failed, MacIntyre decided that she'd rely on the other side, although they regarded her as a traitor. It took her ten minutes of arguing with Rudj Chen to get him to listen to her.

"Cheryl, you're suspended. They could fire me for talking to you. Does the term 'person of interest' mean nothing to you?"

"Ju-Long, if I'm an interesting person, listen to me. Believe me, it will be worth your time."

They again sat at Chen's desk, buried deep in the interior of the Temple of Ma'at. Three other medjau were in the office that day, all talking into phones.

"Can we take this somewhere private? It's confidential," said MacIntyre.

"Sure, why not?" Chen got up and took MacIntyre into a small conference room and shut the door.

"All right, Cheryl, give. Convince me you're not the dirtiest medjat in the organization."

Thinking this through and taking the measure of the man, MacIntyre stayed calm. Knocking him senseless wouldn't help. She needed him alive and talking if she was to find out what she needed to know.

Chen added, "I can save you some time. You went to see Marya Semionevna, and you're not taking money from her. Sources in her organization. That doesn't mean you're not taking money from someone else, Russian or otherwise."

"How about Pyotr Semionovich Podgoronov? He's her brother."

"Yes, we have an extensive file on him. Is he the one paying you off?"

"No, he gives me free samples of his oysters. Look, will you stop saying that? Just for now? It makes me crazy."

"As opposed to…?" The man supposed he had a sense of humor.

She snorted. "If you think I'm crazy, you don't get out much. Anyway, unpacking all the careful lies and hints and evasions, I'm pretty sure there's somebody in the medjau on her payroll. I've got information that implicates the Temple of Bastet. If we can uncover that person, and their connections with the higher-ups at the temple, I might make some headway on the murders there. It's all connected. Financial priests murdered, hidden scandal, payoffs galore, that kind of thing."

Chen gazed at her with a quizzical expression. "My sources never turned up any sign of such a person, and the Temple of Bastet is not a criminal organization."

"Innocent organizations don't have murders, Ju Long."

"What do you know, and how?"

"I know nothing more than what I just said."

"What you just said is pretty fucking vague."

"Which is why I need a professional investigating it. You've been investigating organized crime and corruption your whole career."

"Huh. Flattery won't do it, Cheryl."

"This is my career as a medjat. Have a heart, help a teammate. Aren't medjau supposed to have each other's backs?"

Chen grinned. "You're lucky I'm not internal affairs. Those guys don't have your back, they stab you in it. If you're clean, I'll clear you."

She said, "If you'd just—"

"Cheryl, you're suspended. Lay off. Let me do my job."

"I'm just taking a few days off and exploring the countryside. The Slavyanka Reka is very nice this time of year. Lots of water sports. Since you like river metaphors, you should approve of my explorations in my free time."

Chen got up and opened the conference room door. "Feel free to go soak your head, Cheryl. And don't hold your breath." He paused and smiled. "Unless you're under water. Goodbye, Cheryl."

MacIntyre walked out of the Temple of Ma'at into the bright sun, her mind working furiously. No help from Yaotl, he wouldn't give up his corrupt connection in the medjau. And even less help from Chen, who wanted her to lay off. Djehutymes would not reinstate her anytime soon. And then there was Karkin's admonition to Shes to keep her out of it. The professionals in her life had failed her. Her badge and gun were still in a property locker somewhere. Henutsenu was still a prisoner in the Temple of Bastet. And she was out of ideas.

Except one: call Shes. He wouldn't solve her problems, but he'd at least listen.

She turned on her phone, which she'd silenced during the session with Chen. And there was a voicemail from Shes.

"Hi, Cheryl. I'm off to Milaya to deal with Sennedjem. I'll bring him back to Menmenet and give him to the Henet Baket. Maybe that will get me off their hook. See you tonight? Call me."

MacIntyre's medjat intuition kicked her in the stomach. What was the man thinking, driving into a lonely village filled with Russian gangsters and wanted thieves? The situation screamed backup!

She pushed the "call" icon. The phone rang four times and went to voicemail.

"Shes. What are you doing? Are you OK? Call me!"

She stood stock still in the sunlight, annoyed clerks and medjau walking around her, scenarios rushing through her head. None of them were pleasant, and some were dire.

Milaya.

CHAPTER NINETEEN
Shesmu Follows the Money

I HAD IMPLICIT FAITH IN MacIntyre's investigative abilities, but her diplomatic skills left something to be desired. Pyotr Semionovich was still one of my major suppliers. Oysters don't grow on trees. Oysters, Russian gangsters, and money required finesse—not MacIntyre's strongest point. I decided to go it alone in Milaya.

I drove across the rolling hills, live oaks scattered here and there among the rain-green grass. The mid-morning sun made everything shine. There were very few people in this area, one reason the Russians could set themselves up without too much worry.

I parked at Pyotr Semionovich's bar in Milaya about noon. The little town was quiet, with no people around. Before I got out of my car, I called MacIntyre to let her know what I was doing. She didn't pick up, so I left a short voicemail and got on with it.

I pushed the wood shack's door open and peered in. Pyotr Semionovich was behind the bar with his back toward me, fussing with bottles on a shelf. He wore a black rubber apron over a black knit shirt and jeans. As the door closed after me, the spring creaked. Pyotr Semionovich looked around and reached down below the bar.

I raised my hands. I said, "Don't worry, I'm not armed, and I'm not a threat. Whatever you've heard, it's garbage. I'm the person I always was, the certified Best New Chef of Menmenet." Pyotr Semionovich looked at me, his huge face and beard obscuring his emotions, and his hands still below the bar.

"Sure," he said. "Come over here, and keep your hands where I can see them." He grinned. "Pazhaluista." He still had his hands under the bar. I walked over and sat on a stool.

I said, "I need a drink. Vodka?"

Pyotr Semionovich took one hand from below the bar, scratched his beard, and used the other hand to bring up a bottle from his bar refrigerator. He plunked two small glasses down on the bar and said, "First of the bottle." He poured two drinks. We saluted each other and drank.

"Excellent," I said. The emotional atmosphere cooled to room temperature as the ice-cold vodka shot through us. He poured two more.

Pyotr Semionovich reached again under the bar and brought out a bowl of mollusks. He picked up an oyster knife from the bar. With incredible speed, he shucked four oysters and laid them out, two in front of me and two in front of himself. He picked one up and slurped.

"I'm not here for the oysters today," I said. I showed my hands to Pyotr Semionovich, put one hand flat on the bar, and with the other reached into my pocket for the note from Marya Semionevna. I laid it on the bar, unfolded it, and turned it toward him.

He took in the Cyrillic writing, and his eyes widened. "What the hell is this?" he asked.

"Read it. Pazhaluista."

He did. Twice. I slurped my oysters while he read. He said something that sounded like "Yeb tvoyu mat'" with disgust in his voice, crumpled up the letter with one huge hand, and threw it over his shoulder. It hit the big mirror behind the bar and fell to the floor somewhere. His eyes were on mine.

"So you aren't a master criminal after all. At least, according to my beautiful sister. All that fancy dodging and dancing last time you were here with the medjat, a total waste of time. That sukin s'yn Sennedjem. At least you'll take him off my hands."

He spread a towel out on the bar next to the oyster bowl and reached under the bar to bring out a short-barreled shotgun, which he put on the towel. "We'll need this. But let's finish our drinks first," he said. "And we need to get clear on something."

He untied his apron and took it off and pulled off his black knit shirt. I drew in my breath. Tattoos covered his entire torso, a riot of color and movement. Some were pornographic, such as a flying horse with a naked woman riding it. Some were rude blue marks, stars and crosses and Cyrillic writing. Then there were the grotesques—a cat wrapped in barbed wire. I think I spotted a skull eating an oyster. He had a very large torso; it made for an impressive sight.

"I spent a lot of time in the gulags in Sibir' and Russkaya Amerika. Not political; I was vori," he said, giving the last word the rolling Russian r. "I wasn't very good at it, but I was big enough that it didn't matter. My sister," he said, "was never in the gulags, she was too smart for that. She and her husband led a local business group, don't ask about the business. About the time I got out, when Russia became Russia again, she ran into some trouble with her competition. She wasn't smart enough for that. There was a little fighting and a lot of dying. Her gang died more than the other one. Her husband too. She soon ran out of money. No money meant no payoffs, so the militsia stepped in and ended the war by slapping her in a cell. The winners suggested she leave town and not come back, giving her the alternative of an extended tour of the local graveyard. They were nice enough to include me in that suggestion. We came down here rather than stay and join the ranks in the morgue. We had a little money left, emergency funds. I used mine to start the oyster business. My sister bought a rundown dacha. I'm making more money from oysters than she's making from crime, but she's growing her business in Menmenet now. Or was."

"Until..."

"Until she signed on with Sennedjem's scheme, the money went missing, and you got involved as a competitor." He grimaced. "Or so we were told."

"Told by whom?"

"Who do you think? Himself."

"And how about MacIntyre being a corrupt medjat in his pay?" I asked.

"All part of the story. Besides," he grinned, "she looked corrupt enough the last time I saw you. Consorting with a master criminal, after all. Nothing in her car worth looking at, though, when I searched it. Nice little thing, that car."

"Fits her personality."

He grinned again, pulled on his shirt, and picked up the shotgun. "Let's get to it. I want to see the last of that yebonat Sennedjem."

We walked up the hill toward the guesthouse, Pyotr Semionovich in the lead, me behind. The trees loomed above us, shadowing the path. When we reached the guesthouse, I thought we were going in. But Pyotr Semionovich walked around to the side of the house along a little path that curled through the trees. Behind the house there was a smaller cabin, undecorated and a little run down.

Pyotr Semionovich stopped a dozen paces away from the cabin and whispered to me, "I'll go in first, with the gun. Come in after me, and don't get in between the gun and our friend." I nodded, resolved to go in after him and stay in a corner, out of the way of shotgun pellets.

Pyotr Semionovich advanced to the door and opened it without knocking, then ambled in, holding the shotgun in one hand. Over his shoulder, I saw Sennedjem sitting by a fire, the picture of relaxed domesticity. He looked up when we entered, straightened as if to rise and sank back as he took in the shotgun that Pyotr Semionovich held, then saw me.

"What would you like to do, Shesmu? I can kill him for you, or you can kill him yourself."

Sennedjem rose to his feet, eyes big.

"No need for that. What are the alternatives?" I asked.

"I give him to you, you give him to the medjau. Or you can take the money and let him go."

"Money sounds good. Let's ask him about it."

"Time to talk," said Pyotr Semionovich. He walked over and gripped Sennedjem's shirt collar from behind with a huge hand. He lifted the small man up, spun him around, and tossed him toward the wall like a bag of onions. Sennedjem hit the wall face first and slid down, but Pyotr Semionovich lifted him back up and pressed Sennedjem's face against the wall. "Go ahead, Shesmu, ask him whatever you want to."

"What's this about?" Sennedjem mumbled.

"Masha has cut you loose," said Pyotr Semionovich. "She's made a deal with the master criminal here," he pointed at me with the hand holding the shotgun. Sennedjem was a sad sight, mouth and nose bleeding. Repulsive, but sad.

"She can't do that," he whined. "What about the money?"

"I think," said Pyotr Semionovich in a detached tone, "you shouldn't have talked so much about money without giving her any. Things like that annoy her in underlings."

"I'm not an underling. I'm her partner!" He was getting red in the face now.

"The partnership's dissolved," I said. "I can't promise anything for the authorities, but why don't you just tell me where the money is? Maybe we can get you off the hook."

"It's my money," he stated. Pyotr Semionovich banged him against the wall. His nose bled more profusely, dripping down on his shirt.

"It's the R'ames Society's money, not yours," I said.

"It's mine. I just used the Society to store it for a while." Sennedjem's whine annoyed me.

"A laundry," said Pyotr Semionovich. "That's why my sister made the deal with him. He ran a scheme for cleaning the money she's making from her businesses.

A service, so he said. Then he stole all the money." He banged Sennedjem against the wall again. "Stop bleeding on my floor."

"This isn't getting us anywhere," I said. "Tell me where the money is, and we can solve all our problems. Why make it harder on yourself?"

"No!" screamed Sennedjem. He swung his head, spattering blood over Pyotr Semionovich, who threw him to the floor. He scrambled to his feet. We gave way to let him get up, and he took advantage of the distance to stagger past us toward the door. As he passed, Pyotr Semionovich lifted the shotgun and clubbed him on the side of the head, with a smooth, arcing swing of his huge arm. Sennedjem cartwheeled across the room, crashed into the far wall, and fell like a stone.

"I didn't want to waste the buckshot on him," explained the vor. "Damn. Now we can't ask him any more questions until he wakes up."

"We better take care of that nose."

Pyotr Semionovich put his shotgun down and walked over to a cabinet. He bent over, rummaging around. I stepped forward and picked up the shotgun. He turned, holding a roll of gauze, and took in the new situation.

"It would be better if I held this for you," I said, hefting the gun. "Would you stuff some of that in his nose to stop the bleeding?"

I could see his smile through the dark beard. "Kanyechna, tavarishch," he said. He walked over and applied the first aid.

"That ought to do it," he said. "Had to do a lot of this sort of thing in the war."

"The Great Patriotic War?" I asked.

"Fuck, no. I was a baby. The great gang war in Novoarchangelsk. A lot of blood spilled there, some of it mine," he explained. He walked over to a couch and sat down.

"Look, I don't want to cause any trouble for you," I said.

"But...?"

"But I need Sennedjem back in Menmenet, in the hands of the Henet Baket. I need your help to get him back to town. I don't want to call in the medjau up here. Who knows what would happen?"

"True. But I'm allergic to medjau." He grinned. "Your girlfriend excepted, of course. What are you going to do about the money?"

"The tax people can't seem to get it through their heads that I'm not involved. They think the bomb has something to do with it. They drew their own conclusions. I need Sennedjem to convince them otherwise. If they can dig the money out of him, so much the better for everyone involved."

"Not everyone. Sennedjem didn't express a strong wish to help you there, Shesmu."

"The Henet Baket has more persuasive means at their disposal."

"More persuasive than me?"

"Different, anyway."

"What's in it for me?"

"How about staying out of our gulag?"

"So, you'll turn me in to your girlfriend? Can I bribe her, maybe with a lifetime supply of oysters?"

"She's off oysters after our visit here."

"And what about my lovely sister? She'll want her money."

"She'll have to find other ways to make a living."

"So will I."

"Not necessarily," I said, stepping back. I lifted the shotgun with what I hoped was assurance. I'd never held one. "My restaurants still need oysters. Will you help?"

"Nyet." He smiled again. "Not in my best interest, Shesmu. I help you walk away with the money, and my sister won't be happy with me. I won't be able to supply oysters from the grave."

"Well, then," I said, "Let's load him into my car. I'll take him myself." I shifted the gun to emphasize his lack of choice in the matter.

"Nyet," he said, and walked toward me. I hesitated and stepped backward. Killing a vor would not help my cause with the medjau. And besides, I liked the guy, tattoos and all.

Pyotr Semionovich smiled and said, "Here's a criminal tip. Always make sure your gun is loaded before you point it at people." He grinned and stretched out a huge hand and took the gun.

"What kind of barkeep puts an unloaded shotgun under his bar?" I asked with some heat.

"I wouldn't know," he replied. He broke open the shotgun, revealing two cartridges. He grinned. Closing the gun up, he said, "Let's head over to the main house, Shesmu. He'll keep." He motioned toward the door with the gun.

Pyotr Semionovich pointed at the door of the guest house with his shotgun. "Go on in, Shesmu."

The turrets stretched high above me. Going into the house reassured me; if Pyotr Semionovich wanted to kill me, he'd do it out in the forest, not in his fancy guest house.

I went into the hall and stopped as Pyotr Semionovich entered and closed the door.

"On into the kitchen." He pointed down the hall with the shotgun. I walked.

"Stand there," the big Russian said, pointing to the sink. Covering me with the shotgun, he maneuvered a key ring out of a pocket and unlocked a door. "On in, moi droog, on in."

"What are you going to do?" I asked. "Marya Semionevna wanted you to help me with Sennedjem. 'Give him any help he needs,' she said. This isn't helping."

"Da. But, you see, that is conditioned on getting her money back. Your plan puts the money in the hands of the Henet Baket. I go back to Masha with that plan and no money, I won't be walking out of her house again, brother or no. Nyet. I have another plan now."

He looked around his kitchen and sighed. "Yeb tvoyu mat'. I loved this place. I'll miss it. Even the oysters."

"You're going to run."

He smiled. "The only rotten thing about it: I have to take that yebonat Sennedjem with me, at least until he tells me where the money is. He will, eventually."

"And what happens to me?"

Pyotr Semionovich waved a hand at the open door. I looked in; a pantry. All the supplies for the breakfasts served to guests. My captor said, "You won't starve. Here's some water, and here's a pot for your other needs. Lyuda, my cook, will come by in the next couple of days to check on supplies. I'll call her to make sure. What a surprise she'll have! Until then, there's nobody around. Enjoy!"

He pointed again to the doorway and waved the shotgun. I walked into the pantry, and he shut the door and locked the deadbolt. The front door of the guest house closed, and things got very quiet.

<h1 style="text-align:center">CHAPTER TWENTY</h1>
<h2 style="text-align:center">MacIntyre Bounces Back</h2>

THE PHONE CALL FROM DJEHUTYMES caught MacIntyre just as she was getting into her little red car for the long drive to Milaya. She hesitated over picking up the call. She wanted to get moving, not get caught up in department politics. But he was still her boss.

"Mes?" she answered.

"Cheryl. Guess what."

"I'm fired."

"No, you're cleared."

"I'm *what?*" Her astonishment at this event was at least as great as her incredulity at the original accusation of corruption.

"Cleared. Chen has sent in his report clearing you of the corruption charges. He fired off a nasty telex off to InterSecPol too, about wasting our time."

"Well, damn. That's the best news I've gotten since my boyfriend told me he was fixing me breakfast." She smiled. "When do I get my badge back?"

"Not yet. The evidence suppression and exceeding authority charges are still there, Cheryl. We don't have the personnel to investigate all this, so I need you to see the Atch-Netjer of Internal Affairs."

"Mes! Those people are crocodiles."

"Hear me out, Cheryl. I've given Atch-Netjer Kasa a call and brought him up to speed on your situation. He has the power to deal with these charges and get you back working. I need you working."

"You've *thrown* me to the crocodiles!"

"Cheryl, you're talking to Kasa, or you're looking for a new job, and I'm looking for a new semety. Your choice."

Sensing that no more good news was coming, MacIntyre took the hint. But she needed to do something first—in Milaya.

"All right, all right. I'll talk to him. First thing tomorrow. Let's just hope he's in a good mood."

"Sure. There's always hope. Let me know how it goes."

"Goodbye, Mes. And thanks." But her boss had already hung up.

MacIntyre started up her car and eased into traffic on the way to the ferry to the north.

The sun was low on the horizon by the time MacIntyre's little red car crunched over the gravel in the parking lot of the no-name Russian bar in Milaya. She parked next to Shesmu's car. There were no other cars in the lot, and there was no sign of any people.

MacIntyre popped her trunk and unlocked the shotgun from its rack. Sticks were fine for some kinds of crime fighting. Russian gangsters the size of Pyotr Semionovich needed just a bit more. She loaded all five rounds and pumped a round into the chamber.

Holding the shotgun at port, she crept up to the door of the bar and stood aside from it. She pushed with one hand; locked. No sound from inside. She walked around to the single side window and peeked in. Empty, nobody at all inside.

MacIntyre walked up the path to the guest house and all the way around it, eyes everywhere. To the side, she found a small cabin with the door open. She looked in and gasped. Blood all over the place. Splashes of it. Not one big pool, though, so it was somebody ambulatory moving around and bleeding. She hoped it wasn't Shes, but her stomach wasn't convinced. She inspected the room from the door; no one there, nowhere to hide in the single-room cabin. She voted against going in. Leave it for the criminalists, if criminalists there would be.

She backed away and looked up at the turrets of the guest house. It was the only other building in sight, aside from the bar down the hill. She walked around to the porch and tried the front door. Locked with a deadbolt. She found a window on the side of the house that looked suitable for surreptitious entry. She looked in. A kitchen. She remembered the nice breakfast they'd had the day before.

There was a nice rock the size of her hand nestled up against the side of the house. She hefted it, then fired it at the window, which shattered. That ought to bring somebody running, but she was ready. She waited. There was a thumping sound, but no one appeared through the open door. She waited. The thumping grew louder, but nothing moved.

She undid the latch on the window and slid it back. She reached through and put the shotgun on the sink, then scrambled up and through. Once in the room, she tracked the thumping to a door on the side of the room—a pantry?

"Shes?"

"Get me out of here!" The voice was indistinct behind the heavy door, but she had no doubts.

"Are you all right?"

"No! Get me out!"

"Shesmu. Are you bleeding to death?"

"Oh. No. Just mad as hell."

"OK, wait up. This door won't be easy to break open."

"What the hell are you doing in my kitchen?" The voice from behind her had her swinging around. A tiny, shriveled apple of a woman in a babushka stood in the kitchen doorway, hands akimbo, face a mask of outrage.

"Um," said MacIntyre. She glanced at the shotgun on the sink; go for it? This woman didn't look like much of a threat. Still. She moved toward the sink, explaining as she went.

"I'm here—"

"Where's Petya?"

"I'm sure—"

"Who the hell *are* you?"

"What going on?" asked Shes, behind the door.

The woman's eyebrows rose high. "Who's that?" she asked.

"Shesmu. My boyfriend. I'm—"

"What, did you two break in to steal food? And he got locked in? I'm calling the—"

"Will you wait and let me talk? Please." She reached into her pocket, then remembered she hadn't got her badge back yet. She touched the feather pin over her breast. "Medjau. Something's wrong here."

"No fucking shit." The small woman looked her up and down.

MacIntyre grasped at essentials. "Do you have a key to this door?"

"Certainly."

"Open it. Please." She picked up the shotgun to emphasize that she was in charge.

The thumping started again.

"I don't think so."

Shotguns weren't enough. The woman needed persuading.

"Look, lady. We need your help."

A sharp breeze blew through the broken window over the sink. The old lady marched over and examined the shattered glass covering her sink.

"You broke a window to get in."

"This is a shotgun, lady. Open the door!"

The woman smiled. "There was a time I'd have just taken the shotgun away from you. But not today." She walked over to the pantry door, fishing out a key ring from a pocket. She unlocked the door. Shesmu popped out, looking very grim.

"We've got to—" he began.

"Who the *hell* are *you?*"

"You've got to be Pyotr Semionovich's cook. Right? Lyuda. Why are you here?" asked Shesmu.

"Lyuda, that's right. Petya called me. It didn't sound right, so I came over to check things. And here you are, the two of you. I'm calling the—"

"Just wait, Lyuda," said MacIntyre. "I'm sure Shesmu can explain everything." She addressed her boyfriend. "Did you know there's a cabin next door full of blood?"

"Yeah. He—"

"Will somebody please tell me what the hell is going on!" screamed Lyuda.

"Better summarize it for her, Shes," said MacIntyre, grinning.

Shesmu grimaced and started in. "Pyotr Semionovich is on the run now. He's been holding a man named Sennedjem here for his sister. You do know who his sister is?"

"Masha? Oh. If she's involved, that explains everything. I'm calling—"

"Pyotr Semionovich decided his only recourse was to run with Sennedjem, to find his money and get away from his sister and the medjau." He stared at MacIntyre. "We have to get after them. The Henet Baket are sure I'm involved, and I need Sennedjem to explain to them I'm not."

"Who's going to pay for that window?" demanded Lyuda.

CHAPTER TWENTY-ONE
Shesmu Confronts the Henet Baket

MacIntyre dragged herself out of bed at the first light of R'a.

"I have to go talk to a crocodile at the Temple of Ma'at," she whispered into my barely conscious ear. "I need to get clothes for it at my apartment. See you later." I recorded this information in my sleepy mind as some kind of dream hallucination. Crocodile? What clothes were suitable for crocodiles?

I nodded and fell back to sleep.

My phone jangled me awake some time later. I groped for it and checked the ID: Khenemset Neferet. My mouth opened to identify myself when her distressed voice blared out the bad news.

"Shesmu! They've taken him! I didn't know who to call! They've—"

"Khenemset Neferet," I said, breaking into her incoherent anguish. "Please, slow down. Tell me what happened."

I heard her gulp down her anxiety. She said, "My poor Nesimen, they've arrested him. Taken him to jail. What should I do? Shesmu, can you help him?"

Nesimen in jail. I can't say this was a surprise for me, given what I'd learned. I also wasn't that distressed; jail was where Nesimen belonged, after all. Baki had caught up with him and his fake resume.

"Khenemset Neferet, take a deep breath," I advised. "Who took him? Was it the local medjau, or was it the sepat?"

"Oh. Let's see. I have their card. They gave it to me. It must be here.... Yes. It was the Henet Baket, the ones who were investigating the Society. A Rudj Baki."

"What did they say?"

"I wasn't paying attention, Shesmu," she apologized. "They pushed past me at the door and grabbed poor Nesimen and took him before I could even think straight." She gulped again. "Something about financial crimes at the R'ames Society."

"All right, Khenemset Neferet. I know Baki. I'll talk to my sehy about it."

"Call me, Shesmu? I'm so worried."

"Yes, all right. Try not to worry, Khenemset Neferet, we'll figure things out."

Before calling Nebemhep, I sat and thought things through. Nesimen had shown little concern for others in what he said to the medjau so far. His primary goal centered on how to dig himself out of the hole. He didn't realize that digging just made the hole deeper, and that pulling in people to help him dig wasn't likely to get him out. He'd implicated me when it was just a matter of questioning. Now they were charging him with financial crimes. He was bound to try even harder to slough off his responsibility to anyone available. I was available, and Baki already thought I was a crook. I needed to get Nesimen out of their hands as soon as I could. He could tell me more about Sennedjem and his money. And about who else might be involved at the Society. The scheme that the Russians had told me about was too big for just Nesimen and Sennedjem. There had to be somebody else.

I called Hep and, after I argued him around to the necessity for immediate action, he agreed to meet me at the Sepat Office Building to work his sehy magic.

"Shesmu? Where are you?" I could sense urgency in Baki's tone.

"At your front door, Baki. I'm here with my sehy. We want to see Nesimen."

"Nesimen? You shouldn't worry about Nesimen, worry about you. The guard at the front desk will direct you, and we'll talk."

We took the elevator up to the offices of the Henet Baket Sepat at the guard's direction. The receptionist there directed us to a cubicle where we found Idnu Baki tapping at a computer. He looked up and directed me to a chair next to his desk. Hep put a restraining hand on my arm and directed me to a separate chair, then took the chair next to Baki. I pulled up the other chair and sat next to him. My mood was dark; I'd had about all the direction I could stand for the day.

I asked, "Can we see Nesimen?"

Hep shot me an annoyed look and said, "Shesmu, as your sehy, I advise you to let me do the talking now. All right?"

Simmering, I sat back in my chair and folded my arms. I didn't reply, just nodded.

"Now, Rudj Baki. About Nesimen—"

Baki interrupted. "Nesimen is right where he belongs. He's charged with multiple counts of fraud, conspiracy, embezzlement, tax evasion, and adultery. He's helping us with our inquiries." Baki smiled, narrowing his eyes at me. "Shesmu, it would be a good idea for you to help us with our inquiries as well."

Hep stilled my immediate reaction. "Rudj Baki, my client would be happy to help with your inquiries if we could understand where you're heading. First, we need to see Nesimen."

"If Shesmu cooperates, I'd be happy to allow a visit with Nesimen. You might even persuade me to not oppose the Promise of Ma'at for him if you have something I can use."

"We would consider that. But, right now, we think there is quite a lot of misinformation surrounding this case. My client wants to dispel any mistaken notions the Henet Baket might have about his participation in it. Are you prepared to charge my client with any crimes, civil or religious?"

Baki pursed his lips. "Charge him? Not just yet. But it would be best for him to clear up any misinformation. We work best if we know what's going on."

Hep smiled. "My client is not at all involved in any of Nesimen's schemes, and his connection to the R'ames Society is only that of membership."

"And yet, we find him popping up at every step of our investigation, counselor. Let me review it all for you." Baki stuck out a hand and pulled down one finger. "One. Nesimen. Shesmu has a history with Nesimen's family. Two. Shesmu gets a financial award from the Society based on Nesimen's recommendation, then is on the scene as we discover massive fraud and theft there. Three. Nesimen tells us Shesmu is close to him and is involved in his negotiations with the board of directors over the fraud and theft. Four. Shesmu's restaurant blows up, and the insurance company refuses to pay out based on their suspicion of arson and fraud. Five. Ownership of the Per'ankh restaurant connects to the board of directors of the R'ames Society. That's a conflict of interest given the award to Shesmu, and it's a very interesting coincidence given the situation."

Baki shifted to his other hand. "Six. Shesmu associates with known members of criminal organizations with connections to Russkaya Amerika. Seven. Informants tell us that those criminal organizations have ties to the chief financial officer of the R'ames Society, who has disappeared, and to the Per'ankh restaurant. Eight. Shesmu associates with a corrupt semetyt in the Menmenet medjau, according to information received. *Closely* associates! Nine. Informants tell us that Shesmu may head up a shadowy criminal organization of his own in Menmenet. And, not least, ten. We have received information from an anonymous source just this morning that Shesmu is involved in a money laundering scheme with the criminal organizations he works with. The source suggests investigating to find money he has laundered through his restaurant and the R'ames Society. We're planning to confront Nesimen with this information to see what he knows about it."

Baki sat back in his chair. "I'm out of fingers, counselor. Your client is up to his neck in this case."

Hep smiled back at him. "But you're not charging him. All this is impressive, but there's no evidence of my client's involvement in a crime. Is there?"

"A lot of smoke but no fire, counselor." Baki waved a hand. "But we'll find the fire, never fear."

"MacIntyre is not corrupt. The medjau have cleared her of those suspicions. Check with her boss," I said. Hep shushed me.

He asked Baki, "What about the Per'ankh? Have you investigated the money laundering information?"

Baki gave a grudging answer. "We've looked into it. The house manager of the Per'ankh has left his job and has gone off somewhere on vacation. We interviewed Shesmu's assistant, Qenna, who told us the charges are absurd but can't back it up with accounting information yet. The investigation is ongoing. We can't get any information from the other owners, a billionaire named Hernefer and the Henuttawy Group. They both say they're 'processing' our request." He looked at me. "Anything you can do to facilitate that investigation will help you avoid charges, Shesmu." He didn't sound convincing when he said it.

"We'll see what we can do, Baki," said Hep.

"Hep, we need to talk. Now," I said.

Hep addressed Baki. "We'll take a short break, Rudj Baki."

We walked out to the hall.

"This is all crap, Hep."

"They're not charging you, Shes. Calm down. They're not like the Russians. They won't blow up your other restaurant based on this crap." He paused and looked me in the eye. "Unless there's something to the Per'ankh business you're not telling me?"

I was vehement. "No, I've told you everything. I don't do the accounting, but I keep track of things, and there's no funny business going on. The only things we've laundered were the chef's uniforms and tablecloths. I don't know what's up with Hernefer and the Henuttawy people. I'll talk to them. Maybe you can work on the insurance company; send them a threatening letter or something. But, look, Hep: this 'anonymous source' with information today. That has to be Sennedjem. He's throwing dirt in their eyes to make them suspect me while he and Pyotr Semionovich figure out how to disappear permanently. Can we get Baki to help us track that tip down? If we can find him and the money, all this nonsense will disappear. And what about Nesimen?"

"Shes," the exasperated sehy said, "Baki won't cooperate in any way unless you have something to offer him. Do you have anything more than you've told me? Because 'crap' is generous for all that story. At least, from Baki's perspective."

"I don't. But I know somebody who might."

CHAPTER TWENTY-TWO
MacIntyre Faces Ma'at

MA'AT HAD NEVER LOOMED SO large for MacIntyre as when she entered the office of the Atch-Netjer of Internal Affairs of the Temple of Ma'at the morning after rescuing Shesmu. Right behind the Atch-Netjer, Ma'at stood at least 5 meters tall, including the feather that stretched up into the shadows.

The Atch-Netjer stood behind his desk, tall and austere himself, mirroring Ma'at. This setup was even more intimidating and discomforting than the homicide interrogation room.

"Hutyt MacIntyre. Please sit," said Kasa. His voice was stern, his mouth was stern, and his eyes were stern. His message, when he spoke further, was stern as well. "Idnu Djehutymes has informed me of the details of your transgressions, Hutyt MacIntyre."

Stern didn't work well for MacIntyre, but when you were up to your ass in crocodiles, you had to make choices, such as which leg to sacrifice first. MacIntyre sat in the hard-backed chair across the desk from the Atch-Netjer, who sat as well. Ma'at glared down at her with hot eyes.

She had to respond, put up a defense. Details?

"Idnu Djehutymes has been very patient with me, lord, but he is not aware of all the details."

Kasa frowned. "More evidence suppressed, Hutyt?"

"No, no evidence, but there is context that explains what I did."

"The lady Ma'at rarely considers 'context' in making the right decision, Hutyt, only right and wrong, ma'at and isfet. But I will hear what you have to say. Be brief, please." He picked up a piece of paper from the desk. "What about this charge of exceeding your authority? We had a serious complaint from Hem-Netjer Paneb at the Temple of Bastet." He put down the paper. "They would be within their rights to charge you with a religious offense. Disrespect for the goddess carries some nasty penalties. Can you explain why you acted as you did?"

Ah, the open-ended-question tactic. Go find a stick that I can use to beat you, a classic technique. Her father had been fond of using it, at least metaphorically. Now she was on firmer ground, and it inclined her to further insubordination. She suppressed that instinct. The man might be just another power-imposing male father figure, but Ma'at wouldn't turn aside when she jousted with the man. She didn't believe in the Remetjy gods, but in this room with this goddess, she came close. She chose her words with care.

"Lord, I have no excuse whatever."

The big man folded his hands in front of him on the desk. "Come on now, Cheryl. All I'm asking is what you were thinking. You're too good a cop to have done this without reasons, and you're not corrupt, or so Rudj Chen tells me."

This got her blood going again. "No, I'm not fucking corrupt!" She gulped. Was that a frown on Ma'at's face or just her imagination? More calmly, she said, "I had my reasons."

"The scales of Inpu weigh even tiny grains of truth against the feather of Ma'at. And, to be honest, I'm interested. I don't know why. Tell me your reasons."

MacIntyre shifted in her seat. "All right. I'm a homicide semetyt, lord. My job is to gather and interpret evidence and catch murderers and put them behind bars. So, I ask about the crime scene, and they tell me that the w'abu there cleaned up the scene, scrubbed it spotless. No bodies, no DNA, no murder weapon, nothing. It got my blood going." Her blood was moving again, just thinking about it. She could feel the heat in her face.

"Go on," said Kasa.

"Then I interview the Hem-Netjer of Bastet, an arrogant son-of-a-bitch who hides behind his facade of religiosity. Excuse my language, please." Her eyes rose to find Ma'at's, and she quickly lowered them again.

The Atch-Netjer nodded.

"And he tells me to butt out, that the goddess takes care of its own."

"As the law permits her to do, Hutyt," said Kasa. "Go on, please."

"That's it. It just got my dander up. They're ignoring every bit of evidence we could use to find the murderer. I don't like murder. And I don't like coverups."

"Nor do I, Hutyt, nor do I. But they are within their rights. You are American and perhaps are not aware of the power of certain gods and goddesses here in Menmenet. The temple's role is to worship and protect their goddess. Our role as medjau is to enforce the civil laws and leave the religion to the temples. It's not a coverup, it's a purification of the precincts of the goddess. I understand your frustration, but it does not excuse offending Bastet."

"No, lord."

Kasa picked up the paper again. "Hem-Netjer Paneb has waived any punishment. Magnanimous. But we have our own problem, your suppression of evidence. That is a transgression against Ma'at. Neglecting your duty to Ma'at is both a religious and a criminal offense with serious consequences."

MacIntyre opened and closed her mouth. She told herself to choose her words with care again. "It was…a misjudgment, lord."

"This woman Henutsenu is a friend of yours? And that relationship led you to your misjudgment?" He put down the paper on the desk.

"A close friend. I told her about the situation, knowing she worshipped Bastet, and she told me she was there at the time of the murders." MacIntyre paused. "I wanted to look into it before she told the temple authorities. I had a terrible intuition about the situation. The attitude of the temple made me angry, lord. I didn't trust them to do the right thing. My friend went to the temple despite my urging her not to. They arrested her for the murders. She didn't do it. I know she didn't."

"But you should have reported what she told you, Cheryl."

"I should have, yes, lord. No excuses."

"As the case falls under the jurisdiction of the Temple of Bastet, Idnu Djehutymes feels that your transgression had no real impact on the duties of Ma'at."

"No, lord."

"So we have several religious offenses and at least one major civil offense before the lady Ma'at, Cheryl. I have a certain amount of discretion in choosing penance, but in this case, it's clear that there must be serious consequences. Any final words?"

MacIntyre smiled. "Final words? When's the execution?"

Kasa grinned. "Sorry, poor choice of language. Do you have anything further to say before I decide the penance?"

Like, how big the stick should be? "No, lord. I depend on your goodwill and the benevolence of the Lady Ma'at. I truly regret my actions."

Kasa sat back in his chair, the huge statue of Ma'at glowering over his head at MacIntyre while he considered her fate. Penalties? A slap on the wrist. A short suspension. Ten years in prison. Her stomach tightened as she awaited the fall of the axe.

"The Lady Ma'at demands that her priests and priestesses follow the path of Ma'at at all times, Cheryl. And the path does not include side roads violating other temples' rules or withholding information from your superiors. Do you agree?"

"Yes, lord."

"But your motives leaned toward ma'at. Yes. You committed these transgressions against Ma'at with no bad intentions, just unchecked impulses. Do you agree?"

"Yes, lord."

"And do you believe you can learn to control such impulses? To serve Ma'at, you must."

"Yes, lord."

"Then I will give you time to consider how best to do that. Two weeks suspension without pay, and you'll have to take the video class on the regulations for conducting investigations during that time. See my assistant for the web page, please." He smiled. "And you'll have to pass the test on it."

Kasa stood up and nodded to her in dismissal. The huge statue behind him had a hidden smile, at least in MacIntyre's imagination. She arose, a burden lifted, but dreading the boring video course and calculating how much overtime she'd have to work to make up for two weeks of pay lost. No, three, counting the week she'd just spent without pay. Sebek would tire of seeing her eating at the Neferti, that was for sure. Still, this penance was much less than she deserved.

MacIntyre, having cleared up her own troubles, now had to clear up the troubles of Henutsenu. She considered borrowing Tikhet the Cat again, but her memories of his behavior convinced her they'd throw her out of the temple. Bastet was not a tolerant goddess, even toward her furry familiars.

So, instead, she got Atch-Netjer Kasa to intercede with Hem-Netjer Paneb of the Temple of Bastet.

"Before I go, lord, may I ask a favor?"

"Ma'at is not a goddess who smiles on those she disciplines, Cheryl," said Kasa.

"I'm not asking Ma'at, I'm asking you, lord." MacIntyre smiled. "You've clarified that I must follow the way of Ma'at, but a friend is a friend. If I can at least talk with my friend, it will help me accept her situation," she lied. "If you could give Hem-Netjer Paneb of the Temple of Bastet a call and put in a good word for me? I would appreciate an appointment to see whether it might be possible to talk with my friend, to give her support in her hours of trial."

Her true intention was to persuade Henutsenu to accept that she had to get out of jail by whatever means necessary. But Kasa, not being the most perceptive of medjau, took her plea at face value. He put in the good word for her with Paneb, who agreed to meet with her.

An hour later, MacIntyre sat on a bench in the reception hall of the Temple of Bastet, watching two black cats circling one another with occasional hisses. Given they were both residents of the temple, MacIntyre could only speculate on the internal politics of cat life as influenced by the powerful goddess Bastet. In MacIntyre's limited understanding, independence was one of the foremost attributes of cats. These two specimens more than likely clashed over the particular space in the hall they both believed was "their" space. Just how much diplomacy versus military action would resolve the situation?

The rotund w'ab Tjay interrupted MacIntyre's budding career as a war correspondent.

"The Hem-Netjer would be pleased to speak with you now, Hutyt MacIntyre. This way, please."

MacIntyre followed Tjay back into the temple's warren of offices to Hem-Netjer Paneb's small and spare room.

"Hutyt MacIntyre. I will not say I am glad to see you, but the assurances of Atch-Netjer Kasa have persuaded me to grant you an audience. I understand you are under Ma'at's scepter of discipline for your behavior. Otherwise, I would not allow your feet on the sacred ground of our temple. And I am not disposed to grant you any favors."

"I'm sorry, lord, I've accepted my penance and my responsibility for offending your temple. But that's what I want, lord—a favor, an audience. With my friend Henutsenu. I have no wish to interfere in temple affairs at all, lord. Her associates have her in mind and want to support her in her trials."

"Ah, a compassionate visit. We have allowed no such visits for the accused sinner to avoid pollution of the minds of the innocent."

He looked MacIntyre up and down. To MacIntyre's mind, he was evaluating the level of pollution she herself was introducing to his temple. This was not going well. Paneb thought Henutsenu was guilty. MacIntyre thought fast—what would make the man see reason?

She said, "My penance has led me to understand the power and importance of the gods in Remetjy society, lord. Being American, I hadn't appreciated the might of Bastet. With the power of the Lady looming over my friend's life, I feel she needs some reassurance. That would allow her to gain perspective on her sins, lord. And it would allow me to atone for mine."

"Your sins, yes." Paneb cleared his throat and pursed his lips. "As you are an American, in my judgment the rule of Bastet does not apply. The sinner's knowledge or beliefs cannot harm you."

MacIntyre had enough Sunday school under her belt to recognize this argument for what it was. Whatever hell Bastet had engineered for those that sinned against her was MacIntyre's destiny. Any atonement would be useless. Henutsenu couldn't pollute her any more than she already was. Paneb's condemnation didn't faze MacIntyre any more than had the fulminations of the Bostonian preachers of her youth.

She pressed her advantage. "So I can see her?"

Paneb considered things, then said, "I will arrange for you to meet our errant congregant for thirty minutes only. Return in an hour and Tjay will take you to her. And, Hutyt MacIntyre…"

"Yes, lord?"

"I must insist you do not enter our temple again after this indulgence."

"I understand, lord. Many thanks, Lord Paneb, for that indulgence." She bowed her head. The hem-netjer smiled with grace and dismissed her. As she left the temple, she found the two cats had progressed to open warfare. Only the prompt intervention of Tjay and another w'ab prevented a major battle. If only such religious intervention could settle human wars instead of starting them, the world would be a happier place.

CHAPTER TWENTY-THREE
MacIntyre Herds Cats

Henutsenu looked elegant even though she hadn't changed her clothes in three days. MacIntyre envied her in this, as she had never managed elegance, even with elegant clothes. Sexy, yes; professional, yes; tough, yes. But not elegant. It had to do with the ba, according to another friend: the way the internal formed the external. MacIntyre didn't want to know what this told her about her ba.

"Henutsenu! It's so good to see you!" She embraced the tall, dark woman, holding her and feeling the love that flowed between them. The two of them had never slept together, despite their mutual attraction, because they were both in committed relationships with other people—Shesmu and Sebek. But they were better than just friends.

"Cheryl, I don't know how you got them to let you in," said Henutsenu.

"A lot of lies," replied MacIntyre, letting go of her friend and sitting down. Henutsenu sat in the only other chair, and the pair looked at each other.

The temple could be listening in on them. MacIntyre said, "It would be best to be as discreet as possible, so say nothing you wouldn't want every cat in the place knowing about."

"I have no secrets from the Lady Bastet," stated Henutsenu, smiling. "None. She is my tutelary goddess."

MacIntyre's tutelary goddess, Ma'at, frowned on any sort of shenanigans, so MacIntyre lied to her all the time. MacIntyre relied on her own skills for protection rather than on any god or goddess. She liked to think that she could protect her friends as well, though not at the divine level. Getting malefactors into trouble was her job, getting the people she loved out of trouble was her avocation.

"Has the Lady Bastet given you any ideas about dealing with the murder charges against you?" asked MacIntyre.

Henutsenu reached out a hand and stroked MacIntyre's hand. "Don't worry, Cheryl. It will all be fine. Hem-Netjer Paneb has been very kind once he'd heard my side of the story. He says it takes a while to get all the rituals completed. He says that Hem-Netjer-Tepy Panekhet is very concerned that the priests perform the rituals correctly, enough to take part himself in some of them. Once the rituals are complete, the trial will clear me, and I can get back to running the Neferti."

"That's what the Hem-Netjer said, did he?"

"Yes. They told me two weeks, I explained that the last time you were here."

"Sebek is worried."

"Oh, yes, I know. I asked the Hem-Netjer to let me talk to him to reassure him, but he said it would pollute the ritual web established by the w'abu prayers." She smiled, then said, "Maybe you could tell him everything is fine?"

"I would if I thought so, but I don't. Paneb as much as told me you're so guilty you'd pollute anyone that spoke with you. Except me, I'm already too polluted for him to care."

"What?"

"Henutsenu. This trial in two weeks. You're in deadly danger there. They're lying to you."

"But I explained…. Cheryl, you've got to accept that the Lady Bastet is a gracious and benevolent goddess. She will punish the true murderer. Even if the priests aren't convinced, the Lady will know and protect me at the trial. Don't worry."

"I'd be a lot more confident in that if I saw the Hem-Netjer and everyone else in this temple trying to find that murderer. As far as I can tell, the only thing they've done is to lock you up." MacIntyre squeezed the hand she held. "I'd break you out of here if I could."

"Cheryl, you must leave it alone. Let it be. Really." Henutsenu withdrew her hand and frowned. "I think you should leave now. This isn't helping me. It will just anger the Lady."

MacIntyre saw her friend was impervious to argument. If there was only a way…but there wasn't. She would have to go along with Henutsenu's beliefs or lose her as a friend.

But she'd be damned if she'd leave things entirely in the hands of the gods.

"All right, I'll leave, and I'll try to reassure Sebek. You'd better step up the prayers to Bastet, though." She stood up and embraced her friend. They exchanged a deep, passionate kiss. MacIntyre watched as the guard took her friend off to her lonely cell. Then Tjay came to show her out.

The fat w'ab was apologetic. "I'm very sorry, Hutyt MacIntyre, but the Hem-Netjer has instructed me to tell you that the Temple can no longer admit you to its sacred precincts. I'm sure the Lady Bastet will forgive you. In time." The w'ab swung the big door closed behind her with finality.

She found her car and got in, then released her frustration with a few tears that she wiped away.

MacIntyre found Sebek in the Neferti kitchen, berating a line cook. She looked around the kitchen and saw very few happy faces among the staff. Time to rescue Sebek from himself, and she knew what was bothering him.

"Come out to the bar with me, Sebek, I need to talk about Henutsenu."

"I can't. I'm right in the middle of lunch prep."

"You're right in the middle of creating a staff revolt." She looked around and saw surreptitious looks from all the cooks. Even the dishwasher girl looked pensive.

MacIntyre spoke up. "How about it, people? Should chef take a break?"

Grins broke out and there were a lot of nodding heads.

"OK," said MacIntyre. "Qenna, take over. I've got to talk with Sebek right now."

Sebek opened his mouth, eyes fierce, and MacIntyre grabbed his hand and pulled him toward the kitchen door. He stumbled after her, turning his ire on her instead of his staff, jerking his hand away.

"Cheryl, what are you doing? I won't have a restaurant left if I'm not in the kitchen!"

"You sure as hell won't have any staff left if I don't get you out of here right now."

Sebek looked at his grumbling staff and threw up his hands. Qenna smiled a tight smile and waved him away. MacIntyre pushed open the door and beckoned. Sebek joined her, and they walked out to the empty bar, which was not yet open for the day.

"What have you heard, Cheryl?" Sebek asked.

"I got in to see her, Sebek," she said. "Let's sit down. I'll tell you about it."

They sat at a table near a window. Sebek pulled down a shade, as the morning sun was bright and strong. The shadow and the shade-limited view gave the empty bar a closed-in feeling that only frustrated her more.

"How are you doing, Sebek? This must be hard on you," she said.

"You saw. My temper is uncontrollable. I can't sleep. I can't focus on the food." He put his head in his hands. "If this goes on, I'll have to take some time off, let Qenna and Khay take over the kitchen, and…" He couldn't finish the sentence.

MacIntyre described the conversation she'd had with Henutsenu earlier in the morning. Sebek looked more and more distressed as she described the conversation.

"Two more weeks! I knew she was a devotee of Bastet, but this is too much," he said. "She's just not seeing what's going on! Can't you get the authorities involved somehow, Cheryl?"

"Not in a temple, Sebek. The religious authorities in the temple have complete power over what happens inside. Nobody can interfere unless the place is burning down. It's so frustrating!"

Sebek held his head in his hands, staring at the table. He said under his breath, "I'd blow the place up to get her out, I swear."

"Good intention, bad idea," said MacIntyre. "Besides, I already looked at the likely blast points, and it's too well built."

Sebek smiled, but his heart wasn't in it.

"How long has she been this zealous about Bastet, Sebek?"

"Zealous," the chef grimaced. "It's only gotten bad in the last couple of years."

"About the time you two got involved?"

"Are you saying I'm responsible for driving her into the arms of Bastet?" he asked.

She placated him. "I seem to recall her saying a cat died about that time."

"Yes, her longtime pet. Oh. Yes. She turned to Bastet for comfort. I'm more of a dog person. It's a personal failing." He smiled. "We don't live together. She's moon, I'm sun. We get along fine as long as we're not staring at each other for too long. The love is separate from that. Intense, just…separate." Contemplating love got his lachrymal glands going again, the gleam catching the dim light in the bar.

Placation having run its course, she tried diversion. "Sebek, I've got some questions I wanted to ask Henutsenu, but in her state, she wouldn't have answered them. Can I run a couple by you?"

"I'll try. If it's about Bastet worship, I'm not the man you want."

"It's about Henutsenu worship."

"That's me."

"Oh, ick."

"Well, it's true."

MacIntyre regarded her friend as a goddess of sorts, but worshipping her wasn't the first thing that came to mind. Sex came to mind. She was sure that was true of Sebek. Did men regard sex as worship? An interesting concept, have to ask Shesmu about that the next time we sleep together. Some small devil poked her, suggesting it would be nice to ask Henutsenu. Her own frustration level rose a notch.

"Cheryl?"

MacIntyre broke out of her daydream and focused on the wreck in front of her. Cheer him up, somehow. Questions. Get his mind off sex. And her own. Detective questions.

"Did Henutsenu say anything about what she did at the temple as a volunteer?"

"Prayed, made offerings to the goddess, volunteered in the veterinary clinic. She also did some business office work on a volunteer basis, financial work."

"But those w'abu...."

"Which?"

"The murder victims. They were w'abu in the finance department."

"You mean—that's why the temple arrested her."

"Could be. She thinks Paneb will somehow absolve her of the crimes, but Paneb told me in no uncertain terms that he considered her guilty." MacIntyre followed the logic a little, then asked, "Did she ever say anything about temple finances?"

"No. I asked, just a casual question. All she'd say was that the Temple of Bastet was the richest temple in Menmenet, next to the Temple of Imen-R'a. Details were confidential, she told me."

"And she was a volunteer, right? She didn't get any money for her work?" Please let that be true.

"Not that I know of. Where are you going with this, Cheryl?" Sebek stared at MacIntyre, eyes narrowing. "You don't think she was involved, do you?"

"Of course not. How could she be?" What if? What if Henutsenu had found out the w'abu were stealing from the temple? Would her devotion to the goddess extend to solving a problem with the w'abu with a heavy statue? That was too horrible to contemplate. Not Henutsenu.

Sebek got even more accusatory. "Look, Cheryl, are you a detective or a friend?"

"Don't, Sebek. Don't make me choose."

"You're doing all the choosing, Cheryl. She didn't do it, she couldn't."

"I want to believe that, Sebek. Look, the temple—they are in charge. They have to have their two weeks of ritual. We can't even give them advice. I only want to help her, you know that. I love her as much as you do." Sebek didn't take it literally. He looked mollified. She wasn't his competition, just a helpful friend. And that was true, it was just—that little devil kept poking her. All she had to do was ignore the unwelcome facts and let Bastet work her magic to get her friend out from under. But she didn't trust Bastet to do that, her being an imaginary deity and all.

"Cheryl?" Sebek was restless and broke into her daze. "I ought to get back to the kitchen."

She gave a defeated sigh. "All right. I'm sorry I can't do more. And, Sebek—"

He had arisen and turned to go. He turned back. "Yes?"

"Go easy on your minions, OK? You can do that for two weeks. Don't destroy what you and Henutsenu have built here. The staff won't put up with it."

"Henutsenu might take care of that all by herself. I'm just channeling the gods' anger. But I'll try to get a grip, at least in the kitchen. It's not their fault. You can help. There has to be something you can do."

"I'll try."

The bartender came in to open the bar for lunch and saw them. "Cheryl, chef. Drink?"

Sebek just waved him away and left for the kitchen. MacIntyre considered a drink: what the hell, she had nothing else to do. Bad habit to get into, though. Instead, she got up and raised the shade and sat in R'a's glorious light for a few minutes, soaking up the sun and looking at the bay view.

CHAPTER TWENTY-FOUR
Shesmu Pursues Sennedjem

Baki waited, drumming his fingers on the table in the interview room.

"Where is this guy?" he asked for the fourth time. It was pushing 2 p.m.. My theory was that his anxiety came from having missed lunch, but I might have been wrong.

The door opened, and Huty Seba looked in. "He's here, Rudj."

"Bring him in."

Karkin entered, wearing his green army jacket, his appearance unprepossessing.

"Karkin," he said, and held out a card case with his InterSecPol credentials showing.

"Shesmu here tells us you can help with our inquiries," said Baki.

"Might," said Karkin.

My sehy said, "I'm Nebemhep, this is Rudj Baki of the Henet Baket Sepat."

Karkin looked at me. "Heard about the tip."

Baki snapped, "What tip?"

Karkin looked at him and said nothing. I said, "The tip about me and money laundering, right?" Karkin gave a barely perceptible nod.

"Heard about it from whom?" asked Baki, sitting up in his chair. "That's supposed to be a secret."

"Sources," said Karkin.

"Not in my organization."

Karkin said nothing.

Baki realized nothing more would be forthcoming and pressed his lips together, then said, "All right, convince me, Shesmu."

"I'm giving you facts, Baki, not fiction. Karkin can back me up."

"All right. We'll see. Talk."

"First, Nesimen. He's a total fraud, top to bottom. He's faked his whole resume. You must have learned that."

"That's one reason he's charged with fraud, Shesmu," said Baki.

"Yes, but it has nothing to do with me. I know his wife, she's my khenemset. She was as surprised as I to find out about his deceptions. You can ask her."

"We will," said Baki in a grim voice.

"All right. Next. Nesimen wasn't cooperating with Sennedjem. I don't believe he had anything to do with the money laundering operation. He's not that kind of crook. A con man, yes, but not the kind that burrows in and launders millions. Have you found any evidence of his direct involvement?"

"I won't reveal details of our investigation to you, Shesmu."

Hep stuck in an oar. "You haven't charged him with money laundering."

Nettled, Baki said, "No, we haven't."

"Well, then," I said. "Karkin, any evidence of Nesimen being involved in international money movements?"

Karkin shook his head.

"There," I said. "So we have Sennedjem, who's disappeared with the laundered money. Guess who supplied a lot of it? And guess who bombed my restaurant because of it? Karkin?"

"Russians," said Karkin.

Baki raised his eyebrows. "I don't believe it."

"See?" I said. "Then I tracked down Sennedjem, but another Russian gangster helped him escape. They locked me up to do it, too."

Karkin nodded. "Right about Nesimen and Russians."

Baki stared. "He's telling the truth about all that nonsense?"

Karkin nodded.

"Who's the Russian in charge?"

I said, "Marya Semionevna Ranukhova. In Gorni. Sennedjem told her I was a criminal mastermind deeply involved in his schemes, so she blew up the Per'ankh to warn me off."

"Who's the Russian gangster that helped Sennedjem escape?"

"Pyotr Semionovich Podgoronov, her brother, in Milaya."

Seba nodded at this name. "Petya, he's vori. Works with us sometimes. I knew we'd be going after him one day."

Baki gave his subordinate a sharp look. I interpreted this to mean that Seba shouldn't be airing his knowledge of informers with the uninformed, particularly an alleged criminal mastermind like myself. Pyotr Semionovich appeared to be playing both sides of the pitch.

"How did you escape?"

"My girlfriend came looking for me and got a cook to unlock the door."

"Aww," said Seba. "That's just sweet."

Baki ignored this and said, "So, Shesmu, what you're saying is that it's all about Sennedjem and his Russian pals. Is that right? Nothing to do with you."

"Right. And I can tell you who your anonymous tip came from: Sennedjem. He's confusing you to give himself and Pyotr Semionovich time to organize a permanent escape. It's how he operates."

"There's too much on the other side of the scale, Shesmu." He held up his two hands and wiggled his ten fingers.

"If you'll give me a chance, we can find Sennedjem. And the money. Karkin and I will run it down. Right, Karkin?"

An almost imperceptible nod, but it was there. Hep stayed quiet, stone-faced.

"I'm not sensing much enthusiasm on your team, Shesmu," said Baki, glancing at Karkin. "Tell you what. I'll assign Seba to go with you. I'll give you three days to find something. If you can track down Sennedjem and his money, I'll reconsider opposing the Promise of Ma'at for Nesimen, and you're off the hook. Otherwise, we'll charge you. We'll find something. And don't even think about running. Seba will detain you if you try, and you'll get the Promise of Ma'at sometime after you're mummified."

Great. An almost-interested, semi-catatonic secret policeman and a muscle-bound watchdog as a team. Who could ask for anything more? I looked at Heb, who nodded.

"Deal," I said.

As we stood in the lobby of the Sepat Office Building, Seba said, "I'll check out a cruiser from the pool, we can—"

"No. Mine," said Karkin. "Equipped."

"Equipped for what?" complained Seba. "The sepat net connects to our cars, they can—"

"Mine," insisted Karkin. "Equipped."

"Let's see," said Seba.

He walked all the way around the old, green car parked by a fire hydrant. Karkin had fixed the windshield, but I could see through the window that the bullet hole was still there on the back seta. The dashboard sported a hand-lettered placard saying "Medja—Do Not Ticket." For anybody but Karkin, I would have said this was optimistic. He had a magic touch, even though everything he touched looked like it came from the leftovers at a homeless encampment.

"Do you have any special tools hidden away in this piece of junk you call a car that might enable us to trace the money back to its source?" I asked Karkin.

"No."

"What's our next move?"

"Sennedjem."

Karkin unlocked his door with his phone and leaned across to pop the locks on the other doors, one at a time. I got into the passenger seat, and Seba opened the door to the back seat.

"No fucking way," he said, looking in.

Karkin cleared the seat of the myriad electronics, weaponry (a nice compound bow and some vicious-looking hunting arrows), and various articles of clothing.

He looked Seba up and down. "Room now," he said.

When Seba opened his mouth to comment, Karkin held up a finger in an admonishing gesture and gave him a stare, and the big man went silent. Seba got in and adjusted his rear end. "Where's the seat belt?" he asked.

Karkin shook his head and smiled. "Too old," he said. He got into the driver's seat and started the engine with a muffled roar.

"Needs to get warm," he said. "Sennedjem?"

"Yah," said Seba. "How we gonna find this guy?"

"Well, maybe he's used a credit card or something," I suggested.

"Nope," said Karkin. "Looked."

"Can we put out a medja alert?" I asked.

"The Henet Baket doesn't do a lot of car chases, Shesmu. Alerts aren't our thing," said Seba.

"So the man has disappeared and there's nothing we can do about it?" I asked. Seeing only blank faces, I got sarcastic. "Does anyone have Sennedjem's phone number? We can call him up and get him to surrender."

"Shut up, Shesmu," said Seba.

Karkin pointed to the smallish computer screen installed under his dashboard in the middle of the car. The screen was blank. He reached across my lap and opened the glove box. He extracted a portable keyboard, unfolded it on his lap, and started typing, and the screen under the dashboard lit up. Karkin grunted, then typed in some more.

"Got it," he said. He twisted and leaned back into the back seat, then rummaged around in the pile.

"Watch it," said Seba, using his hands to restrain the tidal wave of junk from inundating him.

"Got it," said Karkin again, holding a small black box. He took out his phone and plugged the box into the charging port on the bottom. He swiped a few times, typed a little with his thumbs, then held it up. It displayed a map with a small, blinking icon. I looked more closely at the map.

"Sennedjem's phone?"

"Place to start," said Karkin. "Triangulated."

"Is it moving?"

Karkin swiped some more, then said, "There since last night."

"This is a joke," Seba said.

Karkin turned his head and stared again, and the big man again fell silent.

I said, "That appears to be south of Menmenet, a few kilometers down by the airport. It's not moving. I say we go look for it."

Karkin put the phone up on a holder on the dashboard, released the parking brake, and we set off to find Sennedjem.

CHAPTER TWENTY-FIVE
MacIntyre Confronts a Gang War

MacIntyre's phone rang. She glanced at the ID: Yaotl.

She had left the Neferti and wandered across the street to the pier that projected out into the bay. It was a kind of park for romantics and anyone else who wanted air and sea and calm. But Yaotl, the foremost Aztec crime lord in the city, augured little calm.

MacIntyre answered the call. "MacIntyre here."

"Hutyt, I must speak with you at once."

This was a departure from the long, flowery greetings the Aztec crime lord ordinarily used to pretend he was a normal, gracious businessman. This was a fire alarm.

"You are."

"I am what?"

"Speaking with me."

"In person, Hutyt. Now."

"I don't enjoy being summoned, Yaotl. It's not protocol." As a medjat, a crime lord ordering you to his house raised all kinds of red flags. MacIntyre was unconventional, still suspended, and ready to look for anything she could use in her search for ma'at, but this? Red flag.

"I do not care what you enjoy. Come to my house, and keep it quiet."

"OK. But you'll owe me." But the crime lord was already gone.

"It's war."

The Aztec crime lord's face had more and deeper creases than MacIntyre remembered, and his hooked nose seemed more prominent. His eyes, usually hooded and dull, flashed his anger.

"With whom, Yaotl?" asked MacIntyre, smiling pleasantly.

"Who do you think, Hutyt?" The sarcasm in Yaotl's voice was unmistakable. He was far past the point of being polite, even to her, an unpaid consultant with whom he had no current beef.

She concluded, "Got to be the Russians. They're the only ones I know who are running around with automatic weapons and bombs."

"You are correct." Yaotl shut his eyes and breathed deeply to calm himself down. MacIntyre had never seen this side of him. Most days he was phlegmatic, displaying his sarcastic sense of humor at every opportunity. They sat facing each other in a large parlor in his glass pyramidal mansion on the Tjesut. The parlor's glass wall looked out on his immaculate garden and greenhouse.

"What did they do to cause a war, Yaotl?"

"They badly misjudged my tolerance, Hutyt. Badly. They dared to set up an illegal business wholesaling pharmaceuticals in my territory in direct competition with my own efforts. If that were not bad enough, they siphoned money out of my various businesses into their own channels. They threatened people who pay me to avoid threats."

"Why am I here, Yaotl? Why aren't you out chopping up Russians instead of talking to me?" She shifted to get more comfortable. "Can we pick up the pace? I haven't had lunch."

"I need the Menmenet medjau to do their job."

"How about I take you down, fingerprint you, take the mug shots, and record your confession to the twenty murders I am sure you've committed? I'll skip lunch for that."

"I cannot see the humor in the situation, Hutyt," said Yaotl.

MacIntyre, who had been perfectly serious, opened her mouth to reiterate her proposal, but Yaotl's raised hand stopped her.

"Our deal," he said, eyes boring into her, "was that I would provide certain information about my competitors to you. And occasional protective services, at cost. In return, you would use that information to enforce the law. Was that not the agreement?"

"Yes."

"All I am asking is that you do one thing: enforce the laws these Russian interlopers are violating. I am not asking for anything illegal, nor am I asking for anything in return. Just this simple favor, Hutyt, without obligation: do your job." He frowned. "If the medjau fail, I will need to take matters into my own hands. I will need to call on my allies from organizations like mine. Should that happen, Hutyt, there will be blood in the streets such as Menmenet has never seen."

"Have you got something I can take to the relevant people? I can't just walk in and tell them 'Yaotl wants the Russians suppressed because they're impacting his business, and he'll murder everyone in sight if you don't do something.' You know?"

Yaotl raised a finger, looking at a man standing off to the side of his chair. The man fetched a folder from a sideboard and gave it to his boss, who handed it to MacIntyre.

"This file has names, dates, addresses, bank account numbers, and vehicle registrations of everyone involved. We suitably cleansed it of any detail that might show its source. The details will allow any competent medja to arrest everyone involved and send them to jail for a very long time." He smiled his sardonic smile. "And you are a competent medjat, Hutyt, if unconventional. Get it done."

She leafed through the several closely typed pages while Yaotl gazed at his garden. His mouth was a thin line, and his fingers drummed on the arm of his chair. This dossier was gold, seriously good stuff. Actionable. There was the Per'ankh bombing, with full details on the bomb materials and the Russian bombers. Marya Semionevna's name popped out in several places, as did Sennedjem's. So did the Temple of Bastet. She recognized the names of the two murdered w'ab priests. The report identified them as conduits for Russian money.

"What's this about Bastet?"

"Excuse me?" The crime lord startled out of his disgruntled reverie.

"Bastet. What's this about the Temple of Bastet?"

"Hi, Shes." MacIntyre drove down the Tjesut, heading for the Temple of Ma'at, talking hands free. "I have news."

"So do I, Cheryl."

"Where are you?"

"Heading for the airport."

"Why the airport? Are you flying somewhere?"

"No, at least not so far. Karkin has located the signal for Sennedjem's phone."

"Sennedjem! Geez, I forgot about him."

Shes said, "Things are happening. I can't talk right now. Maybe tonight? Call me?"

"OK, sure. I'm about to dive into a gang war up here. Looks like Marya Semionevna has pissed off Yaotl to the point of mayhem. Things may get busy. And let the medjau handle Sennedjem. I'd come help, but I'd better stick with the war effort here."

"The medjau still suspect I'm a master criminal. I've got to find Sennedjem to convince them they're wrong. He's throwing around lies to mix everything up while he and Pyotr Semionovich escape."

"Shes! Let the pros handle it."

"I'm with two pros right now. Karkin and a hutyt from the Henet Baket."

MacIntyre visualized Karkin and a nerdy, eyeshade-wearing accountant. "Get help. Now."

MacIntyre heard voices in the background. Shes laughed, then said, "Got to go, Cheryl. Call me." He disconnected. Infuriating man.

"End call," she told her car in a voice that would not be denied.

CHAPTER TWENTY-SIX
Shesmu Misses His Man

"It's got to be in the hotel," I said.

We'd followed the flashing icon to its source, which was a large building on the outskirts of the Menmenet International Airport, the Wedjit Djerdjer Hotel.

Seba looked up at the twenty-story edifice. "We won't be doing a room-to-room search."

"Desk," said Karkin. He moved toward the big doors of the hotel.

The reception desk wasn't busy mid-morning, and we walked right up to a young woman desk clerk. She took in the disheveled Karkin, the huge Seba, and me and opted for the safe choice.

Addressing me, she said, "How may I help you, lord? Do you have a reservation?"

"These two gentlemen," I said, "are medjau. They're looking for a fugitive alleged to be somewhere in this hotel."

The young woman looked at my companions with circumspection, eyes sliding back and forth. "Medjau?" she asked, her voice quavering.

Karkin grunted, opened his green army jacket, and pulled out his credentials, and the woman started back as though he was exposing himself. Seba grinned with more teeth than I'd ever seen him display and showed a badge. The young woman stepped back another step with alarmed eyes.

"Medjau," I confirmed.

The woman gathered herself together and stepped bravely back to the desk. She looked blank for a moment, then asked, "Could you repeat that, please?"

"We're looking for a fugitive alleged to be here. May I run a couple of descriptions by you?"

She liked me more than my medjau friends. She smiled and said, "Yes, of course, lord."

"These two guys are kind of hard to miss. One is small and thin, dark hair and thin beard, big nose, brown eyes, looks Russian but dresses Remetjy. He's got signs of a fight on his face. The other is large and larger, black hair and huge beard, black eyes, and tattooed all over. Looks Russian, dresses Russian, and is so Russian you'd never forget him. I'll forgive you if you don't know about the tattoos."

"Oh. Them." The young woman's voice was flat.

I smiled to encourage her. "Are they here?"

She checked her computer screen. "Only one checkout. He paid cash for another night for the other gentleman."

"Names?" asked Seba.

"Lords Kuznetsov and Popov."

"Which one is still here?"

"Popov."

"Fake," said Karkin.

"We need to check the room," I said. "Or do you want to wait for backup? We should go ahead. Sennedjem isn't dangerous, just evil."

Seba grinned again and said, "Could you give us the room number? We'll check it out."

"I, that is, we have, I don't know if..." the woman stumbled at the sudden proof that trouble was standing in front of her. "Let me get the manager."

The manager, when summoned, said with authority in his voice, "No Consent of Ma'at, no search. Sorry."

Seba, who'd been fiddling with his phone while we waited for the manager, held it up. "Henet Baket Consent, issued by a sedjemy. We're in pursuit of a fugitive. We need to talk to Lord Popov as soon as may be, or inspect his room if he's not available."

"Well, then," smiled the manager. "Here you go. Send me a copy of the Consent. I'll have our on-duty security let you in." He wrote a room number and an email address on a pad, tore off the sheet, gave it to Seba, and called security. Very efficient. Seba grinned again and sent the document with a flurry of thumbs and a swipe of his phone.

* * *

The hotel hallway was long and narrow, doors on both sides stretching to infinity. The closeness oppressed me; I felt as though I was walking through a tomb deep underground.

House security was a large American woman with extra-short, bleached-blonde hair and biceps that rivaled Seba's. Her tattoos were much higher quality than those of Pyotr Semionovich. She and Seba made small talk while Karkin and I inspected the door. It had a Do Not Disturb sign on it.

I interrupted the incipient romance and asked, "Would you…?" and waved a hand at the door. House security stepped up and knocked.

"Security," she said. "Open the door, please."

We waited, she repeated her demand, and nothing happened. Karkin pointed at the door lock, and house security opened the door for us.

The room was dark, even in the sunny afternoon, the drapes blocking out Lord R'a's brilliance. More tomb-like atmosphere.

"You go first," I said to Seba. He grinned and pushed the door open, and his friend from house security backed him up. Karkin and I squeezed into the small hallway behind them somehow.

The room turned out to be a two-bedroom suite. All was quiet in the common room. No one was in the bathroom to the side of the hallway. Both bedroom doors were closed. Seba marched up to the first one and opened it. We all looked in. Unmade bed and nothing else. Seba turned to the other door and opened it. He muttered a curse and walked in. We all followed.

House security flipped on the light while Seba pulled open the drapes to let in some light.

There on the bed lay Sennedjem, naked. He wasn't going anywhere. Multiple loops of an extension cord wrapped around him and the bed to keep him fastened to it. His eyes bulged and his nostrils flared as he grunted through his gag and struggled against his bonds. On his chest was a mobile phone tucked under a loop of cord. We'd come to the end of Karkin's technological road.

Seba rummaged in his pocket and pulled out a pair of blue latex gloves and put them on. He slid the mobile phone out from under the cord. Sennedjem made louder noises and kept struggling against the cord.

"I would say Pyotr Semionovich has given us a present," I said. Karkin nodded.

"Let's see what he has to say," said Seba. He undid the gag, a hotel towel.

"Get me out of this!" he whined, struggling at the cord.

"Why don't you tell us what happened? You look comfortable enough. We'll leave you as you are for now," said Seba. "What happened, my lad? Deserted by your big friend?"

"That sukin s'yn fucked me over, beat me up, and tied me down here! Let me up!"

"Calm yourself, son," said Seba. "You'll hurt yourself."

House security checked out Sennedjem's equipment. "Not very well endowed, is he?" she asked. Rhetorical question, but true. "Hey, he's a paying customer. We should order room service for him or something." Seba grinned, appreciating her sense of humor, such as it was.

I had more urgent questions. "Why did you tip the medjau off about me, Sennedjem? Why did you tell Marya Semionevna that I was a crime lord?" I tried to keep my voice calm, angry as I was at this turd.

Sennedjem twisted his neck to look at me. "Shesmu. That podonok forced me, it wasn't my idea!"

I looked at Seba and smiled. "Looks like I'm off the hook."

"Ya gonna take your turn with him?" Seba challenged me. Then he laughed. The sound was raucous in the quiet room. I didn't answer. He told Sennedjem, "You're under arrest on suspicion of theft, money laundering, tax evasion, breach of fiduciary responsibility, and..." He paused for effect, looking at his house security friend. "Indecent exposure." His friend snorted her appreciation.

"You don't know who you're dealing with, asshole!" Sennedjem struggled against his bonds again. "No fucking idea! I have friends, powerful friends! Let me up! There's way more involved here than just money!"

"He has friends," said Seba.

"No, he doesn't," I said. "Who would be a friend to somebody like this?" His money had friends, but he didn't. He'd told the lies to Marya Semionevna to get revenge for my humiliating him at the Myu-Myu Club. Small lies become bombs in his world.

House security again checked Sennedjem's equipment and said, "He'd need a lot more than I see before I'd consider it, sure."

Sennedjem's face flushed, and he started shouting in Russian. I'd suspected his Remetjy identity was a cover for a more European origin. That confirmed it. He had to be connected to the Russian gangs. After several imprecations, Karkin—the only one of us who understood any Russian—said, "Shut him up. Filth."

"Sure," said house security. "He'll disturb the other guests."

She picked up the towel, twisted it tight, and gagged Sennedjem again. Blessed quiet descended, with the prisoner back to grunting his displeasure with us.

Karkin wandered over to the nightstand next to the bed and picked up a business card.

"Interesting," he said, and handed it to Seba.

"Huh. Sounds familiar somehow." Seba ignored the frantic grunts from the prisoner, took out his phone, and made a call.

"Rudj Baki, Seba here. We have the Sennedjem individual. He confessed to tipping us about Shesmu's involvement, just like Shesmu thought. Yeah. Well, we found Sennedjem tied up in a hotel room at the airport. The Wedjit Djerdjer, room twelve-fifteen. Yeah. The Russian Podgoronov, had to be. Sennedjem's Russian too. Yeah. So, we found a business card next to the guy. I thought it sounded familiar…somebody named R'aweben, company is the Henuttawy Group." He listened to his phone for a while, then said, "Oh, yeah. Now I remember." His eyes flicked over to me and he smiled.

Karkin said, "Henuttawy?"

Seba returned his attention to his phone. "All right, Rudj, I'll head over there. What about—"

R'aweben. Henuttawy. A director of the R'ames Society. Part owner of the Per'ankh. "I know him," I said.

"What?" asked Seba, distracted from his phone.

"He's a R'ames Society board member and his company is an investor in the Per'ankh. It can't be coincidence. There's more going on here than just Sennedjem."

Seba said into his phone, "Shesmu's figured it out, Rudj. Take him? And Karkin?" He listened, then disconnected. "Shesmu, you and Karkin can help me question this guy R'aweben. Rudj Baki requests your help, all right?" He smiled. "And he wants me to stick with you for a while, until we're satisfied about you."

Karkin nodded, and I said, "Sure. This is hitting pretty close to home for me. And I would bet even money that Pyotr Semionovich left us that card deliberately."

As we exited the bedroom, house security said, "What about him?"

We looked back at Sennedjem, who had stopped grunting, just looking at us with partially closed but still furious eyes.

"He'll keep," said Seba. "Rudj Baki will send somebody to pick him up." He smiled. "Why don't you give me your phone number? I'll check in later." The big medja and the house dick exchanged numbers. The air of romance made me think about MacIntyre. She'd sounded a little miffed when I hung up on her earlier. I ought to check in with her and the effort to free Henutsenu. Later.

We headed out to Dju-Liberty.

The Remetjy financial houses lined a stretch of the waterfront south of Mentju Boulevard, near the Dju-Liberty hill and the American business district. R'aweben's address was a modern, five-story edifice more European than Remetjy. The building had a concrete plaza with benches and a modern, abstract American sculpture.

We walked through the travertine lobby and took the elevator to the fifth floor. The elevator doors opened onto a reception area, but it was deserted, nobody in sight. A man came around the corner and headed for us, looking flustered.

"Yes, may I help you?" He scurried behind the reception counter and blinked at us through small, round glasses.

"Lord R'aweben, please."

"I'm afraid he's not available. Nobody's here right now."

I looked around again. "I can see that. Where is everyone?"

The man was in his early twenties, dressed in Remetjy business clothes that were quite suitable for hanging out at the nearby bars after work.

"I don't know. Everyone just vanished. When I got back from lunch, there was no one here. I walked all the way back to the kitchen just now, nobody at all."

I nudged Seba and said, "Badge."

He looked at me, shrugged, and showed his badge. He said, "We'd like to look around a bit if you don't mind. Something's not right."

"I can't, I mean, I don't, well. Lord R'aweben left yesterday for a trip to Russia. That's what they told me. Everyone seemed nervous about things this morning. Then when I got back from lunch, there was no one else here."

"Don't worry, I'm sure everything will work out well for you. Stick around," I said. "R'aweben's office?"

He pointed back toward the corner around which he'd appeared.

We walked down and around the corner and toward the obvious corner office overlooking the bay, 270-degree view of the northern part of Menmenet. We weren't looking at the view, though.

The office looked as though a tornado had hit it. A small statue of Bastet was in a niche in one wall. Bastet did not appear happy.

Karkin said, "Gone."

"And it looks like he took everything he could carry with him," said Seba, pushing a few papers around on the desk. He took out his phone and started swiping and typing. After a few minutes, he looked up and smiled. "Bank accounts are empty. All of them."

Karkin cleared his throat. "Missed him."

"No shit," said Seba. "Gee, Shesmu, following you around is a treat. You know some pretty savvy people in the money laundering business, and they seem to appear and disappear when you're around. Let's go talk it over with the Rudj."

"Are you arresting me?"

"Might as well. We'll call it material witness until we turn up whatever you're doing, which I'm very sure won't take long."

Karkin said, "Bad move."

Seba smiled. "Tough. You can walk, Karkin; you're not needed."

Karkin shrugged, then walked out. Seba cuffed me and called for transport.

CHAPTER TWENTY-SEVEN
MacIntyre Intervenes

MACINTYRE BREEZED INTO THE ORGANIZED crime squad room and found Chen Ju-Long to all appearances relaxing at his desk. She pulled a chair around from another desk and sat down across from him.

She said, "Hi, Ju-Long. Say, you guys in organized crime sure have a cushy job. Shouldn't you be out stopping the gang war?"

"Cheryl. How nice of you to visit! I'm busy."

"Sure you are. Now you're busier."

"I don't have time to help you get your job back, Cheryl."

"That's OK. Not why I'm here. I'm here about the gang war."

"What gang war?"

"Oh, boy." MacIntyre said this in English, then switched back to Renkemet. "You know, it's a good thing there are some real detectives in this place."

"What would we need real detectives for?" asked Chen. "Now, if you don't mind, I'm busy."

"I've just spent an hour talking to Yaotl, Ju-Long. He's not a happy man. He's using me as a back channel to you to avoid having to kill a bunch of Russians he thinks are trying to knock him over. Don't you think it would be a good idea to do something about that?"

"I thought I told you to stay away from Yaotl. Do you want me to reopen the investigation into corruption on the homicide squad, specifically on you? Is your boyfriend Shesmu involved in this? Are you shilling for him and Yaotl? Is he dirty after all? Or is this just some idiot scheme for getting your suspension lifted?"

MacIntyre breathed a little more deeply than usual. "I'm trying to stop a gang war, Ju-Long. Shesmu is just a chef with privileges. And I don't do idiot schemes."

"Say I take this seriously and assume it's not just you trying to jerk my chain. Say I do that, Cheryl. Why haven't any of my sources raised the possibility of hostilities?"

MacIntyre smiled. "Crap sources. Or somebody on your team's gone bad."

"That's it. Out. Disappear."

"What about the gang war?"

"Out." Chen pointed at the door. A couple of squaddies were looking on, following the back-and-forth. MacIntyre didn't mind providing free entertainment in an open-office environment, but it wasn't getting her what she needed, which was Chen's help in negotiating a deescalation of the coming war.

"You need to listen to me, Ju-Long."

Chen leaned forward over his desk and folded his hands. "I hear nothing I want to listen to, Cheryl. There's the door." He nodded toward the door with his head.

"Marya Semionevna Ranukhova. Bombs. Automatic weapons. Extortion, drugs, and a dozen other criminal businesses disrupted. Yaotl pushed past his red lines. More automatic weapons and macahuitls wielded by head-chopping Aztecs. The only thing that's missing is tanks in the streets. How am I doing? I'm naming names here, Ju-Long." She slapped Yaotl's dossier down on Chen's desk. He frowned and opened it and scanned through the pages. His eyebrows rose.

"Ranukhova? She's moving in on Yaotl?"

"That's what Yaotl tells me. In between threats. This is serious, Ju-Long." MacIntyre put as much earnestness into her voice as she could dredge up.

"There's no way Ranukhova could get that strong without my knowing."

"I'm not saying a word, Ju-Long. Can we set up a meet with Masha?" MacIntyre used the diminutive to convey her utter disrespect for the Russian gang queen. "And there's something going on at the Temple of Bastet. Those murders, remember? Those w'abu were involved with the money laundering. That's why they covered it up and arrested my friend Henutsenu. She's a scapegoat for the Temple's mismanagement. They're going to try her in two weeks and pretend their problem doesn't exist."

Chen had a pained look on his face that told her she'd hit whatever button he had that put him into medja-mode. He said, "OK, OK. Let me meet with my team and discuss it. We'll see if there's any more information anyone has, and we'll set something up and handle it. Have you told Idnu Djehutymes about this?"

"No, I came direct to you."

"Good. Now go home, Cheryl. I'll take it from here."

"I want in."

"You're suspended, Cheryl."

MacIntyre stood up and leaned on Chen's desk, looking him in the eye. "I have skin in this game, Ju-Long. And I've met Marya Semionevna and her brother. They need to be dealt with. I can help. Plus, I can stand in for Yaotl's point of view. A special peace envoy. That's me. And I want to get my friend out of the Temple of Bastet's detention room."

"Why do I distrust your diplomatic skills, Cheryl?" he asked. "Have a seat while I confer with my team." She sat back down and smiled as diplomatically as she could.

Chen took his team into his conference room and closed the door.

"Where are we going, Ju-Long?"

The medja cruiser headed west up the hill toward the Djuy-Benty, the twin hills that dominated the center of Menmenet.

"Ranukhova wants to meet on neutral territory, away from any chance of observation and attack. She doesn't trust the Aztecs, and she doesn't trust us. She suggested a chapel in the necropolis, one with a view so she can see what's coming. That's where we're going."

Chen was in the front seat of the cruiser. One of his men, a European named Ugo Gatti, drove. MacIntyre was in the back, behind the cage. She had balked when Chen suggested she get in the back, insisting on taking her own car, but he'd insisted back.

"Ranukhova wants one car, two medjau only, and you. She's paranoid, Cheryl. Humor her if you want to come. It took a lot of talking to convince her to let you come. I'd just as soon leave you here, OK? Decide."

So here she was, traveling at high rates of speed through the city streets, locked in a cage. She regretted not getting psychological help for her mild claustrophobia when she still had medical insurance. As long as she could look out a window and see movement, she was OK. It wasn't a closet, it was transportation.

Her phone rang, and she took it out. Shesmu.

"Don't answer that," said Chen. "Not during this kind of operation. Let's keep it quiet."

MacIntyre shrugged and let the call go to voicemail. She'd check in with Shes later.

The car crested the hill and started down the other side to the Temple of Inpu, the huge edifice at the top of the hill above the necropolis. The massive pylons of the temple soon came into sight. Chen didn't pull into the parking lot but drove up to a gated entry road and used an electronic card to open the gate. The cruiser drove down into the narrow streets of the necropolis.

MacIntyre watched the big chapels and tombs of the very rich pass by for a few minutes. The car stopped on a relatively level side street in front of a big chapel with four papyrus pillars and a double door. Two men stood on the sides of the doors, armed with automatic rifles, Kalashnikovs from what MacIntyre could see of them. They had arrived.

MacIntyre had to wait for Gatti to get out and open the door for her. She scrambled out of the car, and the medja grinned as he slammed the car door behind her.

Chen came around the back of the car.

"Shall we?" he said, waving a hand at the chapel. They all went up the stairs, where the guards searched them before opening the large, brass doors to the chapel interior.

The chapel was six-by-six meters square. It had a high ceiling and a large hetep altar on the side. The walls had the usual carved life scenes of the Justified One. Lots of glyphs; whoever this man was, he had a lot of life story. The tomb door in the back was some kind of metal with a complex electronic lock worthy of a bank vault. MacIntyre took in these details while the main part of her brain focused on one main fact. Marya Semionevna, looking just as drab and angry as she had in her house in Gorni, sat in a chair in the middle of the chapel. The woman got up and the little group of medjau advanced to meet her. She said something in Russian ending in a question mark.

"Da, da," said Chen, nodding his head.

"Translate for me, Ju-Long," said MacIntyre. She didn't want to miss any nuances of this woman's explanation of what she was doing in Menmenet. But it turned out such subtleties were not important.

Chen and Gatti grabbed MacIntyre's arms before she could react. Their grip was too strong for her Tae Kwon Do escape moves. Before she knew it, they had her sitting in the chair while Marya Semionevna tied her arms and legs to it with nylon ties. All this took less than a minute. It took even less time for MacIntyre to comprehend the dire mistakes she had made in understanding the situation.

Gatti and Chen took up positions behind MacIntyre while the Russian woman got a sponge bag from the side of the room. She extracted what looked like a tire thumper, a nasty looking stick about 45cm long with a nice leather thong through a hole in the bottom.

Marya Semionevna approached. Her usual angry expression had given way to a smile of anticipation. She spoke, and Chen translated.

"Cheryl, Marya Semionevna would like to know many things. Your relationship with the Aztec. Why you visit the Temple of Bastet so often. Why you broke your deal with her. What Shesmu truly is. Where Sennedjem and her brother are."

Marya Semionevna leaned over and lifted MacIntyre's head with a hand under her chin. She spoke again. Chen said, "I don't know all the foul slang she's using. Must be Novoarchangelsk dock talk. I don't think she likes you, Cheryl."

"Fuck you, Ju-Long. And fuck Masha too."

Marya Semionevna, not needing translation for this response, smiled and flicked the tire thumper down on MacIntyre's knee. Pain shot through her leg.

CHAPTER TWENTY-EIGHT
Shesmu Unchained

WHEN SEBA AND I GOT to the Henet Baket offices, we found my sehy Nebemhep waiting for us.

"Karkin called me and told me you needed me here," he told me.

"It's a farce," I said. "They don't have a shred of a case against me on anything. Seba is just suspicious, and it's clouded his judgment, such as it is." Seba grinned as he guided us into an interrogation room.

"Calm down, Shes. We'll work it out. Tell me what happened."

"What did Karkin tell you?"

Nebemhep snorted. "All I got from him was a grunt and the word 'Russians.'"

I gave him the highlights of our morning's adventures. The sehy pursed his lips. Baki, when he started the video for the interview, identified the participants. He looked at me, hands folded on the table in front of him.

"All right, Shesmu, let's get on. Why shouldn't we charge you under the criminal organization laws? You're working with a fair number of terrible people. That makes you a known associate of major criminals."

Nebemhep said, "Name them."

"Marya Semionevna Ranukhova, Pyotr Semionovich Podgoronov, Sennedjem, Nesimen, and R'aweben." He smiled. "It's really quite a list."

"My client has explained all of this. What criminal organization do you mean?"

"The R'ames Society, for a start."

"Did you charge anyone at that organization with maintaining a corporate entity for the purpose of the commission of crimes?"

"No. Not yet. It may happen any time."

"Even if it happens, my client is not involved in any criminal activities as a member of that organization."

"We believe he has his own criminal organization that's involved with the R'ames Society and the Henuttawy Group. R'aweben's disappearance revealed the scope of the conspiracy."

"A nice theory, Rudj Baki. Have you charged anyone in that network?"

"They all seem to have disappeared, other than Sennedjem. Shesmu had a lot to do with those disappearances. And they've made Sennedjem the scapegoat."

"What about R'aweben?"

"Until now, he's appeared to be a legitimate financier. He's an ex-hem-netjer-tepy of Bastet. And he's invested in Shesmu's restaurant. Now, he's vanished with his ill-gotten gains. Let's start with the arson and insurance fraud at that restaurant. The Henuttawy Group connects all the dots now. Prove to me that Shesmu knows nothing about all that."

"We don't have to prove anything. You do." Nebemhep smiled. "You can't prove either knowledge or intent by my client. I insist you release him."

"If I agree to that, will your client give us information that we can use to further our investigation into the R'ames Society and the Henuttawy Group?"

I looked at Nebemhep and shook my head. He told Baki, "No."

I said, "May I explain? It's quite simple." Nebemhep pressed a sandaled foot on one of mine, and I nodded at him reassuringly.

Baki half smiled in return and said, "Sure, why not? Confess."

I cleared my throat. "I know nothing other than what I've already told you, Baki. You already know that the whole thing is more complex than I thought. Now that you have Sennedjem and a reasonable expectation for finding at least some of the missing money, I can't contribute much more. I just want to get my restaurant fixed and back up and running. With new investors."

Baki drummed his fingers on the table in indecision. Then he said, "All right, I'll let you go."

"Boss!" said Seba, perturbed. "He's guilty as hell."

"Of course he is, Seba. Can you prove anything?"

"Not right now, but he's got too many fingers in this pie. When we interrogate Sennedjem—"

Nebemhep interjected, "Rudj Baki, I formally ask that you release my client. There is no evidence against him."

"All right, all right. Seba, we can't charge him. Take off the cuffs. You're free to go, Shesmu. For now. Until we find the evidence to put you behind bars. Oh, and a sedjemy has set the Promise of Ma'at for your friend Nesimen. You can take him with you if you can find the money for it."

Seba took off the cuffs, then glowered at me. As I rose to leave with my sehy, Seba pointed to his eyes with two fingers, then pointed the fingers at me in the classic warning of ongoing scrutiny. Nebemhep clucked his tongue and took my arm to persuade me out.

I stood on the sidewalk with Nesimen. I'd called Khenemset Neferet to come and pick up her husband, and we waited, saying nothing to each other. He had been profuse in his thanks when I paid his surety to Ma'at, but once he ran down, we had little to say to one another.

It had been a busy day, and I still had MacIntyre to deal with. I tried her phone again, but again went to voicemail. As I disconnected, a familiar sight pulled up in front of me: Karkin's junker car. Nicely timed, but Karkin never showed up unless there was something very wrong somewhere. He wasn't the type to do me favors by driving me home from the lockup.

Karkin rolled down his window. He said, "Emergency. Get in the car."

I responded, "We're waiting for Nesimen's ride. What's the emergency?"

Karkin rolled his window up and pushed open his passenger-side door.

I said to Nesimen, "Are you all right here, waiting for Khenemset Neferet?"

Nesimen, disheveled and tired, grimaced but said, "I suppose so. Thank you again, Shesmu. I appreciate your help, and so will Taneferet."

"Sure. All right, be seeing you."

I got into Karkin's car. "OK, what's the emergency?"

"MacIntyre. Marya Semionevna has her at the necropolis. Could be bad."

I redialed MacIntyre's number. Again, no answer. "Talk to me, Karkin. What's going on?"

"Informer in Gorni. Marya Semionevna thinks you broke the deal, took MacIntyre to find out how. The hard way."

The necropolis was about as far as you could get from the waterfront. Karkin sped across town. For an ancient car, that thing had plenty of zip; we sped straight up vertical hills with no strain.

"We should call the medjau."

"Not a good idea. Chen took MacIntyre for Masha."

Now, that was a complication. Rudj Chen, head of the organized crime squad, kidnapping MacIntyre on orders of Marya Semionevna. No, calling the medjau would not be a good idea.

"Back seat." He nodded in that direction. I looked back and saw my bow case and a bundle of arrows.

"Are you going to tell me why I have my bow?"

"Might need it. Good arrows, too, your size."

I reached and lifted the bundle of arrows. The tips were black, four-sided metal, and needle-sharp. Vicious. The arrows themselves were carbon fiber. War arrows.

"What the hell are these?"

Karkin grunted. "Bodkin points. Dagger on a stick. Carbon steel. Go through anything, like Kevlar."

"We're going after bear, then. Russian bear?" He just kept driving. Another hill, another swift descent that didn't help my stomach much.

"Come on, Karkin. I need to know what's going on if I'm going to be of any use! What's your plan?"

"Find the Russians. Do something."

I wasn't a natural hunter, despite my interest in food. As an archer, I liked targets that didn't move or weigh on your conscience when you killed them. MacIntyre being tortured changed all that.

The car flew over the top of the hill, landing with a thump in an empty intersection. We sped down the broad avenue that led to the Temple of Inpu and screeched to a halt in the temple parking lot. The temple loomed up out of the mist on one side. A parapet looked out over the chapels and tombs. On a sunny day, the white and gold was dazzling and majestic. That day, it just looked like a place full of dead people. I hoped I wouldn't join them too soon.

We jumped out of the car and got our kits together. Karkin put on a pair of thin, black gloves. I put on my jacket, but I had no gloves. We unpacked our bows and arranged our bodkin arrows.

"Ready?" asked Karkin.

"As I'll ever be."

My face and hair dripped with water that coalesced out of the heavy mist surrounding us. Karkin wasn't even out of breath as we trotted along the long necropolis street that snaked down the hill to the ocean. This area of the necropolis served the very rich, with big chapels and tombs that extended far into the rocky hill. On a good day, the views were spectacular; but today was not a good day.

Karkin knew where we were going, and I followed. He slowed, then stopped and looked around the corner of a chapel. He pulled back and whispered, "Big chapel. Two guards. Take them out quiet, see what's what."

We arranged extra arrows for quick access, readying our bows with nocked arrows.

"I'm left, you're right," Karkin said. We walked around the corner of the chapel making no noise, bows half drawn.

Across from us, about 40 meters away, stood two bored Russians in front of the big chapel. They wore European-style overcoats and had assault rifles. They weren't paying attention. We were. Our bows hummed as they raised there guns, and they dropped to the ground with only a slight metallic clatter as one of the rifles hit the concrete path.

Within seconds, we were standing on two sides of the closed door of the chapel. It had a lever handle and opened inwards. Karkin nocked another arrow, and I did the same. I concentrated on the fact that MacIntyre was inside undergoing who knew what, not on the fact that I'd just killed a man. Karkin signaled, asking whether I was ready. I inhaled and nodded. His hand stretched out to the top of the handle.

Karkin's neck muscles bunched, and we burst into the chapel, drawing our bows. The room was large, well lit, and decorated on every wall, the gold glinting from the many gods shown blessing the ka. I got a quick impression of all this, but my attention focused on a chair in the middle of the room. MacIntyre, face bloody, was heaving against her bonds while Marya Semionevna hit her with a billy club. The Russian's looks had not improved since I had last seen her. I shot her without hesitation, and she fell to the floor as the stick flew out of her hand.

There were two men in the room. A large European man stood behind the chair, and Rudj Chen stood off to the side. Karkin's bodkin arrow, directed at the European's chest, took him in the arm instead as he raised a large pistol. The arrow pinned his arm to his chest, but it didn't take him down. He held onto the gun somehow and got off a shot that destroyed some wall paintings. I shot him and hit him in the neck as he twisted away, and he too fell to the floor.

Karkin covered Chen with another arrow, and the medja raised his hands and backed up to the wall. I walked over to MacIntyre. She was smiling through bruised lips, but her eyes were not happy. She said, mumbling a bit, "Nice shooting."

"Thanks."

We looked at each other. She shifted in her seat, then said, "I'd appreciate it if you'd do something about my hands. Right now." Her voice was warm and inflected with humor; her eyes were just about as hot as I'd ever seen them. I walked around behind the chair and saw her hands tied with black plastic ties.

"This might take a while," I said.

Karkin said, "Get his gun."

I looked over at him, and he motioned toward Rudj Chen. I put my bow on the floor and walked toward Chen. I said, "Turn around against the wall." I kicked his legs apart as I'd seen MacIntyre do and searched him, getting his gun from a shoulder holster. Karkin put down his bow and picked up the European man's pistol.

"Check his legs and back," he said.

I followed instructions and found another, smaller gun in his back waistband and a thin knife strapped to his ankle.

"Just what I need," I said, extracting the knife from its sheath and testing its sharpness with my thumb. Chen turned a little pale, and I grinned and told him to sit down against the wall.

I carried the knife back to the chair and cut MacIntyre's bonds. Her wrists were bloody where she'd strained against the ties. She sat still for a minute, then got to her feet and staggered a little as she got her balance. I embraced her, and she flinched but held me fiercely.

"Thanks, Shes." Her voice was shaky.

"Let's get you outside, to a doctor," I said.

"Just hold me for a minute," she replied, resting her chin on my shoulder. "While I get my breath back. I'm fine."

"I'd kiss you, but it looks like it would hurt too much," I murmured. "You're not fine."

Karkin said, "Medjau. 111."

I released MacIntyre and looked around. Two bodies here, two outside, and a live, dirty medja. Djehutymes was going to have an interesting day. I took out my phone.

"Let me," said MacIntyre, holding out a hand. I gave her the phone. She punched out a number from memory. "Mes? Cheryl. Yes, I'm fine, more or less, no thanks to Chen. He and one of his henchmen on the gang squad, a semety named Gatti, kidnapped me. They brought me to a chapel in the necropolis and turned me over to Marya Semionevna Ranukhova. I'm lucky to be alive. I'm afraid nobody else made it, just Chen. How many?" She raised an eyebrow at me. I held up four fingers.

"Gatti is dead, Marya Semionevna, and two other Russians. That's right. Four. You'll need some serious transportation. Oh, and it's all thanks to Shesmu and a friend of his."

I expected to hear the usual squawk from the phone; Djehutymes didn't like surprises, and he didn't like me. But there was nothing.

"Where are we?" she asked, looking at me.

"We're in the rich-family tomb area of the necropolis, tomb of—," I went over to the door and read the glyphs, "tomb of Pentaweret za-R'ahetep." MacIntyre relayed this information to Djehutymes, then hung up.

"He's coming?" I asked.

"Yeah. Right away."

"You're sure you don't need a doctor? I don't like the way you're holding your arm. You're limping, and your mouth looks terrible. Why don't you sit down?"

"I've been sitting down all day, thanks," she said. "And that chair is uncomfortable. I'll live. Thanks to you," she said, embracing me again. "And Karkin."

Karkin acknowledged her thanks with a nod, but he kept the pistol rock steady on Chen as we waited for the forces of Ma'at to arrive.

CHAPTER TWENTY-NINE
Shesmu Helps MacIntyre Recover

DJEHUTYMES, AFTER INSPECTING THE CARNAGE and getting the story from us, sent us home in a cruiser. During that ride, the effects of her beating caught up with MacIntyre. Getting her out of the cruiser was a trial. So, a long, hot bath and a slow, relaxed evening followed, during which we caught each other up.

"Did he really do that? Point at his eyes to say he was going to watch you?" MacIntyre was incredulous at Seba's police tactics.

"He did. The Henet Baket prides itself on its ability to suspect the worst in people."

"Like our Homicide Squad, I guess," she said.

"Well, death and taxes…." I smiled. "More wine?"

"Better not. I'll ache enough tomorrow without a hangover to add to it."

"What's tomorrow for you? Bed rest, I hope."

"Got to talk to Yaotl again, and see about a cat."

"Bastet?"

"Bastet. I'll go right to the top this time. They're going to have a show trial for Henutsenu in ten days, and I need to get the hem-netjer-tepy to see things straight about their coverup. How about you?"

"Well, I need to talk to Nesimen again. He's got to know something more about what was going on at the R'ames Society. I need to connect all the dots between the R'ames Society, the Henuttawy Group, the Russians, and the Per'ankh."

"Finding Pyotr Semionovich will help with that, too."

"I'll leave that to Baki. He has more resources for that sort of thing. The long arm of the sepat. I need to concentrate on the restaurant and my supposed criminal activities there. Once I know what's going on, I can convince Baki I'm not involved. But I need more information."

"How is the restaurant progressing?"

"Dead in the water. The insurance company won't pay because they think the bombing is a fraud. We both know it was gang-related, but they don't believe it."

"What are you going to do about it once you resolve the insurance issue? Demolish it and sell the land?"

"I wish I could do that, but I can't."

"Because you still want to be chef of the best French restaurant in Menmenet?"

I weighed that question and asked, "If you had everything you ostensibly cared about blown up and felt nothing but joy, what would you think?"

"Therapy. Lots of therapy."

"Yeah. I probably do need therapy. But even without that, I've concluded that I don't want to keep doing what I was doing before the bomb."

"Tell me you don't want to be a chef anymore, Shes. Then make me believe it."

"Well, no. I do. Just not a French chef. It doesn't fit. But…that's not all of it. I wasn't at the Per'ankh only because it's the best restaurant in Menmenet."

"Neferaset and Nekhen, right?"

Neferaset, my former lover and Nekhen's wife, had done everything she could to stop me from taking over Nekhen's restaurant—the Per'ankh. But I'd fooled her with a complicated investment scheme and partners that kept my name out of the transaction. Over the last year as executive chef, I'd fully atoned for my transgression against Nekhen, and I'd lost interest in French cooking.

Then came the Henuttawy Group.

I told MacIntyre, "Since the Henuttawy Group put their money in, my billionaire partner, Hernefer, insisted that we incorporate into a zau. He wanted us to take the whole business to another level, have a board of directors, and start franchising. Turning my restaurant into a massive zau with shareholders and a board. Did I want to become chief executive of a massive worldwide empire? A pera'a of the culinary world? No—I did not. I wanted to cook."

"That's who you are, Shes. Just as I'm a medjat. We both care a lot about what we do."

"Well, blowing up the Per'ankh wiped all that clean. But not having the Per'ankh had its issues, too. The business is three-quarters of my income. And I have a hard-nosed partner, complicated by the Henuttawy investment. The gods alone know how to resolve that mess."

"The insurance will help rebuild it, right?"

"Sure, but somebody's got to run it, and run it right. I can't let Nekhen's legacy turn to dust. His ka would never forgive me." I smiled and reached for her hand. Squeezing, I said, "So it's joy, not grief. But finance still chains me to the place."

MacIntyre rubbed my hand. "Bombs can complicate things, or they can simplify things. Let's explore, find out what's going on, deal with the feelings. I love you. I want you to be happy, but I want you to be you more than anything else. You're not Nekhen. You're you. And the restaurant will be fine without you as chef. Why not let Qenna take over after resolving the financial mess?"

I nodded. "I'll ask him. Add that to the list for tomorrow."

MacIntyre swung her legs off the couch. "I've got to go to bed. I'm just dead."

"Fortunately," I said, "not."

My eyes snapped open. It was pitch black. A hand was on my mouth. It was MacIntyre's hand, smooth as silk. Then I heard a rustle outside the closed bedroom door. I used sleepy logic: if I was here, and MacIntyre was here, then neither of us was making the noise. So, something else was making a noise in my house at—I looked at the clock—3:30 in the morning. Not good.

I touched her hand to show her I understood, and she released my mouth. She got out of bed in total silence. I followed. We didn't bother with clothes. MacIntyre took only one accessory: her gun.

We crept out into the hall and silently approached the great room. A small light flickered over the walls. MacIntyre stretched her hand around the entry and flipped the light switch. The lights blazed on, and MacIntyre was into the room in a crouch, gun held straight out in both hands. She shouted, "Medjau! Don't move! Medjau! Keep your hands in front of you."

In the middle of the room, a man dressed in black stood, hands at his sides, his expression blank. He was European, about 2 meters tall, with longish black hair and reddish lips. He raised his black-gloved hands in front of himself, one palm out, the other hand holding a small flashlight, and said something in what sounded like Russian. MacIntyre glanced at me, saw that I didn't understand, and said, "Speak Renkemet." The Russian said something else, again in Russian.

"Great. Fine." She motioned with the gun toward the wall. "Hands against the wall, please." He didn't move. She used her left hand to show what he should do, and he turned and splayed himself out against the wall. MacIntyre stepped forward, put her hand on his back, and kicked his legs apart with her bare feet. She said, "Shes, search him, and be careful."

I took the flash out of his hand and put it in my pocket, then patted him down. I was getting used to this routine. He wore a thin, black jacket over a black jersey and black trousers and shoes. I backed away and said, "Nothing. No identification in his pockets."

MacIntyre kept the gun pointed at the Russian while she droned through the recitation of rights with the Wings of Ma'at. "We can't question him until they get a Russian translator, though," she said. "Wouldn't be ma'at. Go get my phone from my jacket. It's on the chair in the bedroom. And the handcuffs."

I complied and brought her the phone and cuffs. She said, "Hold this on him," and gave me the gun. She pulled the Russian's arms behind his back and fastened his wrists together with the cuffs with a practiced flick of the wrist. She guided the man over to the couch in the middle of the room and sat him down.

"OK, hold the gun on our burglar while I take care of business," said MacIntyre. She called the medjau for reinforcements, then stalked off to get her clothes on.

When she came back, I gave her back her gun and went to get my own clothes on. When I returned, I noticed a black bag on the floor in the entry hall, the top open. I looked in and saw a small collection of iron pipes. I backed away without touching it and said, "Cheryl, look at this."

She came, pushing the Russian in front of her, looked, and said, "Crap. Outside, now!"

Thirty minutes later, we were out on the street talking with Djehutymes while the medjau from the bomb squad were dealing with the black bag's contents. The bomb squad medjau were the first I'd seen that hadn't traded jokes or insults with MacIntyre since I'd known her. They were intent on their job and didn't seem interested in anything but the bombs.

The Russian said nothing. Djehutymes had rousted a Russian translator out of bed. She had repeated the Wings of Ma'at to our suspect in Russian, but nothing had changed in the Russian's face. Djehutymes stuffed him into a police cruiser and turned to us for information, just as R'a's first light came.

He said, "We'll get him down to the Temple of Ma'at and put him through it. He'll talk. Right now, you need to tell me what happened here."

MacIntyre related the events of the night to Djehutymes. The idnu grimaced as MacIntyre described her impulsive confrontation with the Russian. I let MacIntyre describe the bombs. The bomb squad came out of the house carrying a large box, presumably with the black bag inside.

MacIntyre offered a suggestion. "Mes. You should find that big Russian, Pyotr Semionovich. He's got to be responsible for this. He must have taken over the gang once his sister was gone. And he still thinks Shesmu is involved."

"Leave that to us, MacIntyre. You're suspended. And you're in no shape to help."

The bombs gone and the suspect in custody, Djehutymes left after warning us not to do anything stupid. I had to help MacIntyre up the short steps to the front door. Not a good sign. We sat alone, looking at each other across the small kitchen table. It was light outside.

"Well," said MacIntyre, "I won't get any more sleep. Maybe we can find something else to do for an hour that's not too stupid. If it doesn't hurt too much." I reached across the table, and she took my hand.

CHAPTER THIRTY
MacIntyre Wields a Macahuitl

MacIntyre called Yaotl right after breakfast and got his butler Eztli, who scheduled her into the crime lord's busy morning. She looked in the bathroom mirror and groaned. Of course, Shesmu had no makeup to cover the bruises. But then, she didn't have any makeup at home, either. She shrugged, called a cab, and went to her appointment.

The winter fog had crept out from the east during the night and spread over the top half of the city. She hated the winter ground fog. It smelled of the dank corruption of the river delta and was often so thick you couldn't drive without taking your life in your hands. That day, the fog hadn't cleared by the time she set off for Yaotl's place, but it had lightened up enough to see the road, at least. The cab drove down and up and down the hills across the top of the city to reach the Tjesut with ten minutes to spare. Eztli let her in and took her to the great room to wait.

Yaotl appeared at the appointed time and greeted her with the same sour expression he'd worn the last time she'd seen him. After they had seated themselves, he examined her for a full minute. His face didn't soften, but the creases evened out a bit and the mouth looked like it might break into a smile if given a chance.

"So the rumors were true, Hutyt. You had an adventure. Russians lack subtlety, I've found. You look as though a full herd of Russian bulls has trampled you. I hope you took medical advice?"

"Let's focus on your problems, Yaotl, not mine."

"I am sorry, Hutyt. I had become accustomed to enjoying the vagaries of your beautiful Anglo-American face, and the coloring effects of your adventure are startling."

"Thanks for the compliment, I guess. Now, about this gang war." MacIntyre sat forward. "Marya Semionevna is gone, and you need no longer worry about her incursion into Menmenet."

"Ah, Hutyt MacIntyre, I see you do not comprehend the elastic nature of business organization. It is perhaps because your exposure to real business has been so limited by your career in civil and religious government."

This was too much for MacIntyre's tired brain to absorb and understand. "I don't know what you mean, Yaotl. Spit it out."

"I cannot imagine that you are here just to report on the demise of a Russian gangster. What other matter have you come about?"

MacIntyre sat back in her chair, but despite its comfort, grunted in pain. Keep the movements small and easy, that's the ticket.

"May I offer you some Aztec brandy or perhaps an analgesic, Hutyt?" Yaotl's voice filled with a sham concern.

"No, you may not. All right, yes, there is something else. My boyfriend Shesmu and I encountered a Russian gangster last night. He broke into Shesmu's house in the early hours of the morning. He had pipe bombs with him. So they're still trying to scare Shesmu off."

"And yet you persist in thinking that poor Marya Semionevna's demise has halted the onrushing train of Russian brutality." Yaotl smiled. "There are many Russian gangsters who are quite willing to step up to replace her. I am sure that one of them ordered up the bombs. I am afraid it is more likely they wish to remove your friend from the scene rather than—what was your phrase? 'Scare him off?'"

"I suppose that's possible. I'm sure that Masha's brother has taken up those reins. What do you know about that?"

"I know many things, Hutyt. I speak about few of them, especially to medjau."

"Why be coy, Yaotl? It's in your best interest to have us—meaning the medjau —take care of the Russians."

"Ah, if only you might assure me of such an action. But I did ask that you start such an effort, did I not? The result sits before me, barely able to stand. I overestimated your competence, Hutyt."

"I ran into trouble. It turns out that one of our lead officers was corrupt, and he kidnapped me before I could do anything more about your problem."

"Rudj Chen. Yes, unfortunate. I had not realized that the man was dealing so intimately with my enemies."

"Was he dealing with you, then? We have charged him with corrupt practices, kidnapping, and attempted murder, and that's just for starters. He won't be of much help in the future."

"That is another thing I would never discuss with a medjat, Hutyt."

"Damn it, Yaotl, I'm trying to help stop a gang war here!"

"And failing, Hutyt."

MacIntyre shifted to see if she could get herself into a more comfortable position. She couldn't. Her temper frayed, but blowing up on Yaotl would not be productive. She changed tactics.

"I need your help, Yaotl. If the Russians are trying to kill Shesmu or me, that's going to impact your business. The heat will be on. Every medjau in Menmenet, even the corrupt ones, will be after you and the Russians. Help me stay alive, and help me stop this gang war. Stand down. Please."

"A very nice and well-reasoned speech, Hutyt. But it changes nothing and will not divert me from my efforts to preserve my business. As we speak, my associates are building their strength and working out armaments and tactics needed to finish the task. I am sure you may take comfort because the war will be short, if bloody. My best advice is to warn your superiors to stay out of it. That will avoid any unnecessary bloodshed among the worshippers of Ma'at. And now, Hutyt, I wish you a good day. I have much business to attend to. Eztli will show you out."

The butler appeared at MacIntyre's side. He helped her out of the chair and supported her until she got her footing. But she had enough pride left to shake off his helping hand as they made their way to the front of the big glass pyramid.

She called a cab and waited patiently for it, getting her breath back. Damn that Russian psychopath! She couldn't afford any downtime, not right now. She punched a familiar number into her phone.

"Mes? Cheryl. I'm at Yaotl's. Now, don't go ballistic on me, but I just checked in with him on his intentions. He's moving on the Russians, but he's being coy about naming his targets. I'd suggest you preempt the attacks by arresting him and his main associates before they swing macahuitls at unsuspecting Russians."

"I can do that. Chen has a lot to answer for, Cheryl. Do you know any of the Russians?"

"Just Podgoronov. He must have taken over the gang from his sister. But I don't know where he might be."

"We'll find him, or Yaotl will. He's finished. And the Henet Baket has Sennedjem under lock and key. All we need now is to arrest your boyfriend."

"Oh, ha, ha. Anything from the Russian you arrested last night?"

"Nothing. He wants his sehy, and we're trying to locate her, but she's turned off her phone."

"Busy strategizing with her paying customers."

"Look, Cheryl, I can't reinstate you. Kasa won't let me. And you ought to be on disability anyway, from what I saw last night. But why don't you come in and observe our interrogation of Chen? He's waived his right to have an attorney present. He wants a deal. Two things: will it traumatize you more, and can you keep yourself from killling him?"

The cab drew up. She said, "I'll be there in ten minutes."

Chen Ju-Long sat in the prisoner's chair in the small interrogation room at the Temple of Ma'at. He appeared smaller than she remembered; deflated, or it might be a trick of the one-way window.

Djehutymes, standing next to her, refuted this idea. "No, I've seen this before. Something happens to the muscles in a medja when they get caught doing something terrible. A huty from internal affairs is going to interrogate him. You sure you're OK watching this?"

She looked at Djehutymes with what she considered a look of scorn. But from his quivering lips trying not to smile, she deduced it had little effect because of the bruising.

The huty from internal affairs came into the room from a separate door and sat down, then started the interview. The preliminaries took a little time, then Chen got specific.

"I want witness protection and immunity, or you get nothing."

"Why should we do that, Ju-Long? We have you on half-a-dozen major offenses, including attempted murder. We have plenty of eyewitnesses to it all."

Chen smiled and said nothing. Djehutymes said, "Kasa assumed Chen would ask for either witness protection or immunity from prosecution or both. Right, as usual. The huty has instructions to string him along to see if he'll give up any-thing without them."

He didn't. After a half hour of haranguing the man, the huty realized he wasn't getting anywhere. Chen had been a medja for too long to take the bait.

"All right, Ju-Long, immunity, as long as you don't lie to us and you tell us everything. And we will know whether you do, believe me."

"And witness protection. Somewhere far away from here."

More negotiations followed, but the huty had his instructions, and things wound up to Chen's satisfaction. He had balked at being paroled to Kashia, up north. "Too close to the Russians." He had balked at the little town of Kimike, far down on the lower peninsula. "Too close to the Aztecs." They settled on Tjeny, on the south coast. All MacIntyre knew about the place was that it specialized in fancy pigs and ran on water distilled from the ocean. Good luck to the man.

MacIntyre stirred, restless. "Is this going anywhere soon, Mes? My butt hurts." And her face, and her legs and knees, and…

"Should be soon, according to the interrogation plan I saw."

"Say, we better tell that huty about the Russian gangs still being active."

"Already done, based on what you told me last night and this morning. And I put out an all-points on Podgoronov. Nothing." Djehutymes stared at Chen. "It gets my goat to see that bastard smiling, after what he did."

"Thanks, Mes, I appreciate the thought."

"Oh. I didn't mean to you, but that too."

MacIntyre smiled and shook her head. What the department needed was more women in the higher ranks. Like her. People sensitive to the feelings of others. Like her.

"Say, what about the other medjau on Chen's squad? We'd better—"

"Kasa's already had them all locked up until we figure out who's bent and who's straight."

Chen finally stated a name. Yevgeny Ivanovich Strel'sky. Who the fuck was that?

"Did I miss something?"

"He said that's the name of the guy who took over from Ranukhova."

"Not Podgoronov?"

"Apparently not. Strel'sky is her second-in-command."

"So where the hell is Podgoronov, and what's he doing?"

"Shut up and listen, MacIntyre, and you might find out."

She settled back in her chair. But she never heard Chen mention the big Russian's name, just a few higher-ups in the medjau and civil administration of the city, who would soon get their just desserts.

"Say, what about Bastet?" she blurted.

"What?"

MacIntyre realized that the only medja who had seen Yaotl's dossier on the situation was Chen. And that dossier had disappeared, according to Mes. No doubt shredded while she waited for Chen to set her up for Marya Semionevna.

With urgency, she said, "Mes, get the huty to ask about the Russian connection to the Temple of Bastet. It's important."

He glanced at her, then looked back at Chen. "This is about your friend, isn't it?"

"Yes, but it was in the dossier I got from Yaotl."

"The missing one?"

"Yes. It said the Russians were running money through the temple as well as through the R'ames Society and the Henuttawy Group."

Djehutymes picked up a microphone and requested the huty to take a break and come talk with them. The huty stopped the interview and soon was in the room with them. MacIntyre related what she knew about the connection to the Temple of Bastet and tried to convey her sense of urgency about the matter.

"That temple is powerful and well funded," she said. "If they're tight with the Russians, it's not on the up-and-up. Chen can tell us who and why."

The huty agreed to spend some time on the subject and went back to the interrogation. Chen proved reluctant to talk about Bastet.

"That wasn't part of the deal," he said.

"You tell us everything. That was the deal. You don't tell us, you're in prison for life, locked up with all those Russians and Aztecs you've just been telling us about."

Rattled, Chen stared at his hands, folded in front of him on the table. Then he looked up and said, "All right, all right. The hem-netjer-tepy of the Temple of Bastet, Panekhet, is the contact for the Russians. I learned about it through an illegal wiretap and used it to get more money out of Ranukhova. She didn't want it known. I destroyed the recording and 'forgot' the name until now. Just make damn sure the bastard never learns where you got his name."

"The name isn't enough, Ju-Long. We need details, money movements, anything else criminal."

"I never investigated. Those temples, especially Bastet, are clams. Way too much money and power to cross. And Ranukhova paid me to leave it alone."

"So you don't have any evidence for us about the temple's doings."

"No, absolutely not. I'm telling you, the guy is dirty, but you'll have to prove it yourself."

"Gee, thanks, Ju-Long," muttered MacIntyre. "Mes, how do we crack open the Temple of Bastet to empty the kitty litter and get my friend out?"

Djehutymes shook his head. "Getting access to temple books is damn near impossible without at least three smoking guns, and Chen hasn't even given us a water pistol. The gods take care of their own."

MacIntyre groaned in frustration. There had to be a way to shake it all loose at the Temple of Bastet and get Henutsenu out before her trial. She just didn't know what it was. Yet.

CHAPTER THIRTY-ONE
Shesmu Feels the Pressure

THE CONNECTION BETWEEN THE HENUTTAWY Group and the R'ames Society bubbled up to the top of my mind. Baki had ranked that connection as a major factor in his suspicions, and I had not really understood the relationship through R'aweben. I walked down to the R'ames Society office the first thing after breakfast to talk to somebody there about it. The office had reopened, so I walked up the stairs from the big hall and back to Nesimen's old office. His assistant was there, but he wasn't, and wouldn't be.

"Lord Shesmu," acknowledged the assistant.

"I'd like to see whoever has replaced Nesimen, if that person's available."

"You can speak with the acting executive, Lord Shesmu." He went into the inner office. He returned with a mid-sized, middle-aged woman who introduced herself and bowed. I bowed back.

"My assistant tells me you're Shesmu? How fortuitous that you should come by. I needed to speak with you. Perhaps it would be advisable to come into my office so we can talk?"

"Certainly."

I followed her in, and she shut the door behind us and sat behind the large desk. She folded her hands on the desk and looked at me.

"Lord Shesmu. The Henet Baket, a Rudj Baki, has communicated several interesting things to us."

"I know him," I said.

"He knows you too," said the acting executive cooly. "Well enough to warn us about you."

"Warn?" I asked.

"Warn." She unfolded her hands and folded them the opposite way. "Distinct-ly. And the Board of Directors has given me clear direction about the situation."

"So it was Baki who told them about the fake resume."

"Nesimen? Yes, true. And about you."

"What about me?"

"The Board wants me to inform you they have rescinded the Best New Chef award and your membership in the Society. That means you can no longer use the award or refer to it or to the Society for commercial or personal purposes. Am I clear?"

"As dishwater in a good restaurant," I said. "Which mine is. Or was until it got blown up."

The acting executive put her hands palm down on her desk and frowned. "Because of your connections to organized crime."

"My…" This sally startled me into inarticulate surprise.

"The Board asked around once Rudj Baki had informed them of his suspicions. They confirmed your ties to Russian gangsters and to Lord R'aweben's financial company. We can't have the Society associating with any such people. The Board was quite clear with me—"

"Who on the board? Panekhet?"

The woman stopped, nonplussed, and just stared at me for a moment. "That's none of your concern. The decision was unanimous, if you must know."

"The same unanimity that hired Nesimen and Sennedjem? Were they unani-mous about R'aweben as well? I'm in good company. And none of *them* could cook worth a damn."

"Those men are no longer part of the organization, Lord Shesmu. Nor are you."

"Yes, but I need to understand exactly how R'aweben joined and what he did when he was here. If you—"

The woman rose from her chair. "We're finished here. I'm very sorry it has come to this, but our decision is firm."

Fixing my reputation would take some serious work because of this. I had to talk to Nesimen to get him to divulge what he knew. And I had to talk to Panekhet to change his mind, or at least to find out what was in it. He must have known R'aweben, his predecessor as hem-netjer-tepy of the Temple of Bastet. Nesimen might give me something to persuade him to walk back this decision.

The acting director waited. I took my time to preserve what little dignity remained to me, decided against any verbal ripostes, and stalked out.

* * *

The bus dropped me off half-way up the wrong side of the hill on the Tjesut, two blocks from Nesimen's house. I bet there was a view of the city and the mountains to the south, but I never saw a thing: I was too mad. This whole situation wasn't just out of control, it was crashing and burning.

I rang the doorbell of the neat little house. After a wait, the door opened, and Khenemset Neferet peered out at me and smiled. She said, "Shes, how nice to see you." She embraced me, then added, "I am so thankful you could get Nesimen out of that awful place."

I held her hands in front of me, keeping the connection to her. "So am I. But things are happening, Khenemset Neferet. I need to speak with Nesimen."

The smile disappeared. "He's out in back, sitting in the garden. He's...." She couldn't finish the thought, but it was clear that Nesimen wasn't doing well.

"I need to see him. He can help me deal with Sennedjem and the Society's problems."

"He's left the Society, Shes. He thought it would be best. Now that he has to deal with all the charges against him."

Left. She didn't know they'd fired him. What else didn't she know? I resolved not to leave the house until she knew everything. She deserved to know.

I said, "I need some information from him, Khenemset Neferet."

She showed me into the small sitting room I had been in before. She motioned me to a seat and said, "I'll see if Nesimen will talk to you."

I heard the murmur of voices for a while, then silence. After five minutes, Nesimen appeared in the door with Khenemset Neferet behind him. I stood. He smiled, a shadow of his former charm breaking through his gray appearance. "Shes, how nice to see you again."

I looked at Khenemset Neferet. "Meet with me alone," I suggested to Nesimen. I wanted to spare her from what I was about to say to Nesimen, but I'd have to fill her in later.

She closed her eyes and tightened her lips, then said, "No, I want to stay." Nesimen shrugged with palms up, smiled, and motioned to the sofas.

Khenemset Neferet asked, "Would you like some tea, Shes?"

"No, thanks."

She sat back, protocol satisfied, her face expecting the worst. I would not disappoint her.

I said, "I just came from the Society, Nesimen." I took out my copy of Nesimen's resume. "This is your old resume. You should revise it, since it's all lies."

All this bewildered Khenemset Neferet. I gave her the paper. Nesimen made a slight movement toward her as if he would grab it away, but he couldn't complete the movement.

She said, "This last one—we were in New York, in America, for several months." She looked at Nesimen. "You couldn't have been working. You said you wanted to take a few months off." She looked back at the paper, then at me. "All of it?" she asked with a quaver in her voice. "Lies?" I nodded. She closed her eyes again and leaned back. She let her hand holding the paper drop to her lap.

Nesimen was still smiling, his eyes looking everywhere but at me or at his wife. I asked him, "How did you think you could get away with it?"

He shook his head. "I didn't, I suppose. It started as a fantasy, I guess. I just sat down and made up a life for myself. I wasn't happy with the real one."

"What was the real one?"

"Just going along, working here and there, sales, some bookkeeping, that sort of thing." He smiled. "I was always pretty good at selling, but somehow the deals never made me enough money."

"Not the way you spend it," I said.

Khenemset Neferet opened her eyes again. "What do you mean?" she asked. "We're very frugal. We don't have a lot of expensive things." She waved a hand at the spartan room. "Nesimen didn't want to spend his mother's inheritance on fripperies. He said so."

Nesimen's eyes were closed as he nodded. More research to do. I was reasonably sure he'd had a mother, but I thought it would be a good idea to check. I focused on expense for a bit rather than income.

"Nesimen goes out a lot, right? Alone?"

"Well, yes, he's a very busy man, always working on Society fundraising and things like that." There was a dampened note of pride in her voice. I shook my head again and turned back to Nesimen.

"Fundraising you may have been, but you were fund-spending too, right?"

He shook his head, still refusing to acknowledge the situation.

I said to Khenemset Neferet, "How do you like your beautiful necklace?" She gave me a blank look. "You remember, the old-style dj'amu collar necklace with the lapis lazuli?" Nesimen's eyes were open now, and staring at me bleakly. I described my shopping trip of a few days before.

She stared at Nesimen. "Where is it?"

"I didn't…"

"Shes says you did. Why would he lie? He wouldn't lie, not to me." She looked at me and said, "You're saying everything's a lie. Not just a little of it—all of it. Our whole life. Our life." She looked back at Nesimen. "There's no inheritance, is there? That was just money you took from the R'ames Society. And all those charges against you. They're all true, aren't they? You're going to jail." Her voice rose in a wail.

Nesimen just stared back at her, eyes shifting, mouth ajar. He seemed to have shrunk like a balloon that had been floating on the ceiling a little too long. He lifted his hands in a negative gesture and said, "I'm sorry."

"Sorry!" Khenemset Neferet seemed at a complete loss for words as she moved from vague unease to utter despair before my eyes.

"I'm sorry too," I said. "To add to it all, the Society fired Nesimen because of the crimes."

Khenemset Neferet turned the bewildered eyes on me. "What?"

"The Board of Directors fired him."

"What?" She had to blink the tears out of her eyes.

"They fired me too. Or, at least, they threw me out. Took back my award, too." Enough of that. I'm not a whiner. But I had to tell them. I asked Nesimen, "Why did you hire Sennedjem?"

He licked his dry lips and answered, "I had to."

"Why?"

"There were, some, that is, there were reasons." He was having trouble forming complete sentences, his heart freezing up on him. Taneferet wiped her eyes and left the room without a word.

"Doubtless. What were they? You need to tell me." It was my chef's voice, the one I used when faced with a plate that was unacceptable. I'd learned that voice from Nekhen. I didn't use it often, but when I did, people did what I told them to do.

Nesimen was no exception. "Sennedjem knew things. My life wasn't what it appeared, and he knew it. He had learned I needed money. He said I'd get it, even more of it, if I put him in charge of the finances at the Society. He told me he'd convince the Board that he was a finance expert. And he did, he did."

"What happened to the previous financial officer?"

"Sennedjem got rid of him somehow. I don't know how. He just never showed up to work one day. I got a letter of resignation, one line." He was still incoherent.

"Let me guess: none of the directors asked for any references for Sennedjem. Or about the resignation."

He turned his palms down in the negative sign. "Not one."

The R'ames Society had been a pirate's dream. Large amounts of money, plenty of dumb, rich people in charge not paying attention along with some smart, rich people taking advantage. Even more dumb, rich people giving lots of money. No fiscal controls and a wide ocean of self-deceit into which it all could disappear.

"Did he ever tell you what he was doing with the money?"

"Going to clubs."

I smiled. Even Sennedjem couldn't spend that much money on clubs, not even the kind of clubs a Sennedjem would frequent. "I meant the money he was laundering. Huge amounts, millions."

"Millions?" His eyes were big.

"Baki didn't tell you?"

"Baki?"

"Yes, Baki. The Henet Baket." Was Nesimen really that dense?

"Oh, him. He got me fired? The Board didn't tell me that. Millions?"

"Millions. And they'll extract it deben by deben out of your hide unless they find it. You'll be in jail for the rest of your life. Help me find it, Nesimen. If we find it, the sepat will take it and let the Society off." Not him, though.

"But I'm not part of that," he said with despair.

"Did Sennedjem ever talk about any of his banks, or any of his banking contacts?"

"Maybe he did, a while back, but I can't remember. Wait; there was one I remember, because he's on the Board. R'aweben, he's the head of a big financial group, the Henuttawy Group. He missed a lot of Board meetings, a very busy man, but I met with him twice. Panekhet, the Chairman, was acquainted with him and liked him. Thick as thieves. Sennedjem brought him onto the Board. It was the first thing Sennedjem did to show how good he was for the Society. How connected he was to the financial world."

Way better than everyone knew, I thought to myself. I said, "And did R'aweben bring a lot to the Society? Money? New members in droves? Access to millions?"

Nesimen was dismayed. "I let Sennedjem follow all of that. I'm not much of a numbers person."

R'aweben brought financial ability and a high-capacity financial infrastructure. Sennedjem must have used it to move the money offshore somewhere. Now R'aweben was gone and his digital vaults were empty. The Henet Baket had Sennedjem and would follow up on R'aweben, but if they found nothing, Nesimen and I were on the hook. And R'aweben had invested in my restaurant—through Hernefer. And Panekhet, R'aweben, and the Temple of Bastet—thick as thieves.

Khenemset Neferet came back into the room. She carried the black case I'd seen at the jewelers. Nesimen stood up and made a grab for it, but she held it away from him. She opened the case.

"This isn't for me, is it, Nesimen?" She lifted the dj'amu necklace out; a thing of beauty. She threw it at him. It hit him in the chest and fell to the floor. "I found it in your drawers, under your socks. Who is she?"

"Just…nobody." He looked at the necklace on the floor. "Nobody."

I needed to nip this fight in the bud or I wouldn't get what I needed here. I put away any compassion I had and said, "I'd take that back to Jean at Maupassant et fils and get the money; you're going to need it for groceries. And you'd better do it soon, before the Henet Baket drops by and seizes it. You should sell the house, too."

That shocked them both, and they both looked at me with bewildered eyes and hurting faces.

"You're going to help me, Nesimen. You're going to call Panekhet, the Chairman of the Board of the Society, and get him to meet with me today. Right now. Tell him I wasn't involved in any of this, and make him believe it. Tell him I want my membership in the R'ames Society back."

I'll have to say this: Nesimen was a great con man. Despite the man having fired him, and despite his thinking that I was a Russian mobster in disguise, Nesimen convinced Panekhet to see me at the Temple of Bastet. Nesimen told Panekhet I was no mobster and was a good member of the Society. If I couldn't follow the money, I could at least try to repair my reputation.

Khenemset Neferet walked me to the door, her face now a mask. I knew our relationship would survive, but she was hurting right now.

I said, "I'm sorry. If you need anything, need help—"

"Yes. Well, I'm sorry too." She looked away and back again. "It's not your fault, is it? You're just the messenger. And you got Nesimen out of jail. But he's going back. And—another woman. Women? Oh, Shes, thank you for your honesty. We'll talk. After this is all over." She embraced me, but her heart wasn't in it this time.

The door shut behind me with a dispiriting thud.

On the bus down the hill, my phone rang: Qenna.

"Shes, the insurance people called. Their investigators are holding open their case on the restaurant. We need to talk."

The Per'ankh was only a few blocks away from the Temple of Bastet, where I was due in two hours.

I asked, "Can you get to the restaurant site right now? I'm on my way there on a bus."

"The Neferti can get along without me for a couple of hours."

"How is Sebek holding up?"

A pause. "Not so well. To be honest, he's pretty useless right now."

"Bring him along, give him something to think about besides his missing love. Turn things over to Khay."

"Right. See you there."

I hopped off the bus a block away from the Per'ankh and walked around the block to view the devastation. The construction people had cleared much of the debris, but the reconstruction was on hold because of the insurance, so the site was accessible but quiet. The city had put up demolition notices, as they contended there was too much structural damage to save anything. I wasn't so sure, but I had not spoken with the construction company or my architect yet. I'd been a little busy.

Qenna's car parked in the empty parking lot as I stood looking at the ruin. Qenna and Sebek got out and came over to me, and we all gazed at the ruin.

"I haven't seen it until now," said Sebek, his hand rubbing his mouth in dismay.

"It's depressing, is what it is," I said. "And I'm not sure I want to rebuild."

Qenna, who had more on the line than either of us, said, "We'll rebuild. Better. The old place grew organically out of the mansion that Nekhen inherited. The insurance will pay for most of it, and the customers will pay for the rest. We'll just raise prices a little."

I'd never seen Qenna quite so assertive or quite so cheerful. He was a somewhat dour presence in the kitchen, a perfectionist in a world that prized perfection. I had worked with him off and on for several years and respected his ability, but I wasn't sure about his architectural judgment.

"How much can we save?"

Sebek cocked his head. "Those steps there in front seem sound enough, and that corner post looks solid." He grinned. "Other than that, not much."

Qenna shook his head. "Funny man. We will leave it to the architect and engineer to decide what we can save. We will then save it and build from it, stronger than before. I have done the numbers, and with the insurance, anything is possible." He looked at me. "The insurance adjuster told me you, Shes, must prove who bombed the restaurant. Have you made progress?"

"I have a verbal confession from the person who ordered it, and her dead body and nothing recorded on paper. There is another witness that has vanished. I'm seeing the Hem-Netjer-Tepy of Bastet in an hour. That will give me a chance to restore my reputation." Sebek's gaze swung around to me at the mention of Bastet.

"That's not quite enough, is it?" noted Qenna.

"No, not quite. And I'm still not sure I want to rebuild."

"Why ever not? The Per'ankh is the best restaurant in Menmenet. You won an award to prove it."

"That's what the appointment is about—the R'ames Society revoked the award because of my gang affiliations."

"No!" Sebek had pain in his voice.

"Yes. So, I'm not sure—"

Qenna said, "We must rebuild. For Nekhen's ka, if for nothing else." He looked at me. "Shes, you must feel the same way. And the restaurant makes you a lot of money as well."

"Qenna, I felt that way for the last year, but I don't feel that way now. Something blew up in me on the day the Per'ankh blew up. I can't explain it, but I just don't feel the drive to push Nekhen's restaurant forward. My heart isn't in it."

"Then let me push it forward for you. You know how I feel about it. We must rebuild."

Sebek interjected, "Does this mean you're coming back to the Neferti? I'm out?"

"You're a partner, Sebek, you can't be out. But...no, I want to do something else, something fresh, something big."

Qenna said, "You must follow your heart, Shes, but there is no reason to abandon an investment that is returning itself many times over. Let me run the restaurant. Just as you let Sebek run the Neferti. And then use the money to create more wonderful food yourself in your own restaurant."

Sebek grinned. "You could get some of your Russian mobster friends to invest. They'd love it."

I saw the humor in it, but I didn't feel it, and I was about to admonish Sebek when my phone rang. MacIntyre.

"Hi, Cheryl."

"Hi, Shes. I just got out of an interrogation session with Chen and I'm hungry. Lunch?"

"Can't. I have an urgent appointment with the Hem-Netjer-Tepy of Bastet, Panekhet."

"Oh, yes? Why?"

"He's Chairman of the Board of Directors of the R'ames Society, and the Board took away my best-chef award and kicked me out of the society. I got Nesimen to con him into an interview so I can persuade him to reverse all that, or my reputation's shit."

"Great timing. I want to come along."

"Sure, if you can get to the temple in forty minutes. You can be a reference for me."

"I think Panekhet may be more interesting than you might think."

"You won't ruin my reputation more than it already is, will you?"

"We'll see." She hung up.

Sebek, no smile, said, "Temple of Bastet? I'm coming. I want to know what's going on there, with Henutsenu."

"Sebek. You're angry. You might screw things up for me."

"I'm angry, sure, but I need to know how she's doing. I need to understand how we can get her out. Shes, I'll be OK. Please."

"For the sake of the gods, Shes, take the man," said Qenna. "Something has to be done for him."

"All right, all right. Come on, Sebek. And, Qenna—I'll think on your proposal." But I'd already decided that Nekhen's ka would approve of Qenna running the new Per'ankh.

CHAPTER THIRTY-TWO
MacIntyre Forces a Trial by Cat

MacIntyre waited in her car across the street from the Temple of Bastet. Her mind churned over the possibilities, but she couldn't settle on a real plan. Shes's appointment with the Hem-Netjer-Tepy, Panekhet, gave her the perfect opportunity to confront the man that Chen had identified as the key conduit of Russian gangster money into and out of the temple. So far, so good: but what to do once she confronted the man was a conundrum.

Djehutymes had been clear after the interrogation and her pleas for him to do something. "No way, Cheryl. All Chen knows is what he heard from unreliable sources. To bust into a temple, you have to have solid, no-questions-asked facts that make a civil case for Ma'at. Anything else and you'll just get thrown into religious prison for sacrilege, heresy, or something worse that they make up on the spot."

And here came her accomplice in life, Shes, with her best friend's lover in tow. Pretty glum looking, the two of them. They came over to her car and stood on the sidewalk next to the little convertible, looking down on her. She smiled. She felt every bruise on her face move.

"Show time?" she asked.

"What did you mean when you said 'We'll see'?" asked Shes. "Are you going to screw me up in there? What are you planning?"

"I am extemporizing, lover," said MacIntyre. "Is it time?"

"Five minutes," he replied.

She looked at the determined face of Sebek and said, "Sebek, you told me they threw you out."

"Yeah. Little fat guy, very apologetic, but he had two bouncers behind him." He looked at her face. "What the hell happened to you?"

She ignored that and said, "You'd better wait out here. You can keep an eye on my car," she said. "I'll make sure to tell you when something important happens with Henutsenu, but just being here for her when she gets out will be so good for her."

"I'd sure like to get a piece of cat hide off those bastards in there."

"Here, let's trade places," she said, getting out of the car and holding the door for him. He hesitated, then gave in. He sat and crossed his arms with a frown.

MacIntyre took Shes's hand and pulled him toward the temple across the street. "You should know," she said, "that Chen has implicated Panekhet in the Russian money scheme."

"What!" said Shes, halting in the middle of the street.

"Come on, come on, we're blocking traffic." Wennefer Street was a busy street, and the light at the intersection had just changed. "Come *on*, Shes. We'll be late." She pulled, and he came. "Just follow my lead," she advised, taking charge. "If things go right, we can pressure Panekhet into letting Henutsenu go. Let me put on some pressure and see what happens."

Tjay was on door duty, and he greeted MacIntyre with a sorrowful look.

"Why, Hutyt MacIntyre. It is good to see you, indeed, and yet the hem-netjer has given clear instructions not to admit you to the precinct of the goddess. I'm so sorry."

"I'm with him today," she said, pushing Shes forward.

"And you, Lord…?"

"Shesmu. I have an appointment with the Hem-Netjer-Tepy, I don't want to keep him waiting. I brought Hutyt MacIntyre along as a reference for certain facts of interest to him."

Tjay examined a small book on a side table and found the name. "Very well, Lord Shesmu. I will conduct you to the Hem-Netjer-Tepy. I will have to inform Hem-Netjer Paneb, Hutyt, that you are here and meeting with Lord Panekhet."

"That will be fine, Tjay. I'm sure the hem-netjer will approve once we meet with his superior."

The rotund little w'ab led them back through the big hall and into the warren of offices at the back of the temple. On the opulent side, the decor showed that the priests of Bastet did not stint themselves or their goddess. The offices were busy with the normal business of the temple, with people walking to and fro carrying papers.

The offices of the Hem-Netjer-Tepy were a suite toward the center of the temple. Unlike her own Temple of Ma'at, the center of power was near the goddess—inward looking, not outward. That translated into no windows and a claustrophobic feeling that wasn't helped by the large statues of the goddess Bastet in human form. Black cats stared at them from every corner. They gave MacIntyre a distinct sense of being watched from all angles as they crossed the outer office to the head man's door.

Tjay opened the door and stepped in. "Lord Panekhet, here is Lord Shesmu, your appointment. He has brought a companion, Hutyt MacIntyre, he says for a reference."

She recognized the man at once, having met him at Shes's award ceremony. You don't forget somebody who radiates power. Hem-Netjer-Tepy Panekhet was a tall, thin man who looked at them with what MacIntyre first took to be disdain. But she figured out this was just a trick of his narrow eyes, down-turned mouth, and narrow chin. That said, his expression was not one of joyful welcoming, either.

But his greeting was courteous. "Shesmu, Hutyt MacIntyre. Welcome to the domain of Bastet. I wish our meeting was under better circumstances."

"Lord Panekhet, thank you for seeing me," said Shesmu. MacIntyre could only guess what was going on inside Shesmu's heart as he spoke to the man who was behind a lot of the nonsense that had screwed up his life.

Panekhet lifted his head and said to Tjay, "That will be all, Tjay. Close the door on your way out."

The fat little w'ab ducked his head and exited, walking backwards, as though from a pera'a. MacIntyre inferred from the command and the response that Panekhet ruled Bastet's domain with a strong hand.

Panekhet showed them to two chairs and sat himself in a fancy lion-paw chair that resembled nothing so much as a throne. He wore a simple linen robe with a cat fur sash, the polished semiprecious gemstone black cat pin on his chest reflecting the ceiling lights that illuminated his chair.

"Now, Shesmu. Nesimen was very persuasive in your defense, though he might not be the best reference given his own offenses against the Society. I have to tell you that the Henet Baket was very persuasive as well. So I'm uncertain I can be of much help to you, but I'm willing to listen."

Shesmu smiled, but MacIntyre saw his eyes narrow in a look she'd seen before when he was concentrating on being nice instead of lashing out. "Thank you, Lord. It has been a strange sequence of events, and I'm afraid the Henet Baket has got hold of the wrong end of the scepter. I'm sure when they question Sennedjem more thoroughly about me, they'll find I had little to do with the whole thing. Sennedjem's duplicity explains it. He told a Russian crime lord that I was a major criminal leader opposing her. He wanted to fool the Russians into concentrating on me instead of on him while he stole their money. Then the Russians blew up my restaurant to warn me off, and things went downhill from there. I'm sure that as the Henet Baket puts on more pressure, Sennedjem will divulge everything he knows."

MacIntyre saw Panekhet's lips contract as he took on the knowledge that the medjau were getting close to his own participation in Sennedjem's schemes. What would he do in response?

Panekhet pursed his lips, hiding his concern, and said, "I'm sorry, Shesmu, but you must realize I have to accept the Henet Baket's advice over your unproven assertions. I think we'll have to end this interview. Again, I'm sorry." He rose from his chair.

He needed more pressure. "If I may add something?" she asked.

"Certainly, Hutyt." But he remained standing.

"The Russians had corrupted one of our key medjau, Rudj Chen of the Organized Crime Squad. He is now in custody." And singing like a trilling songbird, but you don't need to know that. Subtlety is the key here.

The hem-netjer-tepy's face became a little pinched, and his down-turned mouth settled into a grim line. "I'm sorry to hear that, but—"

"I fear I have bad news for you, Lord Panekhet. Chen has suggested that the Temple of Bastet may be involved in the scheme somehow. I was the investigating officer for the w'abu killings earlier this week, and Chen has dropped hints that those killings may result from some criminal activity here. I'm sure we will learn more in the coming days as we interrogate the man." There; a hint to beware, but not a revelation that she knew he was involved, giving him an out. Now, how to connect his concern with Henutsenu?

The hem-netjer-tepy tried his best to look bewildered. "That's nonsense." But he sank back into his chair. He was feeling the pressure now.

She continued, "I can tell you, Lord, that the arrest of the woman Henutsenu has concerned some at the Temple of Ma'at that feel that the arrest was precipitate." Well, at least one person: her. But he didn't need to know that either. Make him think he could deflect medjau interest in the case by letting her friend go.

"Henutsenu? Oh, yes, the congregant who was here that morning."

"May I ask, Lord Panekhet, why there has been no trial?"

The priest smiled. "You may not be aware of our procedures in this temple, Hutyt. For temple desecration trials, we must assemble a panel of five judges from different temples in the Republic, so such trials happen slowly. I'm sure—"

"Are there no special procedures that you could use to investigate and clear her? It may be to the advantage of the temple, you know. Freeing an innocent person would show you are serious about understanding the desecration, and that would please the Lady Bastet."

Panekhet cocked his head and said, "I shall be the judge of that, Hutyt." He rubbed his mouth. "There is…an older trial process, less dependent on corporeal evidence and more on the will of the goddess."

MacIntyre perked up at this. "And would it clear Henutsenu if she is not guilty?"

"It would. We try to be a part of the modern world, Hutyt, but some aspects of our worship are ancient. Older than the pyramids. While we prefer modern tools…yes, I think I can allow the process. And, Shesmu—given these developments, I would not be averse to reinstating you in the society. Perhaps we moved too fast out of concern for the bad publicity."

MacIntyre smiled. She had him in full retreat, now. He wanted all of this to go away.

Panekhet got up and pushed a button on his desk. In a few minutes, Tjay opened the door and entered.

"Tjay, alert Lord Paneb. We are going to perform the Tjau Sekhmet for the Lady Henutsenu."

The rotund w'ab smiled, and there was a gleam in his eye. "Yes, Lord, right away."

"It's highly unusual, Lord Panekhet," said Paneb.

"I have authorized it, Paneb. There is nothing more to be said." Panekhet stood, firm and erect, in the main hall of the Temple of Bastet. Shesmu and MacIntyre waited in suspense for their friend Henutsenu to appear. MacIntyre had fulfilled her promise, and Sebek stood with them.

From a side hall, Henutsenu walked out with two guards, Tjay leading her over to the small group. Sebek, whom MacIntyre had fetched from the car, stepped forward, and one guard lowered the ritual spear he carried.

Paneb said, "Please, no contact with the accused."

Panekhet stepped forward and said to Henutsenu, "My daughter, your friends have persuaded me to allow a special trial ritual. Are you prepared to throw yourself on the mercy of the goddess, who will judge your innocence or guilt?"

"Yes, Lord, I am ready." Henutsenu shot a glance at the little group of her friends.

Paneb stepped forward, a frown on his face. "You must go before the goddess cleansed and purified, my daughter. Tjay, please conduct the accused to the ritual bath. Once cleansed, conduct her to the trial room with none of the trappings of the external world."

"Yes, Lord," said Tjay, ducking his head. "Come," he said to Henutsenu, and the pair walked down another hall and disappeared.

"It is now a matter of waiting for the ritual to complete. Lord Paneb, please wait with the supplicants and handle the post-ritual formalities. Now, you must all excuse me, as I have another appointment." Panekhet bowed and left them.

MacIntyre sighed. More delay, but at least things were moving now. "Lord Paneb, thank you so much for taking the time for this," she started. "Could you tell us about the ritual?"

Paneb grimaced. "I ought to supervise the w'abu in their work. But it is as the goddess wills it, I am sure. Well, Hutyt MacIntyre, the process is at its base 'trial by cat.'"

"By cat?"

"The Lady Bastet uses her animal form in myriad ways to benefit society. One such way is to confront evil. Are you at all familiar with the story of the Great Cat of R'a?"

"No, I don't think so. Shes?"

Shesmu smiled. "I learned that one in school. The evil serpent 'Aapep comes to destroy the world, and R'a appoints his daughter Bastet to battle with the serpent. In her guise as the Great Cat of R'a, Bastet kills and dismembers the serpent with a knife."

"Mythological, of course," said Paneb with a sharp little smile. "I bring it up because it shows the strong relationship between Bastet, R'a, and the battle for justice. Justice, Hutyt, does not always involve Ma'at."

MacIntyre realized he was again telling her that civil justice had its limits: the goddess Ma'at was not a part of this story. She asked, "So, how does the Tjau Sekhmet represent justice?"

"The accused confronts Bastet in her form as Sekhmet, the goddess of the desert wind that blows the world clean of its pollution. As you have just heard, the w'abu cleanse the accused of the secular world by bathing, then put her in a room without external trappings."

"What do you mean by external trappings?"

"Clothing, jewelry, or anything else other than the natural body," he replied.

"Naked? She's going to be naked in her trial?" Sebek sounded outraged.

MacIntyre nudged Shes, who laid a hand on his friend's arm. "Sebek, stay calm. Henutsenu can handle a little nudity." Sebek rolled his eyes but said nothing more.

MacIntyre said, "And then, Lord Paneb?"

"Then the w'abu introduce cats into the room and shut the accused in with them. If the accused emerges unscathed after an hour alone with the goddess, the judgment is for innocence. If the goddess shows her displeasure by her instruments attacking the accused, the judgment is for guilt. Simple and remarkably easy."

MacIntyre saw Sebek relax. Her own thoughts were that Henutsenu was such a strong cat person she couldn't imagine there would be any risk of the kitties attacking her. Even Tikhet wouldn't.

"Ah, here are the instruments of Bastet's justice," said Paneb.

A small electric cart pulled a cage from a side hall and trundled along past them toward the hall down which Henutsenu had appeared. They stood in horror, looking at the three lionesses in the cage, pacing around angrily.

"You—" Sebek was speechless. He stepped toward the disappearing cart and cage. Paneb signaled the guards, who lowered their spears and barred them from going after the cart. Shesmu took his friend's arm and whispered in his ear, but Sebek jerked away. He stood, fists at his side, looking after the lionesses.

"Lord Paneb," said MacIntyre, desperately hoping she had not made everything worse.

"Sekhmet is the form of Bastet representing strength and power, Hutyt. The lioness is strength and power personified. What better aspect of Bastet could be the true arm of justice?"

"What have you done, Cheryl?"

Sebek, head in hands, sat disconsolately on a bench. MacIntyre sat next to him, leaning back against a basalt column covered with hieroglyphs that extolled the goddess Bastet. She had a very different opinion of the goddess, but she kept it to herself for now. Shesmu sat next to her, leaning back against the same column.

Hem-Netjer Paneb had left them to wait for developments, saying he had urgent business with his w'abu. He summoned six more guards to make sure that the three guests of the Temple of Bastet had all the company they needed. The guards had orders to help them to the street if they exhibited any tendency to interfere with the workings of the Lady Bastet's justice. Paneb, understanding their concern for their friend, explained that it might be as much as three hours should the results need a purification ritual for the remains. That was when Sebek had gone out of control, only for the guards to restrain him.

MacIntyre, who sympathized with his action but realized they had no chance of intervening, tried to console Henutsenu's lover. He remained inconsolable. She'd given up after the third attempt. Now she responded to his question with only a sigh.

Shesmu said, "How long has it been?"

This from a man who supervised five ovens cooking many differently timed dishes and knowing when to open and remove their contents. She'd watched him do it. She sighed again.

They waited. Time passed.

A murmur arose in a hallway that MacIntyre remembered as the way to the offering hall, the murder scene. A group of w'abu in their robes came out into the main hall and bustled past them. The guards looked at each other. One reached to stop a w'ab and asked a quiet question. He whispered to the other guards, who all gathered together, then followed the w'abu.

"Um. Should we--" she began. Sebek jumped up and followed the guards. MacIntyre and Shesmu rose and followed him. More w'abu appeared from different hallways and office doors and joined the crowd as it bustled down the hall toward the center of the temple. MacIntyre stood in the middle of a crowd stopped before two large doors.

"What is that?" she asked.

Shesmu pointed at a small sign to the side of the double doors. "It's the sanctuary, the room where the goddess lives. It's the holiest place in the temple."

"What are we doing here? Is this where..." She couldn't finish: is this where her friend had ended her all-too-short life because of MacIntyre's all-too-American lack of religious sense and understanding of Remetjy temple nonsense?

Hem-Netjer Paneb pushed through the crowd of w'abu and laypeople. MacIntyre grabbed at his arm as he pushed by her.

"Lord Paneb, what's happening? Where is Henutsenu? What—"

He looked at her with eyes showing too much white and pulled his arm away. "The goddess, the goddess," he said, and pushed through to the doors. He gathered himself together and signaled to the guards in the crowd. They came forward and formed a line, spears held across their bodies to form a fence. At Paneb's order, they moved forward and pushed the crowd back from the doors of the sanctuary.

"What the fuck is going on?" shouted MacIntyre over the murmurs of the crowd, all of whom turned to look at her, scandalized. Sebek pushed forward, up against the line of guards.

"Where is she, you bastard?" he insisted, pushing at the spear a guard held across his chest. "What have you done to her?"

Hem-Netjer Paneb, having regained his composure, said, "Please restrain yourselves. The Lady Henutsenu, 'ankhu wedjau senebu, is undergoing her transformation. The Lord Hem-Netjer-Tepy Panekhet is conducting the ritual in the sanctuary with the goddess. Please stay calm." He looked back and forth, commanding his minions with strong eyes to stay where they were.

"Did he say alive, sound, and healthy?" asked MacIntyre.

Shesmu nodded, looking worried. "That's what he said, could be just formulaic, honoring her in death. But…"

The crowd fell silent as the doors moved. Two w'abu appeared, pulling the doors back into the sanctuary, opening it wide. No one moved as they peered into the dim recess of the sanctuary of the goddess.

Gasps greeted Hem-Netjer-Tepy Panekhet as he appeared dressed in his full regalia as the primary priest of the Lady Bastet. His robes were the richest linen, draped with a full cat-fur sash and a huge onyx-and-turquoise necklace across his chest. The large, black mask of a cat's head covered his own visage. His voice came from within the mask.

"The Lady Henutsenu, 'ankhu wedjau senebu, the devoted worshiper of the Lady of Isheru, the Lady of the Divine Field, the Eye of R'a, the Lady Bastet, is before you as the Hemet-Netjer-em-Bastet, the God's Wife of Bastet, the Divine Emissary of Bastet in Menmenet, having passed through the scouring Tjau Sekhmet without fear or harm. Venerate and adore this, our most holy Hemet-Netjer, who is before you."

The priest stepped aside, and Henutsenu stepped forward. MacIntyre, transfixed, saw her friend dressed all in white with a black cat-fur sash. Her feet shod in golden sandals, her black hair braided with gold beads, her face rigid with ritual makeup emphasizing her eyes and mouth. She held in her arms a large black cat, which stared at the assembled crowd with blinking green eyes.

A groan went up from the crowd of w'abu as this vision approached the line of guards, which opened to let her through. The w'abu fell to their faces on the ground, leaving the three unbelievers standing. MacIntyre stepped toward her friend. A sharp glance from the masked priest and a tug on her arm by Shesmu had her following the others in giving reverence on their faces. MacIntyre saw the glazed eyes of her friend pass over them and sharpen in recognition. Alive, sound, and healthy, indeed.

"The Hemet-Netjer-em-Bastet will make her offering to the goddess in the offering room," intoned the priest. He followed the lady through the prostrate crowd. The guards formed up behind him, two by two. As the lady passed, the crowd arose and followed to see the offering. The three friends gathered themselves together at the back of the crowd and followed. MacIntyre, hearing a sound, looked behind and saw the two w'abu shutting the doors of the sanctuary. The goddess's work was done for the day.

The beer-and-cheese reception that followed the offering ceremony was the first chance any of the three friends had to talk to Henutsenu. Still carrying the cat, she made her appearance five minutes after the servers had produced glasses for the crowd in the main hall. She made a beeline for Sebek, who took the cat from her and deposited it on the floor, then wrapped the Hemet-Netjer-em-Bastet in his arms and kissed her. MacIntyre gave them a little privacy by looking at the cat, who seemed fine with this development. Doped, she thought. Shesmu took her hand, then they faced the clinch.

Henutsenu broke off the kiss first, looking over Sebek's shoulder at MacIntyre with a smile.

"See, Cheryl? I told you the Lady Bastet would help me."

She let go of Sebek and enfolded MacIntyre; another long kiss followed. Sebek and Shesmu looked at each other and rolled their eyes in unison.

"Would you care to explain how you survived being in a small room with three angry lionesses?" asked Shesmu.

"I like kitties," she stated, "and they like me." And that was all she would say.

"So," complained Sebek, "does this mean you're not coming back to work at the Neferti?"

Henutsenu smiled. "The Hemet-Netjer thing is a volunteer position at the temple. I just have to show up on major feast days, four times a year. You're stuck with me, Sebek."

"Glad to hear it," he said. His voice still shook, and emotions played across his face. Henutsenu released MacIntyre and put her arm around him, which seemed to firm him up. Then the crush of people wanting to congratulate the new Hemet-Netjer-em-Bastet descended on them.

MacIntyre pulled Shesmu aside. "We need to find Panekhet," she said. "He has some explaining to do."

She looked around and saw Tjay over by the hastily assembled cheese spread, holding a tall glass of beer. She walked over to him.

"Hi, Tjay. What a wonderful development!"

"Why, yes, Hutyt MacIntyre, wonderful indeed! The temple has been without a Hemet-Netjer for many years. The last one came to us through a mountain lion attack down south—"

Unwilling to listen to a long story about mountain lions and goddesses, MacIntyre interrupted. "I need to talk to Hem-Netjer-Tepy Panekhet, Tjay, before I leave. Is he around somewhere?"

"Why, I saw him head back to the sanctuary, Hutyt. I believe he has some closure to reach with the goddess. I'm sure that after he finishes, he would be happy to talk with you."

"Thanks, Tjay. Again, a wonderful development."

She left the rotund w'ab to his indecision about which cheese to consume first and found Shesmu. She whispered to him, "Sanctuary, now." They put down their barely sipped beers on a side table and walked down the hall toward the center of the temple.

They found the big doors of the sanctuary closed and unguarded. McIntyre pushed at one door, which swung inward. They entered the dim room and found Panekhet, sans mask, standing next to a plinth, on top of which stood a human-sized statue of the goddess Bastet. The goddess, finely worked, had kittens surrounding her feet, all cast of bronze.

Scandalized, the priest said, "You should not be in here! Sacrilege!"

"Yeah, well, we need to talk, Panekhet," said MacIntyre. "About money. Laundered money. And what better place for a private conversation?" She looked upon the visage of the goddess and saw nothing but a catlike withholding of judgment. "Shes, close that door and lock it."

He did, turning the deadbolt lock with a satisfying click.

"I insist you leave this sacred place," said Panekhet, striding to the door. Shesmu gripped him and turned him around to look at MacIntyre, who approached him.

"Chen has spilled the beans, Panekhet. We know you are behind the money flowing through this temple like a river."

"Money? What money?" blustered the priest.

"What did R'aweben set up? A special set of accounts at Henuttawy for you to access? Or even offshore accounts? Did your w'abu find out about it? Or did they just try to take some of the money by blackmailing you? Is that why you killed them?" MacIntyre advanced toward the priest.

"That call from Nesimen." Panekhet shook his head. "I knew there was something wrong with it."

MacIntyre's phone beeped, and she took it out and glanced at it. A text from Sebek: "armed men busted in heading for u."

"Ah, fuck." She looked around. Her eyes took in the only object in the room: Bastet on her plinth. "Shes, help me." She dashed over to the statue. The plinth, as she'd hoped, was not attached to the floor. Shesmu joined her, and she showed him the message. They dragged the heavy Lady Bastet over to the doors and pushed it firmly against them. She looked at Panekhet. "You called in reinforcements, didn't you? Were you going to make sure we didn't get out of the temple alive? Is Henutsenu included? I don't think the Lady Bastet is going to be best pleased."

For two or three minutes, there was total silence. Then, muffled by the closed door, MacIntyre heard voices, urgent, loud. She saw the lever on the door wiggle; somebody on the other side tried it and found it locked. A furious pounding sounded on the door.

"Don't say a word," whispered MacIntyre, as much to Panekhet as to Shesmu. "Lie down on the floor, now!" She pressed the reluctant hem-netjer-tepy down beside Shesmu, who gripped him from the other side.

The pounding became thuds. After a short time, impatience won out over manners, and a burst of automatic gunfire crackled. The door handle blew off. The thuds resumed when the door still wouldn't open. More automatic gunfire, and the door and the splintered holes riddled the walls to its sides, bullets whining in different directions over their heads.

MacIntyre said, "They don't care that you're in here, do they?" she asked Panekhet. "And here I thought we could use you as a human shield."

Panekhet's eyes were closed and his lips were moving. MacIntyre wondered whether the Lady Bastet was also the goddess of money launderers and hoped the Lady was more tuned in to frantic prayer than the goddess of justice. Useless, the both of them. Ma'at never intervened until you passed into the Duat, which might come all too soon. That left Bastet, and she was directly in the line of fire. The statue had taken several high-velocity bullets and had moved a little toward them with the impacts, and the elegant bronze was now marred with bullet marks. Paneb would have a fit over the desecration of the actual goddess.

The surrounding chaos quieted suddenly. Through the clouds of dust, MacIntyre could see the door, what was left of it, still closed and blocked by the plinth and its statue. These would never be quite the same. There were confused noises and shouts from the hall. Then everything quieted. Shesmu stirred next to MacIntyre. The quiet, after the noise, raised the urgency even more. Her body wanted to be somewhere else, and to take Shesmu with it. Out of the silence, a tinny electronic version of the first bars of the hit song "One Love Five Gods" sounded. Panekhet's eyes popped open and all his muscles contracted. So did Shesmu's.

The song repeated. MacIntyre rolled over and extracted her mobile phone. She listened and answered with uninformative grunts. She said in a whisper into the phone, "We're in the sanctuary, no other doors, they're outside with automatic weapons. Yes, we're fine so far. No idea, we're behind a blockaded door, haven't seen them. At least two, though, from the weapons fire. High-velocity ammo. All right." She closed the phone and said, "Mes and the city tactical team are outside, blockading the hall. He says they're negotiating with the people out there. He says they appear to be Russian. Bad move, Panekhet." She rolled over again, back next to Shesmu. "Isn't this cosy?" she asked with a grin. Panekhet groaned. We waited.

An age passed, then somebody knocked on the door and said, "MacIntyre? Are you all right?" It was Djehutymes.

Leaving Panekhet prostrate on the floor, MacIntyre and Shesmu got up, brushed themselves off a bit, then moved the plinth. The door was in shreds. One bullet had gone all the way through the cat's head of the goddess, tearing a huge hole out of the back. MacIntyre unbolted the door and opened it. Pieces fell off the door as Djehutymes's face appeared.

"I see you've made good use of your week off," he said. "Who's this?" He stood over Panekhet, looking down.

"Panekhet," said MacIntyre. "Chen said—"

"Yeah, yeah. You're under arrest," he said to Panekhet, helping him up with a strong arm and reaching for his cuffs with the other hand. "Looks like the temple rules don't apply any more."

Sebek's face appeared at the door, peering into the sanctuary. Then he came in, followed by the new Hemet-Netjer-em-Bastet, who was followed by the appalled Hem-Netjer Paneb. After a brief explanation from Djehutymes, Paneb rushed to the statue of the goddess. Sebek and Henutsenu gathered together with MacIntyre and Shesmu.

Sebek said, "When the armed men busted in, we hid, then I texted you and called the medjau. Three guys in balaclavas with Kalashnikovs. What a day!"

"My poor goddess," said Henutsenu, looking at the statue.

"Clear all these people out of our sanctuary. We must clean and purify the home of the goddess at once!" shouted Paneb.

"Sorry," replied Djehutymes, smiling. "We're locking down the scene for a full civil investigation. And we'll be going through the temple's books as well."

"You can't do that! The goddess—"

"The goddess will have to put up with it this time," said Djehutymes.

MacIntyre, happily aware that Ma'at had taken charge in front of her, caught sight of the large black cat with green eyes. It sauntered into the sanctuary, looked around, and padded over to Henutsenu, rubbing against her leg. Henutsenu picked the cat up and scratched its head. The cat's purr was raucous in the silent sanctuary.

MacIntyre said, "The goddess is at peace."

CHAPTER THIRTY-THREE
Shesmu Pays His Taxes Forward

"I SHOULD TAKE THIS CALL," said MacIntyre.

"Right now?" I asked. I had been engaged for the last few minutes in preparing to take off her clothes and explore parts of her I had seen before and liked. Not going to happen this time.

"It's Yaotl. Every time he calls me, rather than me calling him, it signals an absolute disaster in the crime world."

"Let the medjau worry about it."

"I'm the medjau."

"Not. Right. Now."

"Off." She pushed me away and picked up her phone and answered. "Yaotl?"

She listened for a minute, then said, "We'll be right over."

Putting the phone down, she said, "Get dressed. We're heading to a conference."

I surrendered my passion to justice, and we headed off in her little red car to the Tjesut.

I had heard about Yaotl's mansion from MacIntyre, who had visited it several times. The reality of the thing so outstripped my imagination that I had to stop and look at it.

"How did he get that through the planning commission?" I asked.

"The same way he gets everything else done, money in the right pockets and, if that doesn't work, threats or blackmail. Or killing. With a macuahuitl." She looked at the mansion in front of us. "I must admit I haven't seen it at night. Spectacular. And he's having a party or something."

Yaotl's mansion was a large Aztec pyramid made of glass and concrete. During the day it would stand out dramatically against the sky and the northern hills across the bay. The much more staid Remetjy mansions surrounding it on the Tjesut were pale shadows of it. I'm sure the Aztec sun god lit the building with reflected light to dramatic effect. The blaze of lights from the inside was enough to give the moon above a little more luster. The glass shone out into the neighborhood with no apologies for its origin or existence, just like Yaotl.

"Come on," said MacIntyre, and we marched up the path to the large front door and pushed the doorbell. An Aztec servant opened the door.

"Hutyt MacIntyre, how nice to greet you again," he said, bowing. "And your friend must be the illustrious Lord Shesmu."

"Hi, Eztli. Yep, that's him. We're here—"

"To speak with Lord Yaotl. Yes, he's expecting you in his office. Let me take your coats."

The butler guided us through several halls. I could see through the glass walls the many people drinking and laughing. One room had casino-style gaming spread out with an enormous crowd gathered around the tables.

"Party, Eztli?" asked MacIntyre.

"Indeed, Hutyt. A gathering for our great festival of Xiuhmolpilli, which we celebrate every cycle of our calendar, fifty-two years in your calendar." He opened a door and ushered us through. "The priests completed the sacrifice in Tenochtitlan twenty minutes ago, starting our celebration, and the sacred fire is on its way."

"Sacrifice?"

"The priests started the celebratory fire on the chest of the selected prisoner, then cut out his heart to feed the fire. It is all quite dramatic and now televised so that all Aztecs worldwide may watch. Then the fire travels to all the Aztec communities all over the world to feed their fires." Eztli smiled. "Lord Yaotl was at the last one in Tenochtitlan and volunteered to host the fire celebration here." He opened another door. "Please find a seat. I will bring xocolatl, and Lord Yaotl will be with you within fifteen minutes." The butler bowed and left us alone in the great room. While MacIntyre found a seat, I looked at the antiques mounted in glass cases—jade masks, gold statuettes, ceramic skulls, that sort of thing. A nice double-headed snake made of spotted jade. This took my mind off the image of the sacrifice for a minute or two.

We sat, sipping our excellent xocolatl drinks in silence, until Yaotl arrived. He was a small man with a hawklike nose and fierce eyes, the creases in his face suggesting many years of hot sun.

"Ah, Hutyt MacIntyre. And you must be Shesmu. I regret to say that I have not yet eaten at your restaurants, and my sympathies on your unfortunate experience with the Russians and their ridiculous bombs. I have had similar unfortunate experiences with them." He sat across from us on a couch.

MacIntyre asked the question at the top of her mind. "Is the Xiuhmolpilli sacrifice for real?"

"Ah, Eztli has been boasting again. I shall have to talk to him about that. He takes excessive pride in our traditions and in my celebrations of them, which would not be possible without his excellent efforts. Now, I'm sure you're wondering why I called you here on such a night when I am supposed to be carousing with my friends. And why I suggested Lord Shesmu come along."

I speculated he was going to persuade me to be the local sacrifice. MacIntyre cocked an eyebrow in response. "You talk too much, Yaotl. Without saying anything."

"And yet always to the purpose, Hutyt." He looked at me with a predatory gaze. "I see Eztli served you xocolatl, doubtless fearing you would not care for our celebratory drink." He lifted his cup. "Octli, fermented cactus juice. Perhaps an acquired taste, but I can summon some for you if—"

"Let's get to it, Yaotl. We have things to do." She looked at me with quirked lips, making me more resolved than ever to continue my explorations later in the evening.

Yaotl smiled and leaned back on the couch, sipping his octli. He pursed his lips, then said, "What would you say if I told you, Lord Shesmu, that I could help you trace the monies extracted from your city by the criminals Sennedjem and R'aweben?"

That made me sit up and take notice. "I would be interested in that, Yaotl. Very interested."

"I suspected as much. As interested as, say, twenty percent of the amount?"

I smiled. "Not my money to give."

"Think of it as a fee-for-service, Lord Shesmu." Yaotl was persuasive. "Think of it as a way of avoiding spending several years cooking in the prison kitchens of your Republic."

I considered my options. Could I blackmail Hernefer into financing this? The fat billionaire's sour face filled my mind. No. He was too cheap. He'd go to jail before he'd pay off a gangster. But that got me thinking about the Henuttawy Group and R'aweben. They'd put a good chunk of money into the Per'ankh, all legitimate. Baki couldn't prove otherwise. Why not? Natural justice.

I smiled and said, "A counterproposal. I will personally pay you one-and-a-half million debenu for the service you're offering, Yaotl. That's fair. And if you can make any of the rest of the money stick to your fingers, so much the better. I won't complain." That would put the financing of the Per'ankh right back where it was before all this started, which was fine with me. Qenna wouldn't like it, of course, but he'd understand when I explained it all to him. Making him executive chef of the restaurant would help a lot with that, too. Hernefer, after having a fit, would see the logic of it all. And, if my suspicions about him were correct, I might be able to persuade him to other things.

I looked at MacIntyre, and she looked at me. I said, "Do you see anything wrong with it?"

She laughed out loud. "Aside from the obvious? No. I'd hate your confinement to cooking in a prison kitchen. And I'd starve to death. This is the devil you know, and I'd grab the opportunity, Shes."

So I did.

I walked into Baki's office the next morning with a smile and an extra bounce in my step. A part of those came from a lovely night with the woman of my dreams. And after all, my business affairs were looking up too.

Baki wore a frown on his middle-aged face, and Seba was grim. They led me back to their conference room, where I explained the big picture to them.

"So, let me get this straight," said Baki, folding his hands on the table. "You're not confessing. You're telling us we can get the money returned if we just create an account. And you won't tell us where the money is coming from, but you have got all the significant criminals involved either killed or jailed. Except R'aweben."

"Yeah, that sums it up pretty well."

"Fucking bullshit," commented Seba.

"Is not," I said with a smile.

"I need to think about this." Baki sat back in his chair and stared at me, concentrating.

"What's to think, chief? This guy has strung us along by the nose the whole way. Nothing he's said or done has come true."

"We have Sennedjem."

"Who isn't saying a word and has lawyered up and is going to walk. What I see wrong is that you're one of the significant criminals, Shesmu, and you're not in jail or dead. You're not dead, right? Just checking."

"Not yet, anyway. No thanks to you." I kept the smile on my face, but I was boiling inside. "Look at it from my perspective, Baki. Here I am, working away at being the Best Young Chef, and suddenly I'm up to my ass in bombs, Russians, stolen money, more Russians, and lionesses."

"What have lionesses got to do with it?" demanded Seba.

"Never you mind." I hadn't told them the story of how the Temple of Bastet got its latest God's Wife. "Everything I've said and done is consistent with that, isn't it? And the whole story hangs together. I want your agency off my back, Baki."

"What about R'aweben?"

"Ultimately, he's got the money, he's in Russia, and he's going to send the money to the new account for reasons I won't divulge."

"I want him. There's a Red Notice out on him."

"What the fuck is that, and why would he care? I can tell you he's not stupid enough to put himself in the way of being arrested unless this deal goes through. He's going to have a lot less money to live on. He will find going to a Ta'an-Imenty prison is a better deal than what his hosts will do to him when they find out he's dumped all their money back on us. So you may hear from him."

"I don't know, Shesmu. All this seems too good to be true."

"I have to say I feel the same way, Baki. But trust me, get this done, and you'll have a lot of happy citizens when you give them their money back."

"What about Panekhet? What about Podgoronov?"

"Podgoronov is long gone. Back in Russia is my guess, and good riddance. Panekhet has confessed to two murders in his own temple to the Menmenet authorities. He's also admitted his responsibility for desecrating the precincts of Bastet. The new Hem-Netjer-Tepy, Paneb, took his confession and has confined him for trial. But talk to the prosecutors at the Temples of Ma'at and Bastet and see what kind of deal you can do. Maybe you can notch up a few points with your bosses for him too, but he's going to be busy elsewhere."

"This isn't about points, Shesmu, it's about ma'at."

"Sure, and ma'at means creating that account and getting the money back." I smiled. "Oh, and here's my insurance agent's card. Talk to him."

After a long silence, Baki nodded once.

CHAPTER THIRTY-FOUR
MacIntyre Gets Her Reward

MACINTYRE SAT IN KASA'S OUTER office, waiting for Djehutymes. She checked her watch again and only two minutes had elapsed since the last check, and there were still five minutes to go before the appointment. She'd been there for a half hour. Nothing, repeat nothing, would thwart this appointment, because she was so bored with being suspended that she feared her excellent vision would never recover from her eyes crossing. She'd rearranged her small apartment five times and shopped till she dropped, but after resolving the problems with Bastet, life had become intolerable. Henutsenu was too busy with her new position at the Temple of Bastet and her job to have lunch. Shesmu ran around getting quotes for construction work and talking to architects. And he came home too tired for social outings, at least most of the time. So she got to experience him for brief periods late at night, and that was it. He swore their date that night would be special, and she'd scheduled an early drink or two at Nebu's place with Henutsenu.

"Cheryl? You look depressed."

"Really! Thank you, Idnu Djehutymes, for your support."

"Come on, let's go in."

MacIntyre got up and walked into Kasa's office next to her boss, and at the atch-netjer's invitation, they sat themselves down. The big statue of Ma'at seemed glad to see her.

"Well, Cheryl, and have we learned our lesson?"

"You've seen the test results, Atch-Netjer. What do you think?" She'd spent two days last week doing the police procedures course online and taking the tests. That was a big part of the boredom.

"You're up to speed on police procedures, no question. But I want to know if the goddess Ma'at can count on you to follow the rules in the future."

MacIntyre grinned. "Yes, Atch-Netjer, the goddess can. Say, did you know you don't need to conduct field sobriety tests on mummies caught driving irresponsibly? You can just arrest them."

"Right. What do you think, Mes?"

"She's a good medjat, Kasa, despite it all."

"I believe you're right. OK, give her the badge and gun."

Djehutymes extracted the named items from a deep pocket and gave them to MacIntyre, who scrutinized them and put them away.

He said, "Be in my office bright and early tomorrow morning, Cheryl, and we'll see what cases we can put you on." Djehutymes smiled for once. "We're working on a murder in the Asian quarter. Might be a political killing."

"What happened to the Aztec-Russian gang war?"

"Nothing. Vanished from the radar. You sure your information was correct?"

She shook her head. "I guess it was just a bad rumor. What does OC say?"

Kasa folded his hands on his desk and shook his head. "We've dissolved the whole OC squad for now, reassigned a few people and fired more. The bent ones we couldn't prove had taken money. The others are in jail awaiting trial. Chen's the principal witness against them all. Imy-er-medjau Menna has assigned their cases to White Collar for now."

If there was one thing Yaotl did not have, it was a white collar. MacIntyre smiled. As long as he laid off the macuahuitl, Homicide wouldn't care. She'd get him in the end, though, somehow.

"Have you gotten taller, Henutsenu?"

MacIntyre released her friend from a warm embrace, and the two women sat down at the bar table in Nebu's Place. MacIntyre noted the sideways glances at them from the other tables and knew they were not looking at her. Henutsenu, if not taller, had become more substantial, spiritually.

"What, precisely, is a God's Wife?" she asked.

"It's a little hard to explain, Cheryl, and it's different for each god or goddess."

"Does it involve…er…" She blushed and sipped some wine. Why did this woman make her behave like a shy schoolchild?

"Sex? No. At least, not so far, but Bastet is a goddess with deep knowledge and mysteries. No, it's about ceremonies and festivals and rattling sistrums. Oh, and it's inherited along the female line, so if I have a daughter at some point, she'll be a God's Wife of Bastet, too."

"Well, I'm very sure they well bestowed it upon you. About those lionesses, though—"

"The Lady Bastet protects those who worship her with honor," said her friend. "And that's all I'm going to say. They were beautiful animals."

"Are there any other perks to the job?"

"Well, the Hem-Netjer-Tepy decided that the black cat liked me so much, I should have him."

"The big one?"

"Yes, his name is—"

"Don't tell me: Blackie."

"No."

"Darkie?"

"Cheryl."

"'Kitty.'"

"No. Cheryl, you have no respect for the spirituality associated with kitties."

"Right."

"No, I named him Wepwety-Neb-Kem-Netjeret, or Wepu, for short."

"Wepwety?"

"In English, 'Noble Black Envoy of the Goddess.'"

"Noble."

"I'm sure he is kitty nobility. The goddess would not have bestowed him upon me otherwise." She smiled. "Just kidding."

"So he's going to be the king of your apartment?"

Henutsenu's face grew long. "No, I have to keep him at the temple. I persuaded Tjay to take care of him when I'm not there, and not to feed him sugary treats."

"Why?"

"The Lady requires her divine animals to be available to her at all times. So they have to live in the temple." She smiled. "It's just as well. Sebek, er, Sebek—"

"Doesn't like cats. He told me." Not the best time to mention that she didn't like cats, either.

"Well. He's allergic. One minute with a cat, and he starts dripping and sneezing. Not pretty."

"Ah."

"And I need him more than I need a kitty in my apartment."

"Right."

"And that does involve sex."

"Right."

The two friends burst out laughing and drank a toast to Wepu, then another one to Sebek, and then one to the Lady Bastet.

MacIntyre arrived at the Neferti about ten minutes late for her dinner with the owner, Shesmu. She'd spent some extra time with her clothes. She chose the same ensemble that she had worn to Shesmu's award ceremony. He had expressed his pleasure at it several times, so she presumed it would generate similar feelings now.

Shesmu showed up twenty minutes later, full of apologies. MacIntyre was in the bar on her second glass of wine.

"Sorry, sorry," he said. "I lost track of time working with the architect. He's got some great ideas for the new restaurant. And I had a little talk with Hernefer, my partner."

MacIntyre used her detective abilities to examine his clothes and manner for clues. Biggest clue: he was wearing an old shirt and American jeans. He dressed for construction, not dinner. She narrowed her eyes a little and probed.

"Did you go home and change?"

"Change?"

Bingo. Not a clue.

"Change. For dinner."

He looked down at himself. "Ah…no, no, I did not have time to change." He looked up at her, smiled, and continued dissembling without a pause. "My, you look as though you had a lot of time to go home and change. You're wonderful, a sight for sore eyes, the most beautiful—"

"Don't push it, Shes. Let's eat." She smiled, picked up her half-finished wine, and took his arm.

"I arranged for the chef's table tonight. Hope that's OK," he said, guiding her toward the kitchen. "The private dining room is reserved for the Aztec ambassador and his wife. Good customers, but they don't like to dine in public."

"Afraid of being assassinated by Russians," said MacIntyre.

"Ah, maybe," said Shesmu, a little taken aback. "How is all that going, by the way?" He slapped his head. "You were going to meet with your boss today, weren't you?"

They went into the kitchen. Sebek came over to greet them, eyebrow raised.

Shesmu said, "Sorry we're a little late. Is the chef's table set up for us?" He stared hard at Sebek, smiling a little too forcefully.

Sebek, quick on the uptake, said, "Uh, sorry, we thought you'd canceled, but I can have it set up again, right away."

Shesmu smiled more naturally and nodded, and Sebek hurried off to find a server.

MacIntyre said, "Yes, Shesmu, I did meet with my boss today, and I'm celebrating being a full-service medjat once more," said MacIntyre. "And you're not fooling anybody. You forgot, didn't you?"

"Can't fool a real detective, I guess," said Shesmu, shaking his head and grinning. "It's just that I'm all caught up in the Per'ankh and the Wenmyt."

"The Wenmyt?"

"My new restaurant. We've located a suitable space, and I spent the afternoon there with the architect. The concept is the Remetjy grill and everything it can do with local ingredients. A total complement to the Neferti and its New Two Lands cuisine." He grinned a wolfish grin. "And I blackmailed Hernefer into giving me full control of the Per'ankh. I'm dead sure he's involved with R'aweben in the money laundering, and I said I was considering bringing it to Baki's attention."

MacIntyre could tell it was going to be tough to get a word in this evening, so she resolved to make the best of it and be a good listener. And Sebek knew what she liked. She'd eaten here enough. So he'd keep the food rolling along without her having to interrupt her companion's distracted thought processes. She sat cross-legged on her cushion, through several courses, enjoying herself, while Shesmu described his new concept, the architect's ideas, and the renovations to the Per'ankh.

"Qenna is supervising most of the design work for the new kitchen and dining room for the Per'ankh. The contractors could save over half the building, and we're going to build it back just the way it was, an old Remetjy mansion, but with the interior rearranged to enhance the kitchen space and make service easier."

"I can hardly wait to try it."

"Opening night. Don't know when that will be, but we'll be there."

"Will we?"

She could actually see the light dawning on him. The fact that it came from the fixture above the table, reflecting on him as he leaned back in dismay, did not detract from her satisfaction at having landed her point. Having brought down her prey, now she needed to attach the tag and release him to the wild.

"It's been, what, nearly two weeks since you saved my life? It seems like ages ago. I guess I just need some reassurance that it meant something to both of us, Shes. Did it?"

"Cheryl, you know it did." He waved away the server, who was also quick on the uptake. "I didn't realize until now how much I've been distracted. And I don't think I thanked you properly for getting Yaotl's help in resolving the money situation."

"Anything else?"

"I love you, Cheryl."

"And I love you, Shes."

"What are we going to do about it?"

"Try harder? Less food and more feeling?"

"That sounds wonderful to me. But—"

"But?"

"I'm not ready to live with someone else, or get married. There's too much to do, still."

"I can deal with that. I've got my own set of things to do. We need to put Yaotl behind bars, for example."

"But he's such a helpful guy…"

"It's OK, Shes, really. I think we're doing fine, as long as you look up from your work from time to time and breathe."

Shesmu scrambled up from his cushion, and she followed, and they embraced and kissed. The kiss was engrossing enough that it shut out the catcalls and whistles from the line cooks. When she was hearing properly again, MacIntyre realized the kitchen had gone completely silent. She turned and saw Sebek and Khay holding up their hands. Then Sebek smiled and started clapping, and the kitchen erupted in applause.

Shesmu hugged her and said, "Back to work, people. We have orders to get out."

CHAPTER THIRTY-FIVE
Shesmu Sees Off a Friend

I SPENT THE REST OF the evening forcing myself to concentrate entirely on MacIntyre. It was too bad that became impossible once I got home. We walked around the corner near my house, and MacIntyre said in a conversational tone, "Looks like your houseguests are having a party." The lights at the front of the house shone out, as did the interior lights through the open front door. Music—techno swing, played loud—blared out through the door as well. As I had no houseguests, I overreacted.

MacIntyre drew her recently restored gun. She led the way in through the door. We walked down the hall into the great room. Sitting, slumped in a large armchair, tapping his large toes to the music, was Pyotr Semionovich. His eyes were closed, and he had a half smile on his face. Across from him, sitting up straight on the sofa, was Karkin, still wearing the green army jacket he had worn at the necropolis two weeks before. His hands rested on his knees. He did not appear to enjoy the music, but since he had never appeared to enjoy anything, I couldn't tell.

MacIntyre said, "We should have ordered in food instead of eating out. You never know when friends will drop in." As the danger seemed less than imminent, she put away her gun.

Pyotr Semionovich opened his eyes sleepily. His gaze passed over me to MacIntyre, and he smiled his full smile. "Dorogaya, privyet!" I took this to be a greeting and replied with the most formal Remetjy greeting I could think of. Twice, for emphasis. I use the word "greeting" euphemistically.

"I'm not your dorogaya," said MacIntyre after shushing me. "What are you guys doing here?" She had paused before the word "guys", and I guessed she'd suppressed a stronger word. "We need to sleep."

"We have some unfinished business," said Pyotr Semionovich.

"My interactions with the Russian community don't make me want to prolong this," replied MacIntyre. "What do you want?"

"Closure," said Pyotr Semionovich.

"Revenge?" I asked.

He didn't seem upset, but I'd never seen Pyotr Semionovich angry. He laughed. "Don't worry, I'm not here to revenge my family. I haven't got one, haven't for a long time. My sister didn't approve of the choices I made in life, because they were the right ones. I wasn't up to her standards as a master criminal. More of a petty thief," he said with a happy smile.

He looked at MacIntyre. "From what Karkin tells me, my sister thought you were getting too close to her money. She hates—hated—it when people got between her and her money. It's that mother-bear-cub thing. Sennedjem is alive only because she thought he could tell her where her laundered money was. I have no idea why you're alive at all."

MacIntyre shut her eyes, then said, "She kept asking what I'd learned from Sennedjem, so I'd guess you're right."

"And you didn't tell her."

"Didn't like the way she asked."

"Dorogusha!" He shrugged. "If I could stay around, I'd marry you."

"If you were staying around," she replied, "I'd put you in jail. Tell me you're staying. We can get married when you get out in 30 years."

"No, there's a steamer leaving for the Far East in a couple of days. I'll be on it as a deckhand. I'm a seaman. I'll always be one."

"Why are you here?" I asked. "Not just to tell us your travel itinerary, I hope."

"No, as I said, unfinished business. Closure. And Karkin insisted." He looked at the Ramaytush with narrowed eyes.

Karkin said, "Russians."

MacIntyre looked at me and I looked at her. "What about them?" she asked.

Pyotr Semionovich lazily scratched his beard, then said, "He wants me to fill you in. See, Shesmu, after I left you locked up in my dacha, in Milaya, I took the comatose Sennedjem down to the airport in Menmenet. I wanted to get him to tell me where his friends had taken the money, then leave him for you to find. There I was, sitting peacefully in the departure lounge, when five podoniki in official-looking uniforms surrounded me, then this guy Karkin appeared. Said I had a choice: I could go to jail, or I could help him wrap up the Russians in Menmenet. No choice—I was already in the deepest kind of shit with my brothers. This yebonat pointed out that I wouldn't live long in Mother Russia, or anywhere else once my sister got done with me. Then Karkin got a phone call, and I got the news that my sister had managed to, erm, compromise you, dorogusha."

"I know all about that, and I'm not your dorogusha."

"So I spent some time in a lockup at the airport while my friend here dealt with the situation. I understand it was you, Shesmu, who helped my sister into the next world."

"Sorry about that," I said, not sorry at all.

"Not to worry, this world is better off. I am. Or was, until my friend here extracted me from the lockup and updated me on the new order in Menmenet."

"Complicated," said Karkin.

"Very. It turns out my sister had a viper in her midst, the good Gospodin Strel'sky."

"Informant," said Karkin. "Very useful."

"Yes, well, I wouldn't use that word. Strel'sky seized the day and took over my sister's gang, then stepped up operations in Menmenet."

MacIntyre smiled. "I know all about that, too."

"Dorogusha, you know everything; I'm humbled before you." Pyotr Semionovich grinned.

"Get on with it. And I'm not your dorogusha."

"Karkin here gave me another choice. Take down the gang or find out whether they would welcome me back with open arms when he told them where I was locked up." He shot a not-very-warm glance at Karkin, who was unmoved. Karkin reached into a bag by his side, extracted a folder, and gave it to MacIntyre.

"Details," he said. "Warned Strel'sky, to get him out of town. Fast. Told Aztecs about R'aweben."

MacIntyre looked through the pages inside the folder. "Very nice. Is this official?" She held up the folder.

"Approved by Genève."

"I'll thank you once I've found the words," MacIntyre replied. "None that I know really express my feelings. I really ought to just throw both of you into the first jail cell I can find. But I'll make sure the relevant medja gets this information." She packed away the folder. "Now, you two can leave. We've got things to do. Things that don't involve you."

Karkin said to Pyotr Semionovich, "Give you a ride to the piers."

The two men rose, bowed half bows, and left. I switched off the music and most of the lights, and a blissful silence descended on my house. I locked the door after them, tried the locks, and we attended to the things we needed to attend to. We even got some sleep later.

The next morning, I awoke with one thought dominating my heart.

"Oysters," I said.

"What about them?" asked MacIntyre, turning over in the bed to look at me with a smile.

"I'm going to need a new supplier."

Glossary

Note that Renkemet forms the plural by adding the suffix "u" or "ut" to a male or female noun, respectively.

'ahamedu	the sport of stick fighting, similar to fencing
akhet	the horizon, out of and into which R'a rises and sets, symbolizing death and rebirth; a place of great magic
'ankhu wedjau senebu	"alive, sound, and healthy"; a ritual wish for the continued well-being of an important person
Aset	powerful protective goddess; Greek Isis
ba	the aspect of a person representing the soul or spiritual force
Bastet	cat goddess; a powerful protective deity
Bes	protective household god; specifically protects pregnant women
Boston	the capital of the state of Massachusetts in New England
bozhe moi	"my God" (Russian oath)
Consent of Ma'at	a warrant from a sedjemy authorizing search of a person or location
deben	unit of money, about 3 to the USD
Didiresy Open Space	a Menmenet city park in the south-central part of Menmenet; site of the city archery range and many other recreational opportunities
dj'amu	a natural amalgam of gold and silver used in jewelry; Latin electrum
Djehuty	ibis-headed god of wisdom, husband of Ma'at; patron god of scribes, accountants, and diplomats; Greek Thoth/Hermes

Djehutymes Street	"Born of Djehuty", a street in the Menmenet shopping district; location of the palace housing the R'ames Society
Dju-Keta	"The Wrinkled Hill," a hill in the northeast corner of Menmenet
Dju-Liberty	"Liberty Hill," a hill in the east central part of Menmenet that slopes down to I'ahmes Creek; landmark for the American district of Menmenet
Dju-Seret	"The Hill of the Nobles," a hill in the middle-northern sector of Menmenet
Dju-Setaseta	"The Burned Mountain," a mountain to the southeast of Menmenet
Dju-Tepy	"The Principal Hill", a tall hill filled with residential mansions in the north-central area of Menmenet between Tjesut and Dju-Keta
Djuy-Benty	"The Two Breasts Hills," a two-peaked hill in the center of Menmenet
dorogaya	"dear," term of endearment (Russian)
dorogusha	"dearie," overly familiar term of endearment (Russian)
drug	"friend" (Russian); moi drug "my friend"
druz'ya	"friends" (Russian)
Duat	the path leading to the judgment of Inpu and Ma'at in the underworld
dyer'mo	bullshit (Russian slang)
Gorni	a small town north of Menmenet toward the border with Russkaya Amerika
haty'a	mayor of a city
hekasepat	head of state (singular and plural forms)
hem-netjer	priest, prophet
hem-netjer-tepy	high priest, the priest in charge of a temple
Henet Baket Sepat	Inland Revenue Service of the Ta'an-Imenty Republic
Henuttawy Group	"Mistress of the Two Lands," a large financial corporation headquartered in Menmenet
hetep	an altar for making sacrifices or offerings to a god

Hut-'Ankh-Tepyt Hotel	a large tourist hotel in downtown Menmenet; "First Palace"
Hut-Her	powerful fertility goddess, Greek Hathor
Hut-Her-Sekhmet	syncretic goddess combining Hut-Her and Sekhmet, a lion goddess; her remit was public health, and her temple contains the medical examiner and morgue
huty, hutyt	sergeant, a police and military title (male, female forms)
huty-er-semetyu, hutyt-er-semetyu	detective-sergeant, a police title (male, female forms)
idnu	Lieutenant, a military or police rank
idnu-er-semetyu	Detective-Lieutenant, a police rank
Imen	the great god of Waset; the Hidden One; Greek Amun
Imen-R'a	the great syncretic sun god of the Remetjy Empire, its state god
imy-er-medjau	Superintendent of Police, a police rank
Inpu	jackal god of the necropolis; Greek Anubis
ka	the aspect of a person representing the life force; subject of worship after death
Kemet	an ancient country and empire in North Africa; Greek Egypt
Khenemset	female companion, "auntie", "bestie"
Liberty Street	a street in south Menmenet near Iahmes Creek; center of the American financial district; has a square with a replica of the Statue of Liberty
Ma'at	goddess of justice and truth, sister of R'a, wife of Djehuty
ma'at	justice, truth, the right way
Massachusetts	a state in new England, one of the original thirteen states of the United States of America
medja, medjat, medjau, medjaut	police officer (male, female, plural forms)
Mehetet Street	street in Menmenet running east-west along the north bay shore; location of the Imenhetep Club, a number of quays, and the main ferry terminal to the north bay

Menmenet	capital of Ta'an-Imenty Republic, city on Menmenet bay; the word itself means "cattle" or "earthquake"
Mentju	falcon-headed god of just war and military power; Greek Montu/Ares; also represented as a powerful bull; name of the main boulevard of Menmenet
Mentju Boulevard	large street running east-west, main street of Menmenet; named for the god of just war Mentju; Temple of Mentju is on this street near the other city temples in the middle of Menmenet
Milaya	"Sweetie," a small Russian town on the north coast, just south of Russkaya Amerika
militsia	police (Russian)
Myu-Myu Club	"The Cat," a nightclub in Menmenet with a Bastet theme
na zdarov'ye	"enjoy!" or "to health" (Russian toast)
Neferhetepu Street	"Beautiful Peace", street in central Menmenet shopping district, crosses Djehutymes Street where the R'ames Society palace is situated
New England	a region in the northeastern United States of America
New York	a city and metropolitan area bordering New England to the south
Niutimywer	"City of the Great," previous capital of the Ta'an-Imenty Republic, located on a small bay south of Menmenet
octli	an Aztec alcoholic beverage made from cactus juice (Nahuatl); Spanish "pulque"
pazhaluista	please (Russian)
pera'a	emperor; Greek pharaoh
podonok	"bastard" (Russian)
privyet	"hi," greeting (Russian)
Promise of Ma'at	a monetary amount set by a sedjemy as security for the release of a prisoner prior to trial, or an oath acting as such security
R'a	the great sun god; Greek Re
R'ames Society	a professional chef's association in Menmenet, on Djehutymes Street

Remetj, Remetjet	a man or woman of Kemet, Remetjet is the collective noun for people of Kemet
Remetjy	of or relating to Kemet
Renkemet	the language of Kemet
Rossiya	"Russia" (Russian)
rudj	inspector or special agent; a police rank, supervisor of a team
Sebek	a crocodile god, god of water and marshes, symbol of potency and power
SecInterPol	a secret international police organization headquartered in Genève, Switzerland, run mainly by Europeans but with local medjau agents everywhere in the world
sedjemy	a civil judge (non-religious court), usually a sedjemy sepat, state judge
sehy	counselor, attorney
semety, semetyt, semetyu	detective (male, female, plural forms)
sepat	state; nation; Greek nome
Seteh	god of the desert and chaos; Greek Seth
Setetiu District	Asian quarter of Menmenet in the northwest corner of the city, north of the necropolis district
Shesmu	underworld god, the "butcher of souls"; also the god of wine and olive oil
Shetasen	the secret police of the Ta'an-Imenty republic, part of the Temple of Imen-R'a
Sibir'	the large eastern province of Russia bounded by the Arctic Ocean, the Pacific Ocean, and the Bering Strait
Slavyanka Reka	the Russian River, a river that forms the southern boundary of Russkaya Amerika with the Ta'an-Imenty Republic
Spakoinoi nochi	"good night" (Russian)
sukin s'yn	"son of a bitch," a Russian term of opprobrium
Ta'an-Imenty Republic	a republic on the west coast of North America; formerly part of the Empire of Kemet; capital Menmenet
Tenochtitlan	capital city of the Aztec Republic

Tjau Sekhmet	"The Breath of Sekhmet", a secret ritual of the Temple of Bastet; taken from the name for the desert winds of Kemet that blow everything clean
Tjesut	"The Heights," neighborhood in the north-central section of Menmenet, location of the Palace of the Republic and many palaces and mansions with magnificent views of Menmenet Bay
tlaxcalli	thin corn pancakes serving as bread (Aztec); tortillas (Spanish)
vor	"thief", "gangster" (Russian)
w'ab, w'abet, w'abu, w'abut	a working priest (male, female, and plural forms)
Wedjit Djerdjer Hotel	"Foreign Journey," a hotel near the Menmenet airport
Wennefer Street	"Uncovering of Beauty," a street in Menmenet running from Mentju Boulevard to the North Shore
werkhet	master status at Remetjy stick-fighting
Wesir	god of the underworld, primary deity representing death and the afterlife; brother of Aset; Greek Osiris
Wings of Ma'at	a cautionary ritual recited by medjau when arresting a person
xocolatl	chocolate (Aztec); a hot drink made with chocolate, cinnamon, and chile powder
yeb tvoyu mat'	"fuck your mother," a Russian oath
yebonat	"fucker," Russian slang term of opprobrium
zakuski	"appetizers" (Russian); refers to a tremendous array of small-plate foods served before a major meal, with lots of vodka
zau	corporation, a business form treating the business as a single body, with the owners having legal protection of their assets; pronounced "za-oo"

Wiki Menmenet

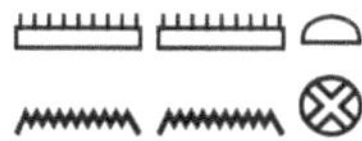

The City of Menmenet is the second most populous city in the Ta'an-Imenty Republic with an estimated population of 502,360. It is the capital of the Semu sepat (nome). Located at 37°46.45.48.N 122°25.9.12.W, the city occupies former grasslands, hills, and sand dune areas at the top of a peninsula and has a land mass of 118 square kilometers. It is the cultural and financial center of the region centered on Menmenet Bay. Founded in 1779 by Remetjy explorer Hormesu, Menmenet has a long and colorful history as a port city in the expanding New World empire of Kemet (Egypt), becoming the central transit point for the establishment of the largest agricultural development in the New World along the central rivers of the territory. The discovery of significant gold deposits in the foothills of the mountains beyond the central valley precipitated both a short-lived gold rush, an attempted invasion from the expansive and determined United States of America to the East, and a political revolution against the Empire. The new republic, founded by the local hekasepat Pr'aemheb after a series of well-fought battles in alliance with the local tribes against both the declining Empire of Kemet and the ragtag opportunists of the United States, immediately took control of the gold fields, which became the source of much of the new Republic's wealth and remained so until the Republic left the gold standard during the depression of the 1930s.

Half of the city was destroyed in the Great Earthquake of 1906 but was quickly rebuilt, resulting in a pleasing mix of modern and classical Remetjy architecture on the rolling hills of the city. Over the years, Menmenet became internationalized with immigrants from the Far East, the United States, and the Aztec and Mayan states to the south. As port traffic declined in the 1960s and 1970s, Menmenet became more of a financial and religious center with culture dominated by the various cults, including Imen-R'a, Aset, Inpu, Bastet, and

Wesir. By 2000, Menmenet had become the world's eighteenth largest producing city and fifteenth in the list of the world's top financial centers. Menmenet's beautiful and expanding necropolis on the western side of the city has become a tourist destination in its own right, along with the cool summer fogs, steep hills, and famous landmarks such as the Temple of Inpu, the ubiquitous ferries that crisscross the Bay, and the spectacular views of the Bay from the hills.

Wiki Bastet

Bastet is an ancient goddess, originally portrayed as a lioness but increasingly as a cat after the ascension of the great unifying pera'a Nebhepetr'a Mentjuhetep.

Role and characteristics

A very ancient goddess, Bastet originally was a sun goddess. With the changes to her character over time, Bastet became the daughter of R'a, often portrayed with the Eye of R'a. At some point, the goddess took on the aspect of Miu'aar'a (the Great Cat of R'a), the vengeful arm of R'a that decapitates the evil serpent 'Aapep, the embodiment of chaos. Bastet is worshipped as a protective goddess, particularly for pregnant women, but her other aspect is a vengeful goddess who enforces her father's rage on the world, particularly on vermin such as snakes, mice, and rats. Early cults worshipped Sekhmet, the fierce lioness goddess, as an aspect of Bastet. A recent tell-all book suggests that this worship has persisted in secret in certain cults of Bastet around the world.

Worship

The worship of Bastet grew strongly in the Middle Empire as the influence of Kemet spread throughout the Great Green Sea. The main cult center of the goddess was in the city of Per-Bastet (House of Bastet) in the great Delta of North Kemet, and the goddess was at one time the primary goddess of North Kemet.

The cult of Bastet became extremely wealthy, with large temples in most cities around the world with significant Remetjy populations. Much of this wealth comes from worshipper donations that pay for specific protection by the goddess. In historical times, the trade in Bastet amulets blessed by the priests of Bastet took on aspects of extortion—buy this amulet or dreadful things will happen to you, your family, or your business. Reforming pera'au outlawed such practices in the 18th century.

The main temple in Per-Bastet, rebuilt and expanded in the 19th century, is a major tourist attraction in modern Kemet. The Festival of Bastet held there each year attracts hundreds of thousands of pilgrims and tourists and is a highlight of North Kemet culture. The priests of Bastet play no political role in the Remetjy state but exercise influence through their great wealth.

Iconography

Scribes and artists depict Bastet as either a woman with a cat's head or as a sitting cat, usually black. From the Middle Empire, Bastet always carries a sistrum (a prayer rattle), signifying her ritual importance in North Kemet. The goddess Hut-her, another major cult goddess, carries the sistrum in the South. Bastet usually wears the menit necklace, a semicircle with multiple rows of beads and a counterweight worn down the back. Bastet figures often have kittens around her feet.

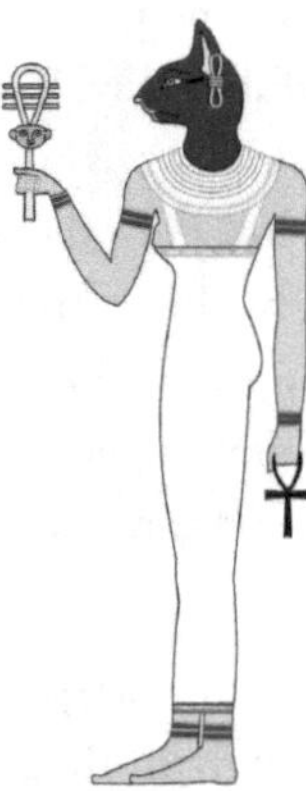

Acknowledgements

I want to thank my illustrator and wife, Mary Swanson, for her willingness to continue to create maps for my strange world.

I am grateful to my writing group friends at the Mechanics' Institute in San Francisco for their thoughtful reviews: Kristina Brown, Bill Carr, Bob Weston, Al Luongo, and John Cox.

The image of Bastet is from Wikipedia:
By Gunawan Kartapranata - Own work, CC BY-SA 3.0, https://commons.wikimedia.org/w/index.php?curid=18165087

Please enjoy the first chapter of *The Bull of Mentju,* the final book of the Menmenet trilogy. Check our website at www.poesys.com for availability.

Cheryl MacIntyre moved from happy to pissed off to a state of incandescent rage, all in the space of an hour of her working afternoon.

MacIntyre had hunted and pecked her way through the case report on a nasty pair of murders. "Dispute" was the accepted police-report term for the wholesale butchery when the Aztec and Russian gangs threw bullets at each other. Both Aztecs and Russians excelled at disputation. She felt she had done a fine piece of work there, and she even took pleasure in writing the report about it for once. Many bad people were going away for a long time. A hard-working hutyt-er-semetyu could take strong satisfaction in a case like this.

"MacIntyre! In the office, now!" Her boss, Idnu Djehutymes, must want to congratulate her.

Her smile was genuine as she put the computer into secure mode, got up, and headed for the idnu's office. She walked past vacant cubicles; the other semetyu were out doing actual work. She stepped into Mes's office. Mes sat at his desk, and another man sat in one of the office chairs, an American from the look of him.

"Shut the door."

This was not a good sign. In MacIntyre's experience with him, Mes liked the noise of his admonitions to be audible to the team, management theory be damned. Usually he waited to deliver his speech until everyone was back in the office, writing up their day of toil. That way, they could all get the full benefit of the lecture he delivered to the chosen sacrifice of the day. She was it today. But he must have something more on his mind than the usual lecture, since there was no one around to hear it. She thought back over the case and found nothing that was likely to have gotten his ire up. Well, there was that incident with the Russian slug and the Taser. That could be it. She had gone a bit outside the rules on that one.

"MacIntyre, this is the United States Consul General, John Smith." Mes's voice was flat and noncommittal.

She smiled and said in English, "Seriously? John Smith?"

John Smith frowned, but said, "Sergeant."

"It's Hutyt, Mr. Brown, Hutyt-er-Semetyu. Sorry, Smith." She smiled. MacIntyre hated the guy on sight. She felt disgust just looking at his sour American face behind his little, round glasses. She could tell from the lines on his face he spent much of his time frowning.

Mes frowned too, but then that was his natural expression.

"MacIntyre. You're fired," he said.

She blinked. "I'm sorry?"

"Sit down."

"Why, if I'm fired? I'm going to dinner, I'm hungry." The queasiness in her stomach wasn't hunger, though.

"Sit down, now!"

His eyes weren't meeting hers. This was another bad sign. Mes always confronted things. He looked you in the eye while berating your stupidity or lack of discipline.

"MacIntyre. Cheryl. This is hard." Now, Djehutymes was the crustiest, least-tolerant supervisor in the whole department. "Touchy-feely" was a swear word to him. MacIntyre knew this was not good; this was a bright red flag.

She sank into the straight-backed chair in front of his desk. He had his hands folded, eyes staring down at them. He raised his eyes to hers.

"I have been instructed," he began, then stopped. He tried again. "Mr. Smith is here because you're American, with a United States passport."

"So what?"

He shrugged irritably. "You're fired because you're American."

MacIntyre stared, uncomprehending.

"American? So what?"

"Don't you read the papers?"

"No, I only read the online conspiracy sites. You can't believe anything you read in the paper. Come on, the president had a bad dinner and blamed it on the hekasepat? Now you're firing all Americans?" The papers obsessed over the details of the incident involving Our Glorious Leader, the democratically elected head of state of the Ta'an-Imenty Republic. John Smith regarded her with unblinking eyes behind his gold wire-rim glasses.

"MacIntyre. He didn't just blame the hekasepat, he threw him out the back door of the White House like garbage. No offense, Mr. Smith."

The unblinking eyes didn't blink as Smith stared at them.

"Do you know what NATO is, MacIntyre?"

"Sure, the North American Treaty Organization. The Numunuu Empire, the Plains Federation, and the U. S. playing war games with tanks and toy soldiers in the desert."

"The government doesn't think they're games anymore, MacIntyre. The Temple of Mentju worries about isfet and going to war. So the hekasepat mentioned it over wine and steak and the President threw him out."

"How does that have anything to do with catching murderers, Mes?"

"It doesn't, except that Remetjet are getting irrational, which you know is like blood in the water. The politicians—and in particular the haty'a—are getting even more irrational than the people that voted for them. So you're fired. Isfet."

The American Consul General didn't know what that meant. "What is 'isfet'?"

Mes explained. "Isfet is the chaos, irrationality, and criminality that the god Seteh brings into the world. It's our primary job to fight it as w'abu of Ma'at."

MacIntyre brought the conversation back to the point. "Americans can be irrational too, trust me on this one. And my being American means what, I'm undermining the Republic? I'm meat to the sharks? Anyway, I'm a citizen of the Republic too."

Mr. Smith stirred. "Your being American means we can help you, Sergeant. The United States commits to helping its citizens wherever they might be in the world."

Djehutymes glared at him. "Don't interrupt! MacIntyre, it all trickles down."

"Until it pisses on me?" MacIntyre was tapping her foot with impatience. "That's not irrational, that's stupid. Power." She laughed without humor. "All the power I wield wouldn't light up a light bulb."

"No doubt." He straightened up. "You're still fired. Gun and badge, please."

She stood and eased the requested objects from her holster and pocket and deposited them on his desk, squaring them up in front of him. The feeling in the pit of her stomach enlarged, and her rage grew.

Mr. Smith said, "If you need any kind of help, I'm here."

MacIntyre scorned this offer. "The last help I got from an American was a ticket out of the place. I don't need any more, thanks." She turned back to her ex-boss. "Thanks for everything, Mes, you know how much I appreciate this special attention."

"Cheryl, please." The idnu's voice was gentle, but his eyes were as cold as ever.

"I know, you're doing what you're told. I don't think that always works out all that well, Mes. Doing what you're told leads to isfet, not ma'at."

"Could be you're right, could be not. You can complain to the haty'a, but I don't think it will do any good." He shrugged.

She mirrored his shrug and put some extra into it as the rage took hold. She didn't trust herself to speak and walked out, leaving Mes and Mr. Smith to console one another.

The window of MacIntyre's small third-floor apartment opened onto a quiet street in the middle of the city of Menmenet. It was quiet the same way many of the streets were quiet in Menmenet. They meandered around or dead-ended in blank walls of Remetjy houses. Her apartment building on the edge of the American district catered to American tastes. Its windows looked onto the street, the exact reverse of the typical Remetjy house. And yet, the mix of different facades made for a quiet ambience. She'd learned to love those streets in the last ten years. She'd even explored several interesting places to see outside of Menmenet, the capital city of the Ta'an-Imenty Republic on the West Coast of North America.

She'd learned to love the fog, natural air conditioning. She'd learned to love the people with their relaxed attitudes, loose clothes, and sandals. She'd learned to love the not-American ways of thinking.

MacIntyre gazed out her window at the quiet street, late in the afternoon of the day Djehutymes had fired her. The rage grew. She turned away from the quiet of the street to the quiet of her empty apartment and sat at her kitchen table, trying not to cry from the rage.

She hated the murderers in Menmenet. But that was—had been—her job: tracking them down and putting them in prison for life. She was a hutyt-er-semetyu on the homicide squad of the Menmenet medjau. It was that sense of ma'at, balance in the universe, that had made her join the medjau in the first place. A scum Aztec lowlife had raped and murdered her wonderful lover R'aia, the most exquisite woman she had ever loved. It was why she had taken the oath of Ma'at, the goddess of justice, to become a priestess, a w'abet of Ma'at, even though she didn't believe in the religion. And she'd become a citizen of the Ta'an-Imenty Republic. Any person with a serious intent to rise in the medjau hierarchy had to be a priest and a citizen.

And she had that serious intent. She had impulsively run from her controlling parents in Boston. Her lover was raped and murdered. Then she took three bullets from a bank robber while on patrol. She needed to be in charge, not a victim. She'd worked her way off patrol, out of the desk job they put her in after the shooting, and up to the rank of hutyt-r-semetyu. She had been looking forward to taking the idnu's exam soon.

Now, the future was bleak. They had fired her. She felt as though they had thrown her off a cliff she didn't even know was there. American. Fired for being an American, even though she was now a citizen of the Republic. Fired for being an American.

Nothing she could imagine came close to this, and her rage knew few bounds as she fell off the mind-cliff.

MacIntyre drummed her fingers on her kitchen table, rage flowing. She hadn't pounded a table in years, ever since leaving her Boston home. This was partly because of self-control gained over years of medjat training and partly because of the memory of the broken hand she took onto the plane out of Boston. Table-pounding had its merits, but mostly it was a waste of energy with too long a recovery time.

MacIntyre saw herself as a strong, autonomous woman. After years of working as a medjat, she'd polished her emotional armor to where nothing got under her skin. But this was like a snakebite. She needed help.

She picked up her phone and called Shesmu, the man she depended on for emotional support, food, and sex. Shesmu would come and comfort her, help her past her rage, feed her, make love to her, and make her feel good about herself again.

This romantic haze lasted less than two seconds after he picked up.

Thank You

Thanks for reading *The Lion of Bastet.*
If you liked the book, please leave a review on the web site through which you
bought it.

Sign up to our mailing list for notifications and get a free ebook!

http://www.poesys.com